Annie's Redemption

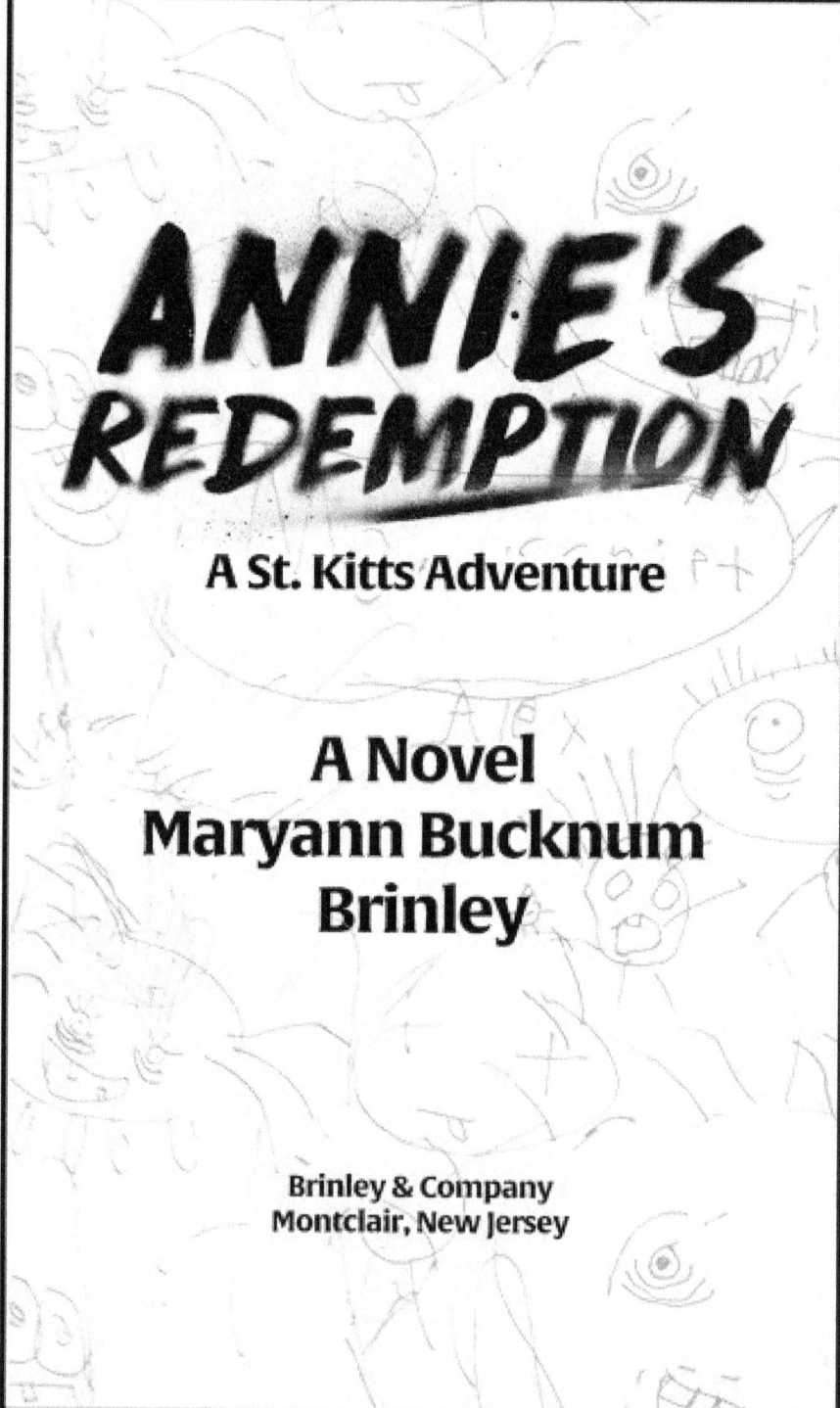

ANNIE'S REDEMPTION

A St. Kitts Adventure

A Novel
Maryann Bucknum Brinley

Brinley & Company
Montclair, New Jersey

COPYRIGHT

Book cover and illustrations: Alex Carr and Mike Lanctot

Map of St. Kitts credit: Shutterstock, enhanced by Mike Lanctot

ISBN: 979-8-9912005-0-9 (paperback)

Printed in the United States of America

DEDICATION

To my spectacular family...

Especially my husband Bob, who listened to each chapter of this story with the keen interest that made me want to continue, and to my wonderful children and grandchildren: Zach, Maggie, Erin, Chris, Finn, Charlotte, Evie, Willa, Alex, and all my Bucknums and Brinleys.

To St. Kitts, the birthplace of our family's life lessons in adventure as well as our extraordinary Brinley Shipwreck Rum Company. (www.shipwreckrum.com).

And, to all the growing-older-and-wiser women, like Annie, true heroines of their own lives.

ACKNOWLEDGEMENTS

I have been a journalist focused only on true stories for most of my life and so I might never have ventured down this path of fiction if it weren't for my so-called 'rogue writers': Silvia DelPriore, Joan Axelrod, Susan Israeli, a slew of others who came and went, all led by Benilde Little, the accomplished author and writing coach who brought us together. Meeting weekly, reading chapter by chapter to an attentively critical audience kept Annie on her rescue road.

Pushing Annie into print has also been a group effort. I must thank my creative graphic designer and nephew, Mike Lanctot, who worked with Alex Carr's dramatic line drawing which overlays the cover photo of St. Kitts and appears inside on the title page. Alex, my youngest grandchild, was only six when he drew these characters. I also want to thank Pat Buikema for nudging me into a new publishing route, Taylor Rockey for making me think creatively about promotion, and Diane Timmons, a Kindle Direct Publishing expert extraordinaire.

Lastly, this fictional story would not be possible without my years of experience on the wonderful island of St. Kitts, home to honest, passionate politicians, honorable, devoted police officers, and thousands of kind, hard-working people.

TABLE OF CONTENTS

MAP OF ST. KITTS

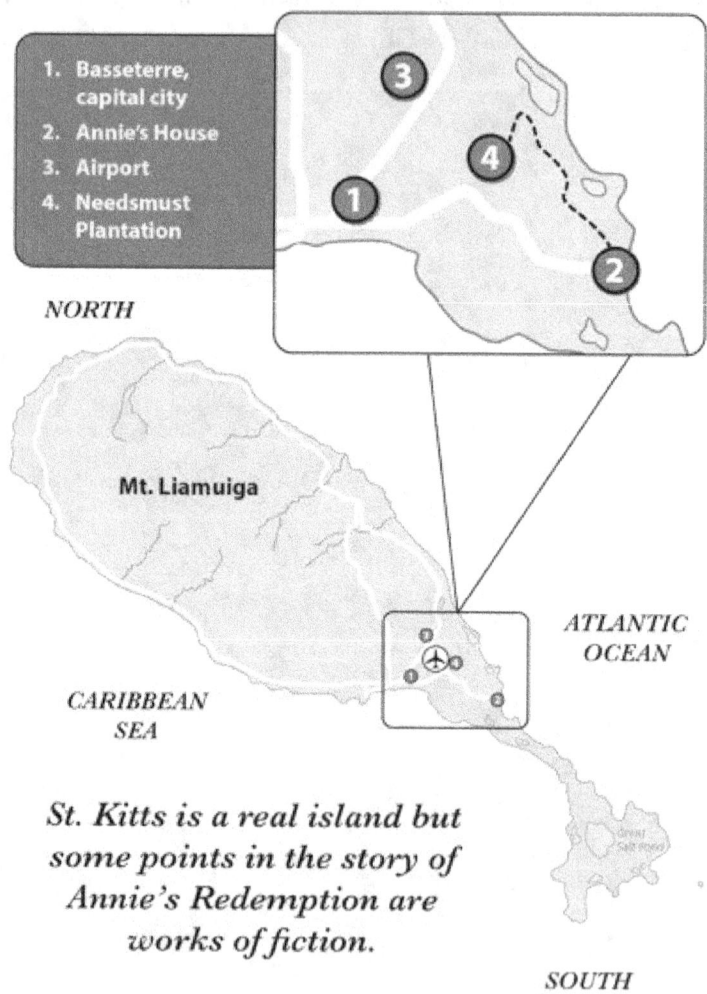

SAINT KITTS

1. **Basseterre, capital city**
2. **Annie's House**
3. **Airport**
4. **Needsmust Plantation**

NORTH

Mt. Liamuiga

ATLANTIC OCEAN

CARIBBEAN SEA

St. Kitts is a real island but some points in the story of Annie's Redemption are works of fiction.

SOUTH

CHAPTER ONE

3:45 AM, November 19, 2021

Redemption: 1. An act of redeeming or atoning
for a fault or mistake, or the state of being
redeemed. 2. Deliverance; rescue

---

*H*e stands in the dark beneath the balcony, one floor up, his whole body vibrating, quivering with anticipation, anxiety, need, all of it. Moon out. Back of the house. Not a sound. Even the sweet nightly melody of the tree frogs has ended. Is it late? No early. Would he? Could he? Should he? Dare he?

But God she was so beautiful. Unlike any girl he had ever seen on the beach at Frigate Bay. That hair. Long, blonde; like no girl on his island.

Yes, he thinks. Go for it. That's what he'd been told to do. Go for her.

He starts to sweat. His palms, his back, his loins, the inside of his thighs, are dripping wet now. His stomach, of late, is rumbling, roiling, all the time. His hands: they are shaking. Don't. No. He tells himself.

Yet again, he thinks, go for her.

Stepping back there in the dark to look up, he can see that the sliding glass door is open just little and just his luck, or not.

∽

Inside the upstairs bedroom above, the girls, all three, are asleep on this trip with their grandmother to celebrate a lifting of the Covid lockdown. The pandemic had made them eager to escape from home, to fly away on a vacation from the real world. And while the virus proved to be unrelentingly tricky with its never-ending variants, they had all been vaccinated by November 2021. Two days before this night, they had flown to St. Kitts from Newark airport in New Jersey. Now, under high ceilings, fans turning slowly above, sheets pushed off, legs out, blankets fallen onto the white tile floors, they are deep in dreams, stirring only lightly, tired after a long day at the beach. It is almost 4 AM. One of them will need to use the bathroom soon.

Annie, let's call her Grammy, is also out blissfully downstairs in the big bedroom with the French doors opening to that gorgeous pool. This long-planned trip had been her gift. And after this day, this remarkably beautiful, sunshine-filled day over at Frigate Bay swimming with these glorious teenage granddaughters in the Caribbean Sea, lounging and lunching on barbecued chicken in bathing suits and bare feet, she had gone to sleep thinking of how precious it was to have them all to herself here on St. Kitts. The girls had loved their perfect beach day. Her 13-year-old had even made friends with a donkey.

The island is one of her favorite places in the world and this house, her home away from home, is teal blue with Caribbean gingerbread trim, tucked into a hillside that slopes up to a mountain. Wow, what color; a shocking shade that would never meet approval in her other, so-very-American neutral shades of life. Oh, that pool too! She swims every morning when she is here; 80 laps even when the water is chilly in the early morning. Cryotherapy! She laughs about her habit with friends. Is she trying to freeze herself into a longer life? Maybe so? she admits. Yet, it is simply sheer delight to have this water right outside her bedroom here on a deck facing across a golf course and out to the blue waters of Half Moon Bay and the Atlantic Ocean. She can see for miles in the light of day.

How about this dream-come-true? Annie certainly loves the place. So does her husband, Buck, her partner for more than five decades of life, two kids and six grandchildren arriving along an occasionally bumpy but substantially smooth road of marriage. Long marriages are so interesting, aren't they? How, and why, they last their length and breadth are certainly lucky in love riddles.

Our couple and this family had all grown to understand intimately how a St. Kitts state of mind could wash away anxiety, especially a never-ending to-do list and too-busy brain. In fact, this place had once helped rescue Annie nudging her out of a deep and very dark well of sadness after a disastrous third pregnancy.

Three generations of family, six adults and six children, had come not once but sometimes twice a year…until the first wave of the Covid pandemic shut down the world in its viral nightmare. St. Kitts had closed its doors to almost everyone, denying entry to travelers and prohibiting local citizens from socializing except during a few hours each day. Stuck back in the states, Annie and her kids knew that the island would always be there and dreamed about returning, planning, then canceling and rescheduling trips, but always determined to get back to their lovely peaceful place. In isolation, unable to be there physically, Annie would find herself mentally floating on her back in the water off the southeastern peninsula, ears below the surface, soundlessly, senselessly, experiencing profound surrender to quiet. It's where she took herself while meditating. Just the thought of her St. Kitts peace of place could calm jumpy thoughts and make almost anything all right in her world.

Annie, our 74-year-old grandmother, is in such a restful sleep this night in November that she might not have woken at all. She's a tall woman with silver gray hair and still athletic in what she never hesitates to describe as old age. How in heaven's name did she get here? It all happened so fast. She hasn't run a marathon in years but is still convinced she could. Hah, her friends say, don't you dare. Your knees and lower back will punish you forever after. Oh they, of the replacement parts club! Everyone espousing, celebrating, commiserating about new knees, hips, cervical screw systems. Exchanging surgical stories is honestly de rigueur for her age category. But not Annie, or as she often says, not yet. She insists on staying fit, attempting to remain immune to those numbers growing exponentially in the passing of years. Call her age what it is, she asserts with a who-care's attitude. She doesn't hide or lie about it. Her motto has been to stay healthy or at least die trying. Along with all the running and swimming, she teaches yoga to an old-timers' group, cherishing life as crazy, convoluted and frustrating as it can be. Her mother lived long and happily until age 104 and Annie has fingers crossed hoping she will follow in those genetic footsteps.

We need to set the stage here with this background on our Annie. It will come in handy as our story enfolds. Our ordinarily fun-loving, optimistic woman is about to experience another side of life, a truth about human nature she has been able to ignore or dismiss until now.

At 3:45 AM, she has fallen into one of those full force REM stages of wonderful unconscious healing. Thank God for her wake-up-instantly ability honed back in those early mothering years and then polished in fear of something going wrong on her watch as a grandmother in charge, the weight of which is always worrisome. What if something happens to a grandchild when you're in charge? Oh God. Don't think about it, she has said before. Tonight, thank God for the extra-auditory, instantaneous hearing alert that can wake a woman in a flash to the sound of a baby crying or child in need. It kicked in for Annie. Thank God. Thank God she would later say.

She sits up instantly awake to a sound coming from the bedroom upstairs. What is that? Hyper-alert, eyes wide open in the dark, Annie can sense something or someone foreign in her space, this home away from home.

Out of her big bed…bigger without Buck there beside her…immediately, she starts to run, bare feet pounding around the corner and up the wide wooden staircase, racing with no clear thought but a flood of panicky fear. What is it? Who is it? She's on duty here. She had assured her daughter, daughter-in-law, son, and son-in-law, yes, all these parents, the children who have grown into parents in this passage of her time, yes, she had vowed that she would take good care of their kids. The girls would be safe. They wouldn't catch Covid. They would avoid crowds, wear those annoying masks, stick together, stay outside to eat, drink or shop on island. She wouldn't let them out of her sight. This is what grandparents do, right? They promise. The three girls, her spectacular granddaughters, would have a perfectly lovely trip.

Hadn't she been promising this vacation for months during the quarantine, the masks, the wait for vaccines, then those vicious viral variants arriving one after another, killing friends, making others so sick that they felt like dying. Damn that Delta, Omicron, and those endless travel restrictions too. They had waited and waited and now the four of them are here.

"Lizzie, Ellie, Abigail!" she screams heading up the stairs. Oh my God. Oh my God. Lizzie is 16. Abigail, her sister is 15, and Ellie, their younger cousin, is 13.

⚜

These girls had cheered when the Covid vaccine was approved for age 12 and older. Lizzie and Abigail crowed with joy on the Zoom call with their cousin and grandmother in a virtual celebration; cheers were screen size only but still better than not at all. "We're going. We're going. Woo-wee. St. Kitts here we come."

"Pack your suitcases girls," Grammy, our Annie, had laughed into the happy chorus and then went with, "We're off to see the Wizard, the wonderful Wizard of Oz."

"Oh my God Grammy no, no, no," they protested. "That song is so old school!" No one remembers who Judy Garland was. These kids are in a generation of girls in love with Taylor Swift, Billie Eilish, and raised on Disney tunes with heroines like Elsa and Anna from Frozen still on their love-that-song list, even as teens.

"Let it go, let it go," they sang on that Friday night family Zoom just a few weeks ago. "The past is in the past." No more pandemic. "We can't wait."

And then they were here, at last, finally, after all the waiting and wanting to get away, to be together. It had been a perfect first full day of island joy; Sunshine, sand, beach chairs...all very glorious...and just yesterday.

❧

Now, rushing toward the upstairs bedroom, too many steps taking too much time, Annie knows that something horrible has gone wrong here in her paradise. Screams. The girls are shrieking, shouting her name, GRAMMMMMMY, as she reaches the landing and turns left into the big bedroom. But there are only two girls screaming.

CHAPTER TWO

3:50 AM

---

*What goes into any decision made in a moment
of panic is complicated. Is it life experience?
Trauma? Love? The mind, the psyche, spirit,
soul, whatever you might call it...is multi-
layered and mysterious. Maybe here on this
night, that invisible bond between a grandparent
and grandchild compels the course of action.*

---

*L*izzie, Abigail, where is Ellie? Where is she?" Annie can
barely get the words out. She is breathing as much logic as
she can muster into her questions. Her limbs feel weak.
Her heart beats like that Goddamned, unbalanced, clothes dryer on
its last legs downstairs when it's laboring under the weight of a
load of wet towels. This can't be happening. This isn't happening.
But yes, sh-t, she curses sliding into a habit that has become more
comfortable, cursing in old age. There is no room for this kind of
disaster in her pretty life and right here on her precious St. Kitts.

But of course, it is certainly happening; the kind of nightmare experienced only vicariously in those tabloids and social media feeds. Right? Wrong. This is hers to own here.

The girls, these brown-eyed brunettes, are hysterical. This grandmother is frantic, fumbling in the dark for the pull switch to the ceiling light. The electrical wiring was updated when they purchased the house but it's still not up to U.S. code. She curses, yes again, that rope pull hanging from its ceiling fixture now. Why can't she have a normal modern light switch on the wall by the door? Not a string. Not a rope. Er. She needs light. Goddamn it. Lots of light to see what's going on here!

"Lizzie, what is this? What happened?" Annie's voice rises in confusion, fear and something else about to break fully through. "Lizzie, my sweet girl, Abby, where is Ellie? What happened to Ellie?" She looks over to the empty bed by the sliding doors trying desperately to anchor this horrible thought into place. Jumpy. Jumpy. Her heart and mind are jumping all over, anxiety and the hormones that push and pull it along are flooding her body. Her youngest granddaughter is gone. Fighting for calm, taking hold of Lizzie's shoulders gently, reaching out to grab Abigail's hand, she is freaking inside but still clawing mentally for even a fake adult calm. Breathe. Focus. Breathe. This 16-year-old in front of her, now as tall as her grandmother, is in a total panic. Annie puts a hand to Lizzie's cheek, willing her to focus. "Look at me, Liz," she says. Lizzie is wide-eyed, gulping big breaths, fear in, fear out, lips parted. As the oldest, she thinks she was in charge, somehow responsible here. Annie's eyes drift again quickly to the open door and the night outside. Open? The door is wide open?

"I woke up. There was a noise. A dog. A big dog," Lizzie says. "I thought it was a dog, a dog there on the floor." She points across Ellie's empty bed, hardly able to get full sentences out. Then

9

she repeats, "A dog or some animal, coming from the balcony," and flicks her hand in the direction of the doors and night outside beyond.

Annie, standing between the two beds, wraps her arms around both girls, drawing Abigail in closer now. Always a hugger, she can feel the girls' hearts beating, pounding against her own thumping chest. The fear is tangible here. There is no hiding it. The two girls had been sleeping together in one of the queens, neither sister wanting to share the other bed with their cousin, blonde Ellie, the girl who always tosses and turns too much. That child takes so long to settle down, Annie has pronounced to Ellie's mom, her daughter Lauren. "What is going on in her brain? What a wonder she is. I can only imagine where she will go in life." Mother and grandmother would always laugh with pride and expectation of their fidgety Ellie's future.

"What? A dog? An animal?" this grandmother asks. "In here? How?" She's looking around the beautiful room, now an unimaginable scene of unseen, unknown violence, but a legacy that is palpable here in this bedroom. Her girl is missing, gone, gone. How stupid, stupid, stupid can you be? she thinks. But whoa, isn't this her Caribbean home? Why shouldn't she have expected it to be fine, just fine and perfectly safe? It's always been that way. Until now.

෨

In 1980, it took a full day to get to St. Kitts from their home in Sleepy Hollow, New York. Annie, still blonde back then, was with Buck and their two children, Will and Lauren. That was decades ago but Annie can still recall that first time they touched down on a barely paved stretch of blacktop. The pilot simply pushed aside the curtain separating the cockpit from passengers in the back of the small twin engine Liat and announced, "Welcome to St. Kitts." There was no flight attendant and certainly no drink service in the tiny aisle.

After that first bumpy landing on St. Kitts, they ducked out the small door and onto flip-down steps that jiggled, bouncing under the weight of feet as they climbed down. Outside in the night air, it was dark and there was no modern terminal, just a small building. A guy waved a flashlight directing them to a hot, muggy, un-air-conditioned welcome center on the side of the runway. They were dragging physically, exhausted after a long travel day but the scent out there was overwhelming, new to their noses and a wake-up call; a green, fresh, sweet, mildly caramel fragrance coming from something un-nameable-growing-right-there-in-the-fields next to this airport. It was sugar cane, they would learn, and the island was once covered in it, fresh fields overlapping the edges of that bare basic runway in fact. In the dark, sweet, hot, humid air, they heard squeaking, chirping, beeping, trilling up and down, so melodious and soothing.

"What's that sound Mom?" Will, her son, asked. He was 7 on this first trip. Yes, she remembers this.

"I'm not sure," Annie admitted.

"It's the tree frogs," Buck added. He was carrying 4-year-old Lauren, her head on his shoulder, awake but sleepy. Annie sometimes thinks back to this night. She had needed to get away from her real world desperately, to get out of her muddy mind and the what-if-only thoughts that plagued her. But tree frogs? Really! Oh my God. How did he know that? Her husband Buck, age 79 now and still her go-to guy, is a walking, talking, frustrating encyclopedia at times. He may not remember birthdays, appointments, or where the scotch tape is kept but esoteric facts are his forte. That time, it was tree frogs.

11

"They live in trees, not in water," he explained to his son. Will took it all in, mesmerized.

Annie laughed out loud right there on the tarmac, feeling weightless for the first time in months. Though she was tired and ought to have been cranky, an unconscious but familiar pressure on her panic buttons lifted. Her body pulled itself off its self-set anxiety pedal. She felt at home in this foreign place, right away, that first night. And when she was handed a free, not-too-sweet, just right citrusy rum punch inside the small passenger arrival area, this immediate dance of mutual admiration was clinched. Island plus Annie; okay now.

"Mmmmmm Buck," she said back then, "this is exactly what I need."

That was so many years ago.

In that upstairs bedroom's rising panic, Abigail answers, a little calmer than her older sister. Yes, that's Abby, the 15-year-old with the shaggy, short-cropped haircut trying definitively to act and look nothing like her sister with the long brown hair. Annie can attest from experience; this Abigail is unruffled in a crisis. She should have started her questioning with her. Abigail's brain and powers of observation are working here.

"Yes Grammy, I saw something too. I think - but I'm not really sure - that I heard a click and sliding sound as the door opened wider. Then, he must have been crawling toward Ellie's bed. On the floor...by the door." She points. "But...I was half asleep. I can't be sure."

"He?" Annie asks. "A man? Not a dog?"

"Not a dog!" Both girls shout in unison and in sudden acknowledgement of the same truth, their voices rising, building exponentially on the growing panic and seriousness of the situation.

"Ellie," Abby shouts, "He took her. He took her."

They rush around Ellie's empty bed to the balcony. The glass door has been pushed almost fully open. When they went to sleep last night, the girls had left it ajar so they could hear the tree frogs and feel the cool Caribbean night air. Now, stepping outside to look out, up and down, all three are blind-sided. How could this happen? Here, in St. Kitts? In this moment, all three are scared but Annie's is a bigger, wider, monstrous explosion of fear threatening to overwhelm her ability to move or to think. This is flesh of her flesh, a child of her child. Nowhere in her 74-year-long timeline of life, travel and experience has she ever imagined this kind of horror. Maybe she should have but Goddamn, what's wrong with optimism? Here at the tail end of her life, she's able to view the whole truth of what is happening with honesty; this is serious, these things do happen to people, other people. You have been so insanely lucky old girl, up until now. Yes, she sees exactly where she is; in a very bad place. Don't cry. Don't you dare cry, she commands herself. Or God forbid, don't you panic. You can't afford to lose it. You know what it is like to lose a child. Not another.

"Ellie," she hollers from the balcony, "Ellie, I will find you. It's going to be okay. It's okay." Then, again in a voice now growing louder with angry determination and resolution, "Ellie, I will find you! It's okay. It's okay." She repeats this line she picked up seven decades ago from her mother, an eternal optimist. It's going to be okay? But is it? That is ridiculous? Is she being stupid here?

Only minutes have passed. Not more than five, maybe ten. Her granddaughter must be right out there, not far. There were no signs or sounds of a vehicle. She would have heard that. Her bedroom is just off the driveway, in the front of the house and closer to the road. It was a quiet night. He must have come from behind. He, this person, oh God, this kidnapper, she names the word for the first time, can't possibly travel fast uphill, carrying her Ellie.

The mountain is dotted with new and older homes, all dark at this hour of the morning, too early in the day and season for activity or signs of life. Is he carrying Ellie? Dragging her? How did he do this? She looks up to a looping, swaying string of streetlights moving gently in the Atlantic Ocean breeze on the road high up there, way above her house. No signs of life. She sees scrubby trees, wind-blown palms, patches of old sugar cane, but no people moving. Could he have gone down around front to the road? Not that way. Too obvious, she decides. She didn't hear anything before that first sound inside the house upstairs. He had to come down from behind and is probably going up now, she suspects. He went up. Yes, yes, she thinks. Having an intuition that feels definitive makes her calmer.

Oh God. This is her safe place. This island. This house tucked into a grove of palms, red flowers of Poinciana trees, and flowering bushes. It's one of several in a line of hillside getaways. She looks up to the top of the mountain behind the house again. She has hiked up there and knows the best way to go. She's still strong, seventy-plus strong but come on, face it, 74 years old after all. Is it do-able? Her nerve wobbles. She can see the roads running horizontally, then some leading straight up. Higher still are those switch-backing, roughly paved, one-car wide, sometimes impassable roads that weave drunkenly into and over the landscape, waiting for builders and investors to come. The St. Kitts government and its local developers, always legitimately desperate for income, operate on the same model espoused in that baseball movie, Field of Dreams: if you build it, they will come. But real construction comes in fits and starts. Sometimes in stops. She's taken a few of the roads with Buck as well as the little trails in, out, up, and over to the other side.

"Oh Ellie, my poor girl," she groans with hands shaking and heart breaking, before turning back to Abigail and Lizzie. "Go downstairs and call the police. The emergency number is by the telephone. Tell them to get here immediately. Tell them that a young woman...a child," she corrects herself, "your cousin has been stolen...kidnapped." That word doesn't come easy at all.

"Grammy, I'm scared," Lizzie says. "Where is she?"

"I don't know. I don't know. Out there, up there. Go girls. You can do this. Lizzie, Abby, I love you both so much. Call for help. Get to the kitchen right now. I'll be down in a second."

Her brunettes with their long legs growing longer by day, dash down the steps, pulling on lights as they run through familiar house territory, heading for the kitchen and the landline, the most reliable telephone for local island calls. Annie pauses for a moment outside on the balcony looking up at the mountain, pushing, shoving her thoughts into order. What once felt quaintly backward about being out of touch without good cell service or reliable internet suddenly turns dangerous here. She takes one more visual sweep for signs of anyone or anything moving on the mountain before she follows the girls downstairs. On the ground floor, she turns to her bedroom, not the kitchen. She has made up her mind.

CHAPTER THREE

3:55 AM

Like Alice in Wonderland, Annie goes down a rabbit hole. She is not exactly the person she was just yesterday.

---

*H*er inner clock is ticking. Loudly. Definitively. If you were there, you might even hear it. That loud. Time is not on her side. The suitcase is open on the floor near the antique wooden dresser. Annie hasn't unpacked yet. There had been no time yet for that and now this; this ugly awful very goddamn personal assault on her Ellie, on her, on her life, on her family. How could this happen? Who is to blame? She stares at the old European wooden chest of drawers and is instantly and irrationally angry. There it is, representing a nasty colonial era in the Caribbean. She growls crazily at this large, ornate piece of furniture as she tosses clothing aside on the floor looking for what she needs.

Goddamn that hardwood chest probably shipped from England when plantations dotted the Kittitian hillsides. It is beautiful. Yes, but... this perfect piece represents rich getting richer, oppression and poverty. Great houses, yes for God's sake, they were called great because that's what they were: great polished hard wood floors, great doors that opened on all sides to catch Caribbean Sea breezes; great wrap-around porches for sipping great rum punch while looking over the beautiful blue water; a sweet dream but only for the rich foreigners. Not so great for everyone else on any small island, so many still poor, still, and maybe always in debt to the rich and famous, like all the small states in the world, island nations searching always and forever for financial stability, begging bigger nations for a way out and up. Why is this so hard?

"Jeez," Annie mutters, searching quickly now through the pile of clothes spilling onto the floor from the half-emptied suitcase. "This is a nightmare." Her mind keeps flashing to Ellie. Where is she now? Who is this madman who took her from bed? Why did he do this? Is she okay? Alive? Wait, wait a minute, why didn't the girls hear a scream, not a single sound of resistance up there in the bedroom? Why, in God's name, didn't Ellie cry out? Is she dead already? Don't go there. DO NOT ALLOW YOURSELF TO GO THERE. Breathe. Think. Even she, with her grandmother-in-charge super hearing, heard nothing from Ellie.

She checks the time.

✆

Of all the English colonies, not just those in the Caribbean Sea, St. Kitts was once among the wealthiest with its fertile volcanic soil and ideal growing climate. Battles were fought over the land rights of soldiers, sailors and settlers from England,

France, Spain, and Holland, while the locals who had lived on this lush green, mountainous island for centuries were enslaved, nearly and sometimes completely wiped out. Fortunes were made in sugar and rum for the landholders who built wealth on the hardworking backs of slaves, perfectly lovely human beings, so many poor souls kidnapped and brought from Africa.

At the National Museum on St. Kitts on that last trip before the pandemic lockdown, Annie was surprised to learn that women - the majority were women! - not men, did the back-breaking work in the cane fields. So many deaths and havoc in the history of this West Indian tropical treasure, not quite a vacation getaway back then, when St. Kitts was the world's leader in sugar cane production. Those crazy Europeans seriously believed that Africans could not feel physical pain in the same way as all humans. But here she is, a rich American woman, taking advantage of this geographically spectacular island too. Is she complicit?

Annie glances around her bedroom, still scared but also raging mad about what is happening here, for everything that once happened here on her island. Is her outrage connected to Ellie's disappearance? She can't think straight, whispering to herself, "I don't know. I don't know." Did it take a personal assault to set her mind straight about this privileged life. Look at the finely carved piece of furniture. It shouts of colonial human catastrophe and what her very own ancestors may have done, not done, ignored, or misunderstood. Stop. Settle. Oh my God, think clearly. Don't go off track. Look forward. Not back. Think now. Focus, she begs herself. Ellie. Ellie. Ellie.

Grabbing the black yoga pants from the floor, she pulls off her pajamas, puts one leg after another into the pants and then tugs her sleeveless black tee over her head before grabbing the cell phone. Take it. Even if it doesn't work all the time, she might get a blip of connection and be able to call for help from the top of the mountain. The airport is right over on the other side. It's wired over there. Maybe there will be Wi-Fi somewhere else along the way. She shoves the phone into the pocket on the side of her pants and puts on her watch. Socks, sneaks, and then she's ready. Wait a minute. Be prepared. She adds the Swiss Army knife from the nightstand on Buck's side of the bed and looks around for any other possible tool or defensive weapon. Ah. She grabs the little bottle of hand sanitizer spray she used on the airplane. It fits into her side pocket too. Protection? To spray into a kidnapper's face? Oh jeez. So lame. But maybe, just maybe.

"Girls, girls, what did the police say?" she yells heading toward the big open kitchen, going around the wide staircase and through the living room.

"They're coming," Abigail says. "The police are coming from headquarters in Basseterre, not the Frigate Bay Road station. That one isn't open until 8 AM."

"The officer told us to stay where we are. They will be here soon," Lizzie adds.

"I don't believe it," Annie says shaking her head. This was St. Kitts after all. No one on this island ever moves quickly, especially at 4 AM. There's even a sign out near her favorite beach bar telling visitors, "Rush Slowly." Looking at her watch, she considers the distance to the main police station in the downtown capital city of Basseterre, 7 miles away, and does the math. At least 10 minutes have passed, and she adds this to the fear that no one is awake enough down there at the station or interested in hurrying; so probably add 10 more minutes, way too long. Maybe even more time, in fact. Nothing good ever happens in this bewitching hour. How often has she thought this back home? How many times has Buck agreed when they were waiting up far too late for one of their children out way past curfew? She hates this time of night. Or is it morning?

The girls suddenly notice that their grandmother is dressed, in black, wearing sneakers, ready for something?

"Oh noooooo, no. Where are you going Grammy?"

"I'm going to get Ellie," she says. "You two stay here and tell the police when they arrive that I have taken the trail out the back of the house, the one going up toward the mountain. I think I can see the house from up there so I may be able to see when they've arrived here. It's only a hunch but I'm guessing that he had to go up that way. I didn't hear a car or commotion out front of the house. So, let the officers know where I am heading."

"Oh Grammy, no," Abigail says again. "No. No. No. Don't do this. Don't go up there alone. Wait. The officer said to wait." Abigail could be so definitive. Her sister calls that bossy. Annie disagrees. There is no time to waste here.

"Time is not on our side here. Ellie is in danger. I need to go now. If I stay until the police arrive, we might never find her. Our girl is in terrible, terrible trouble." Just saying this out loud sends a chilling and maternal message to her entire body, the hair on the skin of her arms prickles up, her stomach lurches. Do all mothers feel this when a child is in danger? Yes, yes for sure. Is she going to be sick? Not now. No time for that.

❧

A memory of the St. Kitts downtown police station pops up. Annie has always appreciated this Kittitian force but…and this is a big BUT. They make choices sometimes. They are understaffed and can be unprepared. It's tough for these gentle guys...and yes, she would call them gentle. There are no knees put to necks here on this island and no Black Lives Matter groups protesting blunt police force.

A former British colony, St. Kitts prohibits guns and ammunition without written permission of the Commission of Police. Even shock batons, stun guns, pepper spray and mace are outlawed. Crime rates are low and worries about homes being broken into or things stolen are insignificant. Yes, there are exceptions, purses snatched, drunken exchanges, drug busts, property disputes, but still not much of a violent persuasion here in her paradise. This is not Aruba where a young woman can disappear, her body never to be found, and a kidnapper nearly getting away with his despicable crime. Or is it?

Keeping order on this small island, 28 miles around, shaped like a plump-bellied fish, with a long, thin tail that tickles out toward its sister island, smaller Nevis, can be complicated. Hordes of drinking, partying tourists land at the airport or arrive by sea on two, three, maybe even four daily cruise ships in the winter season carrying thousands of passengers who often need attention day or night. Busloads of visitors tour around the island and up narrow, local streets into the hills. Annie truly gets the dilemma the local police force faces.

Not long before Covid 19 arrived and the world locked down, St. Kitts set a record with 10,629 cruise passengers arriving in a single day. The island's population is only 34,918. This onslaught of strangers can set off a clash of rich versus poor, an outside world invading the space of these easy-going island folks. The flood of tourists seeking Caribbean dreams and escapist excitement creates a hectic, sometimes overloaded imbalance of power and money that easily tips the scales of justice occasionally. People get lost, misguided, misunderstood and then angry or plain crazy. On her last visit to the island before the Covid lockdown, Annie encountered a naked man out back near her patio wearing just a yellow plastic grocery bag to cover his groin. He must have come from Upper Conaree and had shoved his skinny legs into the handles of the bag – awkward! – for his hike down the hill behind her house. Obviously, he believed that this state of undress was quite okay.

"He was so weird," she had told Buck later that day.

"Aww poor fellow," her husband said while working in the garden that edges up to the stone pavers out back.

"I know, but do you think I should have called the police?" she asked.

"What would they be able to do?"

"Maybe locate his family? Get him help of some kind? Some clothes?" she laughed.

"I wouldn't worry about it," he said. "Let him be, even if it means being naked."

They both chuckled but sighed at the situation, sad but so true about St. Kitts sometimes.

Annie also remembers what happened years ago when her purse was snatched at the Saturday morning market in Basseterre. She and Buck were tourists then, not homeowners on the island. Browsing the stalls for trinkets and a good looking, vine-ripened tomato, she probably did stand out in the crowd of shoppers. Both are tall; Annie is 5'9" and Buck is 6'4". Together, they stand out, perhaps a rich couple on holiday? They could often sense that they were drawing glances from Kittitians as well as the tourists from the cruise ships who come ashore and mob the streets looking for bargains. Her bag was gone in an instant. How stupid, she thought, to have had it draped over her shoulder on such a thin strap, so easily snapped or cut. Too trusting. Annie, she's been told, be more careful. The policeman stationed at the Circus, a downtown roundabout modeled after Piccadilly Circus in London, genuinely wanted to help. Witnesses nearby on the waterfront told this officer they recognized the purse-snatcher and could identify him. Someone thought she knew where he lived, for God's sake.

"Please," Annie had begged, "can't you get the bag back? I don't care about the money. But I need my cards, driver's license, keys, and so much more from that little purse. Please." But all she was offered was lovely lip service. Was that a wink? And a promise that someone would look further into the matter. She, after all, was just visiting the island then. These rich foreigners who jet in, projecting privilege, outsider privilege. The thief? Well, he grew up here and was one of them. Who mattered more here? The outsider or the insider? But that's not a fair way to think. Both are right. All deserve justice, true? Of course. Of course.

Later at the station house on Court Street where they went to pursue the loss, she and Buck pushed their case politely. That was when they met Sergeant Valamine.

In a British accent, this officer apologized for her loss, held up his hands, opening his palms in a gesture of surrender.

"What can I do, Madame? There's not much I can do," he said dismissively, making his choice before making a move to help. This couple in front of him? Hmmm, I don't think so. The young man who snatched the purse? Well, maybe not so much going right for him in this life? Let's go easy here, he didn't say out loud but surely projected.

"Really now, how much cash was in your purse?" he asked

implying that any amount was negligible to Annie. They let it go.
She and Buck turned and left, not as angry as they were sad to see
the way the situation had gone. Where was the justice? Maybe this
was leftover injustice, a payback embedded in Kittitian history? A
part of her wants to complain; why couldn't these people be more
appreciative of the money and jobs outsiders bring to the little
island? After all, tourism is so essential to the economy, isn't it?
Yet her inner moral compass sees the dilemma clearly. All that
injustice? All those years of no justice for all here on the island?
The landowners, outsiders, foreigners had ruled for centuries. Now
the rules had changed.

Nearly 4 AM in the kitchen, Annie quickly weighs this
muddle of memories and impressions left by these local heroes
knowing that she knows best right here, right now. She must go
and she must go fast. Taking each granddaughter's cheeks
separately into her hands (the hands that look more and more like
her own mother's did), one by one, she assures them, "I can do
this. Grammy can do this. Trust me."

CHAPTER FOUR

4 AM

Google "grandmother hypothesis" and the term
pops up in scientific literature. Grandmothering,
it turns out, can help women remain vigorous
beyond their fertile years, forcing them to share
wisdom and vitality.

*W*ithout another word, just another kiss blown to the girls, her lovely Lizzie and audacious Abigail, Annie steps out into the night air on the patio that backs up to the sloping string of hills and mountains behind her house heading for the trail that goes up. She turns back to the balcony and the upstairs bedroom where this nightmare began moments ago. She can see clearly in the moonlight. This moon is huge, one for the record books, but she can't remember which kind of moon: Harvest? Hunter? What is the name of the one that comes after, in November? Beaver! That's it. Her mind is a mess, jumping, darting, flipping frighteningly all over but it's working. Her mental stew stops bubbling over when she sees the wooden trellis on the side of the house that stretches from the ground up to that second floor. Partially crushed, with rungs broken and vines hanging loose, it's a mess now and she shakes her head. Oh God. So that is how he got up there. This guy must be lightweight and sure-footed to have done this! It's not a Goddamn ladder but a trellis for vines to climb. Her house, with the golden gingerbread trim, shimmers in the bright moonlight.

That trellis, built by Buck for their first garden makeover, was never designed to hold the weight of one person, let alone two. The wood is ornamental only and clematis and snapdragons are mangled, trampled, pulled off vine-y footings. Who did this? Oh Ellie, she wants to shout. Why weren't you screaming? Calling for help? That's not like you at all, she decides. She's a tough resourceful kid. So why was she silent this morning? Oh my God, she didn't because she couldn't. Ellie didn't scream because she had been knocked out. If she could have, she would have but she didn't make a sound. What in God's name did this guy do to her?

The steep road up through Lucas and into the Conaree Hills is one Annie has taken before, in a car, on a walk, hiking with family, friends, fellow travelers, but never at four o'clock in the morning and racing uphill or at least trying to go as fast as she can. When they first purchased the place, she and Buck wanted to see their extravagant adventure in Caribbean real estate from high above. They were relishing the reward of living long enough to reach this dream on their bucket list; their Kittitian kingdom, a home away from home in a place they both had fallen in love with over the decades. What did it look like from up there? From the top of the mountain...well it was spectacular with the Atlantic Ocean out front, across a gorgeous golf course with flags on each green flapping gently in the nearly constant breeze, and that superb Marriott over on its big beach. Nice hotel but hard to grasp or love

26

at first because the scale of building and meandering pools outstripped the smaller old Caribbean scale of the Frigate Bay neighborhood. From up there on high above their house, they could even catch a glimpse the Caribbean Sea off to the other side.

Tonight, this Beaver — what a goofy name for a moon, right? a native American namesake — is so full on its way down that she can see where she's going. Her gaze goes everywhere, darting, daring the kidnapper to show up or make a movement. Ellie, where are you? Who has done this? Why? The moon above is a gift, she decides, maybe a little miracle of extra light this night. Just maybe this gift, like the gift of Ellie herself being born on Annie's birthday, will grow bigger. The ground beneath her sneakers is hard. It's been too dry lately here on her green tropical island. She starts to sprint heading for the concrete maze of roads going up and over, instinctively thinking, yes, go up and over. Go. Go. Go. That's where he might take her. Up there, away, to the other side, not here on her side of the mountains. She's okay, a little calmer now, thinking I can do this. I can do this. Thank you, Mom, for those longevity genes. Annie's mother died peacefully at age 104 with oxygen levels that rarely dipped to the astonishment of the healthcare team who watched over her that final year.

This range of low mountains, none here with sharp peaks, reminds Annie of a multi-humped camel curling around the island's eastern edge on this Atlantic side. There's a chunk of one hump carved out near the end, creating a cliff and deep pass to the other side. Higher up now, she looks down toward her house but still can't see movement of any kind. Too quiet. No sign of anyone going anywhere. No police? Where can they be? Listen. Listen closer, you crazy grandmother. Yes, you are crazy to be up here. Where in God's name, do you think you are going? What will you be able to do when you get there? Stop. Stop. Right now. Breathe.

Go girl. Just go. You are wasting time. Bugs biting now.
Damn them. These no-see-ums with their bright nasty red, itchy
bites that can last for days. She stops short with sudden stinging
around her right ankle. Fire ants? Oh jeez. Did she step into a
mound? That's going to hurt for days.

In her sleeveless top, arms bare and free. Staying cool in
your seventies has always been her bugaboo so she opts for
sleeveless even though her days of girlish arms are long gone. Who
cares? She and her 70- and 80-something friends still refer to each
other as girls. Yet why not? When should women stop calling each
other girl friends? Never! They agree. Even her mother would call
Annie, "My girl," with much love until the day she died. And with
a silent thank you to her yoga teacher, she sprints again.

Annie practices yoga every day. Stay strong, she's been
telling herself. Years of working out and running come in handy
now. What she once thought was a gift to herself, a yearning to
stay physically fit and mentally sharp through regular, everyday
exercise, has turned out to be a godsend, perhaps a gift for her
granddaughter.

～

"I'm perfectly okay without grandchildren," she used to say.
"Honestly, I just want my daughter and son to be happy, contented
human beings. They don't need to have children to please me.
Their lives belong to them, not me," she insisted in those years
before her kids' paths to parenting took first place in their busy
lives. Then, with one, two, three, four, five, and then six
grandbabies arriving in a raucous, rapid row, she learned that the
grandparenting gig was exhausting yes, but also so much fun and
enriching that she can't imagine finding her own path to wisdom
without this journey. Being able to see life through children's eyes,

especially your own grandchildren's, is a wonder, and intimately different from parenting itself. She tells others, almost everyone if they let her; just let it happen. Don't hold back or get caught up, mired or trapped in your own adult fears or insecurities. Volunteer to help. Mess up if you must. Say you are sorry. Go when they call. Be there. Don't offer unsolicited advice. Hug. Kiss. Love them unconditionally. She appreciates her childless and grandchild-less friends and family members, wise perhaps but missing pieces of their human puzzles. Empty places in their hearts, minds not stretched to selfless proportions. They are like tapestries with tepid colors, no deep textures, unfinished works, not always by their own choice, of course. And still beautiful but without what she has come to believe are essential ingredients for understanding the fullness of life.

Ellie was born on Annie's birthday, a happy bonus gift she met for the first time 13 years ago. Yet, Ellie was a gift that arrived with strings attached, health puzzles to solve, even before her "birth" day. A prenatal testing prognosis during Lauren's pregnancy had everyone holding their breath with anxiety until this new baby took her first. She was fine, perfectly normal. The test had been wrong and this baby's Apgar scores were off the charts. Sighs of whew, all clear, full speed ahead were tangible, right there in the delivery room. But worries about Ellie's health would never quite disappear. Parents never forget the near misses, do they? Worries bubble beneath the surface of smoothly flowing life, refusing to go away, get lost. Annie's own mother would recall the time her son, Annie's older brother, came up their back porch steps with a knife wound in his head. This was a memory that even popped up just days before she died.

"Mom, that was more than 50 years ago," Annie would remind her.

"I know. I know that. I'm not crazy. Just old," her dying mother would agree, "My memory is as clear now as it was then. I will never forget how scared I was. And why in heaven's name, does everyone assume that old equals Alzheimer's?"

In middle school, Ellie's haunted health returned with bouts of gut pain, nausea, diarrhea. She started losing weight, and all these unnerving symptoms were diagnosed as irritable bowel syndrome (IBS). God bless that pediatric gastroenterologist and the nutritionist who found pathways to a manageable future for this sweet-natured girl. Ellie had become afraid to eat but with guidance, she wised up to what worked, what stayed down, and what didn't. No ice cream? Who cares? Give up pizza? Okay! No problem. Medication did its magic too. This granddaughter, who had been thrown curve balls early in life, grew more resilient, developing a stoic approach to what life can bring.

"Mom," Lauren told Annie proudly, "she doesn't seem to worry about what she can't control and reminds herself that things could be worse. Did I tell you that Ellie has a friend who was diagnosed with bone cancer, a tumor near her knee?"

"No, oh my God. That poor child...and her family," Annie replied.

"Ellie rushed right there to be by her side, went into the hospital, sat by her bed. Brought schoolwork to her. Some of the other kids steered clear, uncomfortable about the situation."

"Oh Lauren, how awful. Why do kids do that?"

"They are just being kids, Mom. But not our Ellie. The doctors think this girl is going to be fine. What I'm most proud of is how Ellie has been with her throughout."

"Oh Lauren. She is so special. My spectacular granddaughter."

"You love that word spectacular Mom," Lauren laughs. "But for sure. This is an experience that is going to stay with Ellie."

∽

At 13, Ellie still sees life with the wonder of a child but colored by what any serious health issue can leave in its wake. If you met her, you'd sense the stronger emotional immune system that has come from her brush with illness. Maybe that's why she's hung onto fairy tales, dolls and dreams. She packed a Barbie for this trip and set it up by the side of the pool yesterday. Her cousins laughed, but in supportive glee. "Why not? El! Wish I had packed Ken!"

Blue-eyed and blonde like her mother Lauren, Ellie memorized each of the Walt Disney Frozen movies and watched them multiple times. All three girls on this Grammy vacation, even as adolescents, can't get enough of this shout-out to sisterhood. Ellie sings each line of every song as if she were Anna or Enya, her heroines, but her favorite character just might be Sven, Kristoff's sweet, goofy reindeer because of her love for animals. For this trip, Ellie has packed her Frozen flashlight. A flashlight for St. Kitts is always on her grandmother's packing list.

"It gets dark there at night girls and we may need flashlights to find our way home after a stroll," Annie reminded all three. Ellie packed hers, a toy with push-button sound effects from Frozen.

"Listen to this Grammy," she had asked trying to show her distracted grandmother this cool little toy. They had just arrived and were unpacking the car. Like any too-busy adult, Annie wasn't honestly paying attention when Ellie pressed each sound tab to

31

demonstrate.

"Awww El, how cute," she nodded with her mind miles away, making a shopping list mentally, planning a take-out dinner order, wondering if the sheets had been changed as she instructed the cleaning crew to do last week by phone. She is not really listening to Ellie. But she does hear the tinny toy sounds.

❦

Thank God for Annie's deep dreaming sleep earlier on this night. A fully REM-rested body has come in handy. Running up, up, up higher still, she is awake, alert and looking ahead with clear eyes. While she can't read a word without her 3.0 red-framed reading glasses, her distance vision is near perfect. So is her hearing which is why she catches the blip of faraway, tinny music. Music? How could that be? Where? What? Then that sound stops. She stops too hoping to catch it again. Hyper-alert, standing still she listens and hears, a cracking, crunching noise...like ice shards snapping in super cold temperatures.

"Whoosh. Whoosh...Crack...Snap." It's high-pitched, strange, wait, maybe tinkling glass? No, more like the sound of ice cracking and popping on a frozen lake, clearly impossible on a Caribbean night with a temperature of 72 degrees. Way too hot for ice anywhere up here. She shakes her head in dismay, disturbed by this weirdly odd noise. St. Kitts' temperatures are almost the same year-round. In late fall now, with a daily, mid-day high of 84 degrees Fahrenheit, the number doesn't dip far below 72 at night. Ice creaking and groaning with expansion and contraction? Incredible. Impossible. Then she hears it again; "Whoosh...Crack...Snap," faint but definitive. Annie catches it a third time and with this third snatch of sound comes a wisp of memory. This is something she recognizes. She has heard it before.

32

But where? Frustrated by her inability to place this sound, she wills herself to let it go momentarily, a skill she has perfected in old age. Let it go so it will come to her later.

"Oh Ellie, Ellie," she prays. "Stay calm. Stay alert. Stay with me."

Annie is too rooted in the real world to believe in telepathic communication but on this fantastical night, all bets are off on reality. Can this actually be her up here on the mountain at 4 AM? No, not possible, she would like to say. But yes, it is! The woman who has always been there right inside herself, is stronger than the stereotypes, faster than those laughable caricatures of old women, so over-the-hill of real life. Hah. She is right here, running as fast as she can and that is pretty-fast indeed. She pictures Ellie and tries sending her a message mentally with every ounce of her being. She whispers, "Come on Ellie. I know you girl. I know how strong you are. Look how far you have come in 13 years. Look inside yourself. You are resilient." And then she considers this person, the kidnapper, a monster, he must be, monstrous, a creep who has taken a love of her life, "Goddamn it. Goddamn you. Take me first."

But there is no time to waste.

CHAPTER FIVE

4:05 AM

How do people get to their personal here and now? So many pieces of experience go into an individual's psyche: the mind, soul, spirit. And let's not forget the pile up of micro-aggressions along the way; those little but catastrophic events can weigh as much as the big.

Ellie is dreaming. She is outside, on the mountain up behind the house, trying to wake up and thinking about donkeys, like the one she petted on the beach. Lady? Was that her name? Our girl can't seem to move arms or legs, let alone focus clearly on her situation. She is way too heavy, outside her body, but moving. She can feel herself swaying back and forth. Is she dreaming of that donkey? Wake up. Wake up. But she can't completely. It's all too heavy. She is too heavy. The dream, or wait, the memory returns; this is not a dream. It happened today. She's in and she's out but somehow, she knows, she just knows that this

34

really happened. This is happening to her. Yes, there was a donkey. There is a donkey here now.

⤚

Yesterday...12 noon...first full day back on St. Kitts

"What's his name?" Ellie asks the guy sitting on the ground under the tree where the donkey is tied. Cute boy, but not so cute. He's local for sure; a Kittitian with dreadlocks but sort of cute. She's not sure about that. Ellie has friends with dreadlocks back home on Long Island.

"Nuh he," this guy mumbles in that island dialect she can never quite understand completely. "Dem is guyl."

Guyl? Oh, he means girl! Kittitians slip easily from American English into a West Indian Creole native to their island.

"How sweet. Can I feed her?"

"E suit yuh. Lady."

Is he calling her Lady or is the donkey's name Lady?

Without waiting for an answer, Ellie approaches the donkey, gently patting her flank with a soft light touch, as if she were grooming the animal, nosing her own nose closer to this soft sweet being. She pulls out the rest of her egg sandwich with the other hand, the breakfast Grammy insisted she bring along when she couldn't finish it back at the house. Our girl likes animals, dogs, cats and now, maybe donkeys?

"Here, here," she says, "Don't be afraid Lady. I won't hurt you." Patting the donkey's flank softly, she coos sweet nothings to the animal instinctively, patting and stroking all the while.

At the sound of this gentle feminine voice...so different from the commands and whacks she's been hearing, feeling, living with for days...the animal turns her head completely around to see Ellie. Peripheral vision is great but only goes straight on, ahead, or down the nose for donkeys. This head turn means she wants to take a closer look. This girl is wearing a pink bathing suit with matching pink cover-up, one of 13 swimsuits Ellie has packed for this trip. Lips pulling back to show big teeth, Lady makes a braying sound that sounds like laughter.

"Aha, you are funny," Ellie laughs in return and when she holds out a piece of that sandwich, the donkey gobbles it up quickly, waiting for more.

"Wow girl," she says. "Lady, were you hungry? Yes, of course you were hungry."

What Ellie didn't know was that donkeys have an acute olfactory sense as well as a superb mental capacity to remember and learn. They love sweets. So, it must have been the sweetness of ketchup on the egg sandwich that appealed to Lady's taste buds. Centuries old misconceptions have deemed donkeys dumb but in contests with dogs and horses, their equine cousins, they are better at problem solving. They remember good and bad experiences for a long time, up to two years, trainers attest. And in terms of olfactory issues, they themselves don't smell bad at all. They'll remember a smell 100 times better than a human.

Mid-day, donkeys don't see well, however, so Ellie was probably blurry to Lady. Standing there under a tree, even in her bright pink bathing suit and coverup, but especially next to a wide sun-high beach reflecting the noon of a cloudless Caribbean day, Ellie was not as clear visually as her good-natured intentions were towards this instinctive animal. Donkeys prefer the dim of early morning for getting things done or better yet the night. With twice as many rods, or photoreceptive cells in their eyes, a donkey excels at night vision, better than humans, especially when detecting certain colors. They see panoramically even if they do have to turn their heads completely around to miss that puddle or rock right in the middle because of that blind spot right in front.

"She is sleepy," the guy tells her. "Dis nap time."

"Okay, sorry I disturbed her."

Then he says something Ellie doesn't quite catch. "Wa sweet a goat mout sour a ee bottom."

Honestly, these people could switch language gears so quickly, going from perfectly understandable English to gibberish, at least to Ellie's American ears. Of course, she knew his dialect wasn't nonsense, it was his rightful native tongue, but what was he saying? Was there a tinge of torment there? She could sense something off kilter in him, not quite right. If she had known that his slangy saying translated, "What is sweet in the goat's mouth is sour at the bottom," would boomerang back and hit him, not her, she might not have been so insulted. This tidbit of Kittitian wisdom means, "Some things which seem enjoyable at first have unfortunate events."

"What did you say?"

He smiles condescendingly, making her feel even more uncomfortable. He's sweaty, and now she can detect an edgy undercurrent. Are his hands shaking? Nose running? Should she be frightened of him?

Turning back to the beach, right over there across the narrow one-way, single lane road, she laughs because this encounter with the donkey made her forget why she'd left her cousins and grandmother over in the sand in the first place; to buy bottles of water at the shack under the palm trees.

"Grammy," she says after returning to their sand chairs on the Frigate Bay beach. "Guess what I did?"

"What?" Annie asks absentmindedly. She's started reading a new novel and is blissful to be on this beach with her girls.

"I met a donkey. Her name is Lady."

"You are so funny, Ellie. Maybe you should be thinking of veterinary school not medical school. You know there's a vet school here on St. Kitts."

"Oh no, Grammy, I want to become a doctor for people, not pets."

"Oh Ellie. You are spectacular," Annie says before adding, "Girls, who's hungry? Want to walk up to the Shiggidy for lunch?"

Annie is still smiling about Ellie's determination to become a doctor, an idea she has shared before, not only to study medicine but to specialize in an issue she knows intimately: irritable bowel syndrome.

Grammy points up the beach. "Let's go!" What a beautiful day in paradise, she's thinking, not a care in our world for five blissful days ahead. "We can celebrate our first full day here with lobster or barbecued chicken!" she announces.

∽

On St. Kitts, this Shiggidy Shack bar/restaurant is legendary, known best for its sunsets but just as much for the divine food eaten on picnic tables with your feet in the sand. At first, Mr. X's

Shiggidy was not much more than a thrown-together piece of cast-off carpentry sitting high in the sand on the furthest southeasterly point of Frigate Bay Beach. This sand bar is called the Strip, a long narrow pinch of land along the Caribbean Sea, now dotted with small eating and drinking spots, with a big salt pond inland and behind, back where Ellie met Lady, the donkey. Squatters rights here! If you build it, you own it. Beachgoers, like our girls this day, can choose from so many new dirty-down bars and restaurants to have lunch, dinner, or a sunset cocktail. Shiggidy is where everyone wants to go. It grew from an ice cream truck that once serviced the customers using Mr. X's water sports and is now a favorite.

By this fall of 2021, it had a roof, a bar that was so high it only worked well if you were tall, a few stools and picnic tables sitting out in the sand right up to water's edge. There were lots of regular customers from the tourists to the politicians, bankers, foreigners including lots of Russian newcomers and long-timers...all flocking to Shiggidy to watch the sun go down. These people would gather not only to drink and enjoy the buzz of island gossip but also to catch a green flash just as the water finished gulping down the last of the day's sunshine. When meteorological conditions are just right, this distinct green whiff of light can be visible briefly on the upper rim of the sun...if you are lucky. Luck must be on your side to see it, some say. The optical phenomenon lasts briefly, no more than a second or two, when the earth's atmosphere causes the light to separate or refract into different colors. The best time to catch it is 10 minutes before complete sunset. Annie has seen it only once there on the horizon.

That day, the girls' plans didn't include trying to catch a green flash or Ricky, the fire-eater, either. Ricky, who really did poke rods of flame deep down into his throat, came after dark and they planned to be long gone, having dinner back at Grammy's

39

house, just the four of them, by the pool, and afterward sound asleep in their beds. They were still jet-lagged from the travel day before.

Right then, they were just hungry for a Shiggidy Shack lunch. "Come on girls. Let's hurry. I'm starving!"

Walking up the beach, Ellie looks back past the small buildings and palm trees lining the Strip to glimpse the donkey one more time. So sweet. Is Lady still tied up there? But there is no sign of her or the guy who had given her the willies. Cute but certainly not so cute at all. The donkey, however? Adorable. Maybe they will meet again? Not a chance, she decides. They are gone.

◆

On the mountain this November night, Lady lumbers along, breathing in the scent of the girl, Ellie, tied to her back with legs down one side, head hanging heavily, obviously unconscious, on the other. She feels this girl intimately, protectively. And this preternaturally stubborn, determined donkey refuses to be hurried, not even by the jerk of a kidnapper yanking a rope, angrily arguing for her to go faster. She won't. Not for him anyway. Some animal lovers point to a historical ornery streak in donkeys but that's not exactly the truth. They simply know their task and insist on moving at a personal pace, whether that be fast or slow. Gently swaying, Lady is savoring the soft, pleasant touch of this girl's cheek on her flank; a memory that will stay with our animal always. She's been high up here on this mountain before and lives with an ancestral sense of ease around here. There is no doubt for her that she's going up and over to the old plantation, the place where they, her kind, were all born.

"Come. Come you dumb donkey," the guy hollers in frustration, yanking harder, trying to get this girl to where he has promised she would be by dawn. His name is Kennedy. Yes, it sounds like a name given in American presidential honor but it's not. And there is nothing honorable or presidential about what he is doing here. In fact, he's not quite of sound mind here and hasn't been for too many weeks squandered in a drug and alcohol-induced haze.

᷍

Annie stops to breathe in the early morning air. Like her childhood cartoon heroine created way back there in the 40s, Brenda Starr, Girl Reporter, Annie followed her high school dreams into the world of women's magazines where she learned all sorts of lessons. Perhaps one of the most important didn't have anything to do with pitching or putting stories on paper when she worked at Ladies Home Journal and Good Housekeeping in Manhattan. The lesson came from Nathan, the dapper decorating editor in the 1970s who shared a wisdom Annie didn't get at first.

"Never look busy," he'd insist imperiously. Impeccably dressed, tall, calm, cool, Nathan didn't bow under pressure, never rushed, or showed hesitation or weakness. He'd shake his head in a tsk-tsk, don't-do-that-way, appraising her piled-high desk with its half-finished projects, mountains of manuscripts, sloping slush piles and frantic energy there in the hallway where she worked. There was a long line of editorial assistants, plugged into hallway desks, leading down to the editor-in-chief's corner office; always a man, never a woman in Annie's experience during those dark ages of males dominating a female world of magazine journalism. Nathan could hear Annie's boss, a guy who believed that flexing his I'm-in-charge-here-I-know-everything muscles was the secret to success. His dramatic directives from that big-windowed office opposite Annie's open-air cubicle would spread out like a frantic emotional virus, infecting all, especially a much-younger Annie. Sometimes Nathan would shake his head at the noise and nod his head at our future grandmother like a parent teaching a toddler.

"No, no, no," he'd whisper to Annie. "Head high girl. Do not react."

"But what else can I do?" she'd defend. "He's my boss."

Nathan would lower his chin reassuringly, smile and try to assure her. By not reacting, she could build strength. Calm, cool, imperious, he would teach her by example. Be cool under pressure was his lesson. His own creative work was always done on time without rushing but most important to his success…and eventually Annie's…was his demeanor, a body language that spoke seriously and knowingly even when his mouth was closed. It took our grandmother years to understand and perhaps only in looking back, that Nathan, an "interior" decorating expert, was teaching her personal "interior" decorating she would be able to use throughout her life and especially in a crisis. Sometimes you just need to hide what's inside.

Here with no time to spare, Annie isn't thinking of this advice, of Nathan, that wise, wonderful man, or any of her childhood heroines. What has kicked in was something only someone facing a life-or-death emergency might understand. In this moment, her adrenaline-fueled fight or flight reflex has gone into high gear. A flood of enzymes and proteins are released. Known as "hysterical strength," the word hysterical is clearly off base. She isn't crazy. This is the only option after all. She can do this. She believes that she can do this. Can fear create a superhuman? Evidence may be scarce, but anecdotes are plentiful. Adrenaline, we do know, affects muscle twitch and endurance. And, with a child in extreme danger, some believe that motherhood and its grown-up twin, grandmother-hood, might be fuel enough to fight for a life.

Annie? Really? She is 74 years old, not young or a superhero by any stretched definition. Yet, think about it: this is her granddaughter, a love of her life, someone especially precious because Ellie, of all her grandchildren, might not be well enough physically to withstand an extreme, physically dangerous situation. Perhaps the drama of tonight is also intensified because of the baby girl Annie lost. Still such a sharp memory, her stomach lurches anytime she lets it return. Back then for a time, she nearly lost sight of herself. Not Ellie now. Please no, no, no, don't take her from us, from me. There would be no over-thinking here, Annie tells herself. No fear. She can't bear to lose another child and she will do anything to find this precious girl and bring her home safely. Wouldn't any grandmother feel the same? The very thought of possible failure here and how it would ripple through her family's life makes it difficult to breathe. Families do fall apart. And if this ends badly, if Ellie is gone forever, she will be at fault, the person who put an end to life as she has known it. Oh my God, and all for a frivolous vacation escape!

What about that science behind the anecdotes and stories of extraordinary ability and super strength in extreme circumstances, when parents lift cars off trapped children, when ordinary people rush into burning buildings to save strangers? Well, she has no time to contemplate it or understand how and why she can keep on running. It is all about Ellie, her fair-haired Ellie. The clock is ticking.

More determined than ever, she picks up her pace toward that tinkling, ice-crackling sound, the woosh-woosh. She heard it before somewhere. But where and when?

CHAPTER SIX

4:10 AM

---

*There are layers upon layers in life. Look
beneath to find another story, a different version
of the same event, and another and another
still...especially when two cultures clash.*

---

*A*t the house, the police arrive. Just one squad car pulls
into Annie and Buck's St. Kitts driveway. Lizzie and
Abigail, waiting, watching, wondering and expecting the
worst, are in the kitchen ready for these rescuers. They race to the
door. Here are their heroes! These policemen will do what's right,
won't they? They will find Ellie. They will go straight up the
mountain following Grammy's path. They will get this guy, the
kidnapper.

"Good evening," the uniformed man at the door says in the
most unhurried tone of voice, as if he were stopping by for a bite
of breakfast. "I am Sergeant Valamine." He smiles and casually

walks around the girls, heading into the kitchen as if he has been here hundreds of times, like he owns the place. Wait. Wait. What is this? Who is this? These sisters hadn't even invited him inside but that's not where their brains are going, they are searching for the signs of emergency in his movements. Where is his hurry? There is a missing young woman, right? Their cousin was dragged right out of bed, right? This is a kidnapping for God's sake. He is very casual, looking...and of all the incongruous emotions in the world under these circumstances...happy to sit down inside. He's looking around, checking out the kitchen.

"Thank God you are here," Lizzie says anyway, shoving aside these first impressions and her apprehension.

Abby turns on the charm too. "Thank you so much for coming!"

With the relief of rescue at hand, both teens start to speak at the same time, words bumping and lapping. They love Ellie dearly. "Our cousin has been kidnapped," Lizzie says. "Our grandmother has gone up the mountain to rescue her," Abby adds. "What are you going to do? How can we help? What do you need to know? Can we show you where she was taken from?"

"She was in the bed right next to us!" Liz chimes in.

"Woah! Hold on, slow down. Let's not get ahead of ourselves," the policeman pushes back, slouching at the counter, perched but precariously on the stool. The pause in this conversation is loaded now. Something is not going to happen. This guy, this man in charge, is not going to be in charge. And the real shocker dawning on the teens with a jolt of sickening horror is that he is all by himself. Alone? One man! Where is the rest of the rescue force? They had pictured a SWAT team. The clock is ticking. It's been almost a half hour since Grammy ran out the back door.

"Now young ladies. May we start at the beginning?" he asks. They hear a bit of a British accent.

"Noooo. Noooo," Abby insists, dumping polite reserve for definitive anger. "We don't have time. Where are the others? the rest of your police force? Our Ellie was stolen from bed right upstairs and taken by a man. Dragged out and down off the balcony. The guy climbed up to a second floor for God's sake. She could be dead. What are you doing here? Why did you even come?"

Lizzie adds, "We think they went up the trail out back, up the mountain." You can sense her trying to cool her little sister back off that cliff of disgust. Maybe they do need his help here. Maybe he won't help them if they aren't nice. This guy, after all, may be their only hope. But she can't stop being upset and blurts out, "There is no time to talk. Where, oh my God, where are the others? The rest of the police?"

"Girls, girls," he says, "it has been a very long night. I'm not going anywhere until I get the full story, and from the very beginning. When did you and your family arrive on the island?" And from here, he launches into a litany of questions leading nowhere good. "Is this trip business or pleasure? Who owns this home? Who else is here with you? When will you be leaving? What exactly is your departure date?" He pulls out a notebook and pen, waiting for one of them to answer his idiotic questions. This is not about Ellie at all. His pained tired expression begs for a cup of tea. His glance has strayed to the kettle on the big stove and the box of Earl Grey Grammy left out. No way is he getting a cup of tea here. Jesus Christ. This is a mess. Then his next comment sets off a bomb that sends rippling waves of fear out in all directions there.

46

"My dears, what makes you think she didn't slip out on her own with this young man?"

"Oh my God," Lizzie hollers, "F--k you." When pushed to a point even she doesn't always recognize or know when it's coming, Lizzie can curse with abandon. Abigail shifts, eyebrows raised in what should be alarm at her sister's language but not at all. She's impressed. Thank you, Lizzie. Go for it, she doesn't say out loud. This is the appropriate time and place to get into a crazy rabid verbal assault, especially if it knocks this guy out of his comfortable seat in their kitchen.

"This is our family home. Shut up with this small talk you idiot," Lizzie shouts again. "How can you propose such a ridiculous possibility? Why are you asking these stupid questions about departure dates and purpose of travel? Ellie is in danger. Up there! She would never ever go somewhere on her own, without us, her cousins, and with a stranger. She is only 13 years old for God's sake," she adds in the same condescending adult tone she uses with her little brother. She points out the door to the back of the house, across the terrace. "Up there. Up there. Please, please," she begs, trying a new tack. "Please help us. Please sir. We need your help."

Apparently unmoved by anything, he counters, "How do you know she is up there? Or, if she is in danger? Maybe, yes, but maybe no. I believe that she went willingly with this man." So there, he says using a dead tired body language, entire being sagging obviously from exhaustion after a long night on the job. Then, with this pronouncement, he ends this line of unreasonable interrogation on an outrageous down note, putting both hands, palms down firmly on the counter to end the debate.

"Jesus Christ," Lizzie says. "Ellie is a child and has never even been on a real date or had a boyfriend. She is not about to go

47

willingly in the middle of the night with a stranger who has scaled the side of a house to a second floor and snuck into a bedroom. We heard the man. He grunted crawling on the floor. We were there!" With these thoughts out in the air now, Lizzie brings back the scuffle of the morning in that upstairs bedroom, sensations she caught mid-sleep and wake, before even opening her eyes. Yes, there was grunting and someone on the floor beside Ellie's bed. What was he doing to her?

In that instant, both girls remember; Yes, they did hear him. He made a noise, a grunt? Then he panted a little. Was he winded from his climb up the side of the house? Oh God, there were no sounds from Ellie. Wait, maybe a slight sigh or cry. Then nothing. Why didn't she scream? How did he keep her quiet? What happened right there in the bed next to them? What did he do to her? Is she still alive?

✍

The air is cool outside in this Atlantic Ocean breeze. Ellie, tied to the back of the donkey, being yanked by a rope up the mountain, is barely conscious, coming in and out, in and out. In her pink pajamas, with flashlight still in a side pocket, she can sense movement, something warm and alive under her slim body. She's in what scientists and doctors call a k-hole.

Ketamine, the big K in that k-hole, is an anesthetic, often used in veterinary medicine and more frequently now for psychiatric and mood disorders. It's a dis-associative drug that acts on various chemicals in the brain to produce visual and auditory distortion and a detachment from reality. A white powder, it can be dissolved in liquid, swallowed, snorted, or injected and its effects can be felt in a single minute. It's been popping up in recent years all over the legal and illegal marketplaces to get high but also as a legitimate treatment for depression. Salons and new companies specializing in ketamine are opening for patients seeking relief from longstanding mental health issues like intractable depression and post-traumatic stress disorder. Patients can enter what's known as this k-hole and come out feeling psychologically lighter, emotionally freer, maybe happier. Depending on the person or animal's size, weight, and existing health as well as the dose, ketamine can last in a body for 30 minutes, an hour, or much longer, possibly affecting senses for 24 hours.

Does Ellie have an increased heart rate or blood pressure? Maybe. Blurred vision? Yes. Vomiting? Not yet. But soon. Anxiety? No, she is too out of it, alternately conscious, then unconscious. But she senses she is with, no on top of, an animal, a creature she knows somehow from somewhere. Lady?

Numbly, distractedly, she fumbles down to her pocket with thick fingers, so unreasonably heavy she can hardly move them, but she finds her flashlight; the little Frozen gem with the four musical buttons still there in her pocket, where she put it before going to bed. As she raps her hand around it clumsily, she falls back to sleep but without letting go. Somewhere in the fog of her dream but not a dream, she knows to hold on, to press one or all the buttons, the musical notes. Don't drop this, someone is telling her. Her light may mean her life.

∽

You pass the main campus of the veterinary school, Ross University, on St. Kitts driving along the southern coast. You'll also run into vet students on beaches or at local bars everywhere. The motto for this Ross crowd ought to be study hard, party hard. The waterfront campus comes up before the turn-off for Trinity and not far from Romney Manor, where the hand-made batik

49

fabric is designed and tourists flock to check out the Wingfield plantation, Thomas Jefferson's ancestors' home with its old rum distillery.

Buck and Annie took an unofficial tour of the vet school years ago with a student who offered to show them around. It's a tough academic program boasting hands-on work with animals. A real plus to this island education is that preparation for surgery is done not virtually on computer screens as it must be in the United States by law, but on large and small, living, breathing animals. Ross graduates do well when they head back home to practice medicine. Annie remembers being impressed by the covered, outdoor operating arena for large animals.

She commented, "This is amazing. Do the cows or horses feel anything during a procedure?"

"Not at all," she was reassured. "We have the best anesthetics."

≈

Ellie has never been to Ross, but on the hillside in the moon's glow, she knows what it feels like to be under the same kind of influence as the animals she loves. She's in a k-hole, out, in, here and then gone, coming up inside in an under-water, I-am-drowning-but-so-unable to move feeling only to dive back down again, and feeling queasy.

Lady, pulled along by Ellie's captor, knows where she really wants to go and it's not alongside this guy holding the rope. Her instincts tell her to race up the side of this mountain and down into the valley on the other side, drawn by a knowledge buried in her genetic code. She has an innate understanding of where she stands in her world of work and what she must do for this semi-conscious girl on her back, the same girl who shared her sandwich yesterday. Lady knows where Needsmust is. She brays softly, not to scare off a predator, but in a sign of attachment. Curious with an empathetic nature, Lady, our donkey, wants to know more about Ellie.

Kennedy curses and yanks the rope again.

"Stoopid donkey. Moov, moov, faster." He doesn't want to be late with this girl. He promised to deliver her on time. He needs the money.

❧

Because of its warm, tropical, even-tempered climate, like the one tonight in November, St. Kitts was once known as Sugar City, the richest colony in the Caribbean with 68 sugar cane plantations, one for every square mile. Tobacco and rain forests were cleared for the crop known as "white gold" introduced to the island in 1643. Plantation owners sold sugar, molasses, and rum worldwide.

Up on the mountainside, new houses dot the landscape, boasting ocean views. Down on the other side, in the valley where Needsmust Estate once operated, the slave quarters, plantation house and outbuildings are long gone. But the land is still called Needsmust...look on any map of modern-day St. Kitts. William Woodley, a member of the British Parliament in England in 1776, inherited these 225 acres of St. Kitts' sugar-land, an unearned prize that came with living, breathing, sweating, dying human beings: his property, his slaves. Those long-ago record keepers noted carefully how many babies were at mothers' breasts as well as the adult population year in and year out, with no way out ever, even in dreams or revolts. By 1817, the number of 140 souls was catalogued methodically at Needsmust, recorded in a flourished, pretty penmanship giving no hint to the horror it hid. In 1831, that number rose to 157. And by 1834, it was 177. The mortality rate was 50% in this hot, hilly, backbreaking place. And by the end of the 17th century, there were twice as many slaves as European settlers on all of St. Kitts, a lousy lopsided balance of power versus no power. By the power of democratic numbers alone, the island should have belonged to the enslaved. But, of course, they didn't count.

❧

In the kitchen with the police officer, Lizzie looks at her sister Abigail with horror. Her eyebrows arch up and her mouth and teeth grimace. What she really wants to do is shout; can you believe this guy?

Sergeant Valamine, with his sagging, sad, negative energy, every move signaling how very tired he is, sits calmly indicating no intention of moving anywhere anytime soon. Neither girl can imagine this man keeping up with their grandmother climbing a mountain in search of their cousin.

Abigail asks point-blank, "Don't you even want to see where Ellie was abducted? Check for clues or fingerprints? Look outside for signs of movement?"

Liz adds, "What is wrong with you? Do something, anything!"

These teenage sisters, aghast at the indifference and lack of help being offered here in a crisis, now understand why Grammy ran out the back door, reasoning logically from the start that they might be on their own here.

"Why are you just sitting here?" Lizzie demands.

Offended, he takes out a pack of cigarettes and they shout in unison.

"Don't you dare light up here in our kitchen!"

❧

Buck wakes way too early up there in the Hudson valley, troubled with a sense of unexplainable dread. There is an hour difference in the time zones. He's in his suburban Sleepy Hollow bed but Annie and the girls are in his thoughts. Something is not right. Tossing and turning, checking that time, he has no logical answer for his unease, a premonition that something is wrong.

"Don't be a fool," he says out loud. "Go back to sleep. Everyone is fine, just fine."

But that is not true at all.

CHAPTER SEVEN

4:15 AM

Could unconditional love, the big forgiving
family kind...no judgments, no put-downs, no
hidden agenda or disguised meanness...be like a
vitamin every child needs to survive and thrive?

*I*f you circumnavigate this green gem, 28 miles around, you'll be driving like a Brit on the left side of a two-lane, bumpy, pot-holed road. Cows roam freely, sometimes with tall white egrets standing on their scrawny backs. Foraging for food doesn't make fat cows but farmers simply put their animals, even the donkeys, out to scavenge on their own. The sea is never far out of sight and fields of sugar cane once grew up those mountainsides as far as fertile soil and incline permitted. Now most of those rows of cane fields have gone to a weedy, wild mess.

That left-side driving has been the only seriously

uncomfortable thing about daily life on the island for Annie. Even after so many years of personal history here, she still has to remind herself when she is on the road, as she was yesterday on the five-minute drive to Frigate Bay beach with her precious granddaughters on board, "Stay left. Stay left." And it's not just the driving itself. Rental car steering wheels are often on the "wrong" side of the front seat so it can be awkward getting accustomed the first few days. You go looking for the rearview mirror, turning your head and eyes up in the wrong direction. American driving instincts honestly do take over especially in the roundabouts. With few traffic lights anywhere, a parade of circles link two, three, four and sometimes five incoming lanes together and around. At least people honk to let you know they are coming through. Kittitian drivers, her neighbors, friends, even strangers, honk one, two or three times in short, crisp beep greetings to one another. One honk means "Hi there" or maybe "Move along," "Go faster." Two honks are something else entirely and she doesn't quite get this, but three or more could be the start of a fight or someone insisting on an extra happy hello. All this beep-beeping is ordinarily a sign of friendliness, not road rage. People are nice, she always insists to anyone thinking of traveling to the island.

"You will love it," Annie has always said when recommending her favorite escape to anyone and everyone. She is this island's biggest cheerleader back home. "Our family has been going for decades and the worst thing that ever happened was a purse snatching. But I wasn't careful. It was my fault."

⁓

This is Ellie's tenth… or could it be her eleventh trip to St. Kitts? Who's counting? Her family goes to "their" island as often as they can sneak away. Lauren and her husband first brought their baby girl when she was two years old, but they stayed at the

55

Marriott then. This was before her parents bought the vacation house. Februarys would find them always leaving from an airport in New Jersey or New York on the way to St. Kitts, maybe even escaping an oncoming snowstorm. It was considered a rite of passage for each grandchild to arrive by plane from the depths of a North American winter, maybe as snow started to fall. Upon landing, they could step outside a few hours later into Caribbean blue-sky, clear-as-day sunshine. Glee would go up a notch if it happened to be snowing harder, yes blizzard conditions, back home. Annie can remember the morning they all sat inside the plane on the tarmac while it was being de-iced. They held hands in the airplane seats, three across, dodging a close call cancellation of a trip almost postponed because of weather.

Ellie has always loved these vacations, even when she was embarrassed and plagued with gut issues that made no sense to her at first as a 9, 10 and 11-year-old. The symptoms were not all in her head, she'd insist, trying to explain how bad she felt. She couldn't wish them away with positive thinking. It wasn't her brain. The pain, cramps and unpredictable diarrhea were real. At 13, she understands that it might have been alarming for her parents and grandparents. But IBS was far worse for her. For 10, 11 and 12-year-old Ellie, it was a real and ever-present physical nightmare especially in school, on vacation, at a friend's house, and God forbid, even in gym class. She'd pack extra underpants in her school bag in case she needed a quick change as the oh-so-familiar stomach and intestinal cramping arrived and signaled toilet terror to come. This was so embarrassing. No matter what she tried, her gut wouldn't go back to her old normal. A previously happy middle-schooler, for a time she lost both her optimistic outlook and precious pounds precisely when so much else was happening to her body hormonally. Was it connected to her soon-to-arrive period as her mother suspected? Oh God. It didn't matter. Always tall and on the thin side like her mom and grandmother, Ellie would be foggy-headed and mentally out of sorts. Irritable bowel syndrome would strike in class so she'd have to be excused. Then, she'd be so sleepy that she could hardly keep her eyes open.

❧

On the mountain, Annie stops to check her watch with a mind racing with all those who, what, when, where, and how questions boomeranging in her brain. Ping. Ping. How long has she been gone? Is Ellie's IBS out of control? Oh God, please no. The drugs, her diet changes...all have been working so well, up until now. Should she have tried to reach Buck before she ran out the back door? Maybe. But honestly, what could he have done from up there in Sleepy Hollow, New York, thousands of miles away? Nothing. Nothing at all. Maybe everything. Then, another idea refuses to back itself down there in her brain. It keeps bubbling up. Stress is one of those IBS triggers they all learned to take seriously after Ellie's IBS diagnosis. What could be happening to her now? Is she sick? Is he hurting her? Don't go there now, Annie reminds herself, don't let those images in.

Glancing back down toward the house, she sees the police car in her driveway. Good. The officers will be on the way up soon. Then, turning completely around to look over toward North Frigate Bay, she can see that the island is unnervingly quiet. Partygoers, night-owls, tourists...no one, no one at all is out and about.

Get going. Keep your eyes open. Find Ellie. She is here somewhere. Annie picks up her pace. Passing below one of the newer stone, multi-terraced houses, she sees lights up there, two streets above and wonders, who's up, who's in there? When did all these newcomers move in? What are they all doing here in her paradise?

It's a big house with foreigners settling into their own brand of paradise, maybe for some of the same reasons she bought her own. And yet? Thinking about who's buying houses around here and all the new people drinking at the beach bars, she recalls the strange "For Sale" sign. It was right on the golf cart path. A month before the pandemic arrived, on the golf course, she and Buck had laughed, noting the misspelled words in the numbered reasons why someone should buy the house. Yet, thinking back about it, the homemade ad spelled something sinister in fact, and while they had laughed about it, it was not so funny in the way it promoted St. Kitts. Against a black background, in bright yellow lettering, it read:

BUY THIS LAND WITH HOUSE AND

BECOME CITIZEN OF ST. KITTS

10 REASONS:

Kittitians are honest and friendly peoples.

This country is for family and grow kids.

Your life will be longer than 20 years.

Stable economy to establish business.

Safe country with respect of privacy.

Safe bank system.

Rispectful government and police.

Confident safe lawyers who will give you new life.

In island present only nobile criminality.

We don't do questions.

CALL, BUY AND ENJOY was followed by a What's App and gmail address. It all sounds creepier than ever looking back now. No questions asked? New lives? What about their old lives? Who was being invited to buy here? People who wanted to ditch their past lives.

She's running, heading up a concrete narrow road unable to stop this storm of thoughts. Did this seller represent something about the island that skirted international law? What did it mean, "We don't ask questions?" Why hasn't she paid attention? Did she put her granddaughter's life in danger here?

Oh God, she is so vulnerable when it comes to grandparenting. But she gets it. Above all, she has wanted each of her six miracles to be so comfortable with her that they could share anything if and when they needed to talk. Maybe it all started when she lost her third baby. Was that dead baby girl the reason why these next-generation pieces of herself, her grandchildren, flesh of her flesh, became even more precious than she could have ever imagined?

Whew. These kids, her kids, and grandkids, have been so lucky, with lives built upon rock-solid love. They were blessed with two parents who loved them as well as one another and double sets of grandparents, a gift not many children get. Her heart breaks sometimes for friends who were not loved enough as babies or others who had been given up for adoption. A good friend searched for her biological mother for years and then found a woman not easy to like, let alone love.

Like extra money in a pocket or a hand, held out to pull you up when you are down, the kind of bedrock of generational parenting in her family offers intangible tools for survival that might come in handy someday. Wouldn't it? Do they? Oh God, she hopes so…maybe this very day for Ellie.

She slows up and wishes she had brought along water.

What is it about being a grandmother that surprised her so much? Not the arrival of the children but the depth of emotion each birth brought. From the moment Lizzie, her first grandchild, was born, Annie fell into a well of wonder.

She kept a Kahlil Gibran poem by her bedside. "Your children are not your children…they are life's longing for itself…" Yes, that's it. That's what's going on here and now. They are my life. If anything happens to Ellie, will I be able to live?

Turning back for another check on police action down there at her house, she misses the cinder block and falls forward, cracking hard right onto her knees. Falling when you are 74 can be among your worst nightmares bringing not just injury but embarrassment, shame and quintessential, intrusive medical history questions. Yikes, it's among the first healthcare points on so many checkups. Healthcare professionals want to know: Are you on the decline? Ready for something worse? How often do you fall? You couldn't have just lost your balance like a patient of much younger years? When you are old, seventy-something, this falling down business becomes big business. Of course, it should be, but it hurts to hear the questions coming all the time. Have you fallen lately? In the past six months? Yes, sometimes falls are serious but not this one, not tonight. I am okay. I will be okay; she insists to no one but herself getting back up.

Now stand up straight, Annie. Don't tell anyone you fell to your knees in the roadway. Get right up. Check for blood. Keep on going. You simply tripped over a Goddamn cinder block while under extreme circumstances. You are not on death's door girl. At least not yet here tonight! You can't be.

CHAPTER EIGHT

4:20 AM

---

*Take a nearly bankrupt island, a few brilliantly
practical moves by local politicians and bankers
so desperate for dollars that they are not allowed
to care where money comes from...add a few
seedy, immoral, international characters and
voila; there is danger in paradise.*

A bit of history here will help this story go down. Years
before the United States abolished slavery in 1865, three
English settlers on St. Kitts pulled off a humanitarian
win that brought slave trading there to its end in 1807. But, if you
look around the island and into the eyes of dear friends as Annie
and Buck have done, you glimpse buried family histories, ancestry
tinged with touches of misery. Until 1983...when St. Kitts gained
its independence from the British empire and became the smallest
nation in the western hemisphere with a seat at the United
Nations...even the tallest volcano, now known as Mount Liamuiga,

or fertile land, was called Mt. Misery. Life had been miserable for generations. Now it was not, of course, but this legacy left bits and pieces behind.

Kittitians are anything but miserable. Perhaps because of all the generations of hard-working, hands-on, physical investment in their land, their own independent nation, thank God, natives take enormous, happy pride in their island. They talk about it. Bask in its successes. Argue about its politics. Face to face, at the Shiggidy Shack, the Lion's Den, the Shipwreck Bar, out at Reggae Beach or sitting on a stool at the lobby bar in the Marriott, you will sense a pride in the landscape, the sea, the mountains, and how they have resourced this little nub in an archipelago of oceanic islands right into the 21st century. This happy place belongs to them now, not some confounding conquering outsider and they honestly want to share it with tourists from everywhere.

Natives, Kittitian born and bred, may fly away but don't often leave for good or forever. Their homeland is priceless, especially if you consider the price ancestors paid. Maybe a long-standing love of place is why there was public grumbling and outrage when politicians started selling citizenship and land to foreigners in the 1980s. Russians especially took note of this opportunity and opened their wallets.

Christopher Columbus claimed to discover St. Kitts in 1493, and outrageously named it after himself. The gall, the hubris, of this guy who was just stopping by is laughable if you think too long about it now. What made him believe he had discovered a place that was already there and occupied by human beings when he landed? Kitts is a nickname for Christopher and it's a gorgeous treasure. Home for pirates looking for treasure then and again now, the treasure of St. Kitts was never buried anywhere but right there in plain sight; landed freedom for anyone and everyone, with a price tag labeled good or evil. Mostly good, but it's that little bit of evil that has sent Annie on the run tonight.

St. Kitts is a rich garden of earthly delights for sure. Annie can see and smell this tonight up here. There are palms, dwarfs, acais, arecas, so many different kinds, flowers and fruits galore. Unfortunately, the only crops that brought in cash when the government coffers hit bottom in the 1980s and the world market for sugar cane tanked for this little island nation, were foreigners who began planting themselves. For a $150,000 non-refundable donation to St. Kitts and Nevis, or a $200,000 - $400,000 real estate investment in a state-approved property, a ticket to ride through the world on a new, wiped-clean passport would be granted. This is Citizenship By Investment or CBI and it constitutes a huge piece of the financial sustainability of St. Kitts. Go on the World Bank website. Check it out. CBI is all over the balance sheet. For those willing to spend, the wait for citizenship and new lives is just a few weeks. After that, you don't need to be officially Russian anymore, at least not officially when going through any immigration and customs checkpoints. Your passport and papers are bona fide Kittitian identifying you as a citizen of the Federation of St. Christopher and Nevis. Called "alternative citizenship," this for-sale option also granted visa-free access to 152 countries worldwide. Entire families were eligible and St. Kitts citizenship came with no tax on income, wealth or inheritance and no physical residency required. Valid for the life of the applicant and family, and transferable to descendants, the operative word here is forever.

Seriously, if you needed a get-out-of-town pass because you found yourself in an indelicate situation in your native country, not necessarily or just the Soviet Union but any dictator-desperate state, this gift of citizenship was a dream come true. St. Kitts, in fact, has the oldest program in the world for a purchase-your-way-into-passport plan, launched in 1984, and inviting foreigners with big checkbooks.

It would take this night in November to help Annie and Buck understand the true nature and ugly impact of this Russian red tide on their idyllic island. Not all Russians are evil, of course, but Buck had suspected that Putin's like-minded pals were planted in so many places around the world. Maybe right in his Kittitian back yard.

Annie thinks back to her first closer look at someone who had taken this fast track to a new life one evening at the Dip N Sip pool bar in the Frigate Bay Resort. This simple hotel tucked into a hurricane-safe valley and wrapped around a palm-tree-encircled pool was the first place they stayed on St. Kitts in the 80s when she desperately needed to leave the real world behind and go someplace safe. What about that little Tiki bar wedged into the side of the big swimming pool? Spectacular! Half the stools on dry land, the other half under water? It became the family's haven, not only because of its signature rum punch but also for the deep dive out of real life that it offered. You must promise that you will go to a bar like this someday. Annie always says that if, like Peter Pan, she was ever in need of a happy thought to help her soar above the everyday menacing morass of life, the memory of this place would be it. Years of taking all her cares away, but especially the memories of her last baby, the one who didn't make it into this world, were invested there.

On the night they met their first Russian émigré, the underwater pool lights were just coming on and Annie had taken a seat on a stool to order her rum punch. She could look through the open-backed bar, across the pool and out to the banana trees that lined the walkway going left down to the Caribbean Sea. There was a full moon just like tonight on St. Kitts. The bartender, Julica, was at her worst best; hardly a smile, gruff, but that was just Julica. Take her as she is but don't take her mood personally. She may honestly like you! Annie's youngest brother Timmy used to call her "Lovey" when he vacationed with them. And for that nickname, Julica would gift Timmy with a sly, one-sided smile.

"When is your brother coming back?" she was always asking. Julica, aka "Lovey," missed Timmy's verbal touch.

"I don't know when my brother is coming back Julica. How are you tonight?"

With just a nod, no verbal response or half-smile, she turned her back to Annie. Yet, to be fair, Julica has always been the bartender who would serve Annie's kids, Lauren and Will, the local grapefruit soda: Ting. They would swim up with a Barbie or a toy boat and then sit up on the underwater stools at this bar where she would pour two cold ones. Years of ingrained habit and perhaps hard experience had simply settled Julica's facial expression into one comfortable direction: smirky. Her eyes rolled on this night they first met the Russian.

He sits down next to Annie, and she turns to him to say, "Hi."

"Yoooleeka gud eeeevningh," he says in a thick, back-of-the-throat, phlegmy, edgy accent, greeting his favorite bartender. His nostrils flair and Annie almost laughs aloud at this comic book version of a person. He's wearing a sailor's cap with a little brim and smiling at her. The scent of his aftershave lotion almost overpowers the cool, fresh night air with its cloud of obnoxious, undoubtedly expensive, artificiality. Annie gags. But just a little. She's having too much fun already with this stranger.

"Wodka," he says with an almost too-funny roll of the

65

tongue, looking at Julica, who obviously knows him well. He's been a regular for months now, she tells Annie and Buck later. His huge house up on the hill overlooks Frigate Bay and out to the Caribbean Sea. Everyone knows him or of him, a guy with an accent who's been telling outlandish stories about an escape from the mother country and what he had stolen to bring along with him when he left in a hurry. Of course, his name is Ivan, had to be something of that sort. Later, after this first social situation, they would see him around the island and wave. On beaches, he'd wear weird tiny bathing suits, too small for his skinny frame and as if he thought he was on the French Riviera, and a silly-looking hat. Ivan, of course, had long tall tales to share with anyone willing to listen. Supposedly, with his new Kittitian passport, he had left a job as a nuclear scientist and walked away with a plutonium isotope. But who could believe that? Not many. What fellow drinkers did notice is that he soon switched from "wodka" to the local rum.

"Give me rum," he said, adjusting his order that night.

"Where does the money come from?" Annie had asked Buck one evening when they left the bar after speaking with him.

"I hate to say it because it sounds like I'm stereotyping these foreigners," Buck answers, "but I think they are up to no good. Seriously, his house up there on the hill was more than a million dollars and he bought it in cash. Unbelievable. Stacks of bills, in fact."

"All cash?" Annie asks surprised by this piece of gossip.

"Yes, that's what my contact downtown at Scotia Bank told me."

"So, he has a lot of cash. But from where?"

"I'm guessing it's coming from nothing honest or worthwhile."

⁊

At home in Sleepy Hollow, Buck can't go back to sleep. So, he's out of bed, pedaling away anxiety and un-nameable fears on his stationary bike. Something is not right on St. Kitts. He knows it. He's called Annie twice, but she is not answering, obviously out of any cell service range. But, the landline, that on again off again telephone, at the house isn't ringing for him either. Where is everyone? Maybe they are still in bed, he wants to believe. But he doesn't. From all his years of intuitive experience in tough situations, he just knows that something is terribly wrong in his island paradise.

⁊

A tall reed of something sharp slashes across Annie's cheek as she races up. Look at her with those bloody knees. Our grandmother startles at this new unexpected encounter with a wild plant and slows to put a hand to face. Whew. That hurts more than it should. But it's sweat, not blood. Skin isn't broken. Good. Her heart's pounding and breathing is deep and fast. Left hip is hurting. Not her skinned knees. But damn that sciatica. Gone sometimes, too often it returns with vengeful pain down the left leg from her backside mid-hip all the way to ankle deep. Why is that? She wonders and then knows where and why it has re-emerged. Thank you not-old spine! No yoga for days, lots of sitting on an airplane and then slouching in a low sand chair. Forget about it. Move through this pain.

CHAPTER NINE

4:25 AM

There is a dark side to so many modern wonder drugs. We love them. We need them. We hate them. Cures. Side effects, all of it. Saving lives, changing lives, sometimes taking lives.

---

*E*llie is awake, jumbling, jerking, swaying. What? Why? Is she is having an out-of-body experience? Can she see herself from above? Is she in a fairy tale here? No, a nightmare! Moving, moving upward, yes, that's it. Awkwardly on the move. Not on her own two feet. Legs numbingly heavy. She is on her belly, head down, lying on something warm and soft, touching her cheek to fur, the soft, hairy coat of an animal. Her gut is cramping, grumbling, threatening. Oh no.

Once again but more focused now, she recognizes the scent of this animal and then feels her belly tightening, lurching with a familiar low-level intestinal turmoil. Then from outside herself she wakes to a mewing sound. Opening heavy-lidded eyes, still so heavy she can hardly do this, praying that her tummy will settle and not simply explode, that these symptoms will pass, she senses this animal right on her face and beneath her body. Is this a dream? Is it the donkey? The donkey she met today? Or was that yesterday? Is she still in her pajamas?

"Lady," she whispers. "Is that you?"

A hee-haw comes back. This donkey remembers her. Then, immediately, she knows that someone else is here. And with a prickly, fearful alert and semi-conscious understanding, she knows she's in the presence of danger. He's turning back toward her now. She can feel, smell, sense the direction of his movement.

"Shuusssh. Shut up. Shut the f--k up," he says, followed by "Please." The voice, she decides, is not as mean as it is frightened, maybe tired, sick, something more.

"Who, who, who..." she asks.

"Stop de talk. Stop. Stop."

Then, he asks again, "Please." He's talking to the donkey, to Lady, her Lady.

He stinks. Whew, a sweaty, unwashed-for-weeks scent. Dizzy, head wobbling, then bobbing up against the donkey's body, she asks, "Who, who are you?"

He is holding a rope that encircles the donkey's neck.

"Whaaat? What do you think you are doing?" she adds in an anger growing more intense as she slips out of her heavy druggy state. "How dare you? Where are you taking me? What have you done?"

He's coming closer but she doesn't give a damn. This is not appropriate at all. She shouldn't be here. He shouldn't be doing this to her. Head turning, she can see that he's just a kid, not much older than her…like one of those boys up at the high school where she will be next year. Jeez. Why is he doing this to her?

Body still tied around the donkey at the waist but hands free, she reaches down for the flashlight, still there in her pocket. Had she been holding it in her sleep? Before? Is that a real memory? Was it in her dream? Did it really happen? Did she push for those little tinny sounds of her favorite movie? Not possible. No. But yes, yes maybe. She's trying to move the top of her body up, wiggling over and down, legs shifting toward the ground, working against the rope at her waist, determined to climb off, to stand up, to stand up to him.

Alarmed by her movement, he stops, turns around, comes closer, gets right up into her face, so near she can smell his rank breath, that awful, stink of his days-old sweat and something else. His fear? He grabs her cheek with one hand, the other keeping hold of the donkey's rope. "Shut up yo guyl. Shut up. Shut up." Yes, he's nervous. Scared? Of her? Hyper-alert, she can sense his trembling, shaking. What's wrong with him? She knows what it's like to be nervous, an anxiety that she lived with for years, a gut-earned wisdom for sure. But his is different. And now with a sharp sense, she gets this guy, understanding his inadequacy here, maybe she has seen him before. Not sure where. But not long ago. Wake up Ellie. Wake up.

Now in a fury about her circumstances, she lurches up at her waist, lifting herself off the donkey's back, as if she were back in that gymnastics class, and screams, scaring him. "I will not shut up, you stupid boy. I will not. I will not." And with that third loud NOT, more awake than she has been for the last 30 minutes, her voice rises and reaches out, "Grammy, I'm here. Grammy, I'm here. Graaaaammmmy!"

He drops the rope to grab her with both hands and push her back down. The donkey, knowing how danger feels and what this boy has been capable of doing...there is no love lost between the two...starts flinging her head back and forth in alarm. Lady has a big horsey head. And it's a hard head. This Kittitian kid...is he the same cute-not-so-cute one from the beach yesterday?...yes, of course he is!...now reaches for Ellie's face again with a rag, a piece of Ketamine-laced cloth, in his trembling hand.

You can't smell the anesthetic Ketamine but you can taste it. On the street, human addicts sometimes call ketamine donkey dust. Ellie would laugh about this if she could. How serendipitous is that? A donkey and ketamine and donkey dust? Who would have predicted? Ellie gets a jolt of this bitter, harsh, awful rush up through her mouth, nose, sinuses and then it travels back down her throat. Ohhhhh. No no, no, she can't say out loud because she is going into that k-hole again. Her nose starts running but she is not aware of this drip. She's out; detached from her body. But thank God, Lady is not and starts kicking in fury, in retribution, in a protective whiplash of crazy kicking. The animal, so smart, assumed to be complacent, without intelligence, turns her head to see this creature whose been breathing sweetly on her back. This is her girl. That man; her enemy.

Ellie's pink pajamas stand out in the moon's light, but Lady wouldn't have appreciated them even in the dark or with her night vision. Though she has extra rods in her eyes, Lady's color vision is limited. She's better at seeing puddles directly in front of her. What Lady recognizes and loves is the scent of Ellie. She picked it up from her brief encounter yesterday at Frigate Bay beach and can even recall the taste of the ketchup-y egg sandwich Ellie had shared under the palm tree. The donkey kicks harder and harder at the kidnapper again and again, braying loudly, throwing her head up, back and then around to pound the man's hand away from her girl. Yes, this human being with the soft touch, the empathetic voice and her tasty sandwich is her girl. Lady is angry.

"Yoaah...F--k, F--k." he lurches back and charges at the donkey's head, hitting her directly on the nostrils, putting his angry bad breath right in Lady's face; a no-no according to any donkey trainer you might ever meet. If you are trying to make friends with a donkey, don't go for a head in. A donkey's nose and mouth are critical sensory centers. She doesn't like to be touched there. She hates it. And her whiskers, well those whiskers are special receptive organs, like her large pointy, powerful ears. Don't mock or knock them. The blood vessels in a donkey's stand-up ears operate like a cooling system on the hottest days and allow her to pinpoint sounds coming from either direction or far away. She is certainly not stupid at all, no no, no.

People sometimes poke fun at donkeys and their hee-hawing but in truth, these animals have supported and carried humans for centuries. Even Jesus Christ rode a donkey to meet his fate and die on a cross. Trainers know that there is a reason for everything a donkey does and the path to a donkey's heart, perhaps like all creatures, is through enrichment, mouth-watering treats and tender grooming touches. Ellie knew this instinctively. Her captor did not. Yes, he had been with this donkey the day before at the beach, but it was not his donkey. Lady...and who knows if that is really her name...belongs to the boss who hired him to watch for and track the right kind of girls, the women who would be worth big money on a hideous black market. That bray? Well, it's not Lady laughing but a warning of possible danger in the surroundings.

Now, Lady turns her backside completely aiming even more

directly at this kid, kicking sideways, leaving him on the ground, breathless, in pain and shocked. A donkey? A stupid donkey? Not stupid at all. A donkey's rear hind legs have always been a powerful defense against predators and tonight, she recognizes that difference between good and evil.

"Eeeeee. F--k. F--k," he curses but Ellie, unconscious now, can't hear. Lady is pleased, hee-hawing victoriously that she's hurt him but justifiably.

With an instinct toward self-preservation passed down through generations, Lady jerks hard and away now, taking off with Ellie, dragging the rope, with her girl out cold and still tied loosely to her back in a race away from danger. She won't lose her girl. She'll be careful.

Angry, fuzzy, out of breath, our kidnapper stumbles to stand up. He has made a mistake assuming that donkeys were docile and dumb, treating Lady with cruelty. What he didn't know is that donkeys may walk at the same speed as humans, maybe four miles per hour, but they can run nearly as fast as horses, up to 40 miles per hour.

※

Down below this scuffle, on the narrow road, Annie hears the commotion in the quiet of the early morning. Was that her name being called? Was it a Grammy she heard?

Like the what-is-it noise that woke her back there in her warm bed less than an hour ago, she could hear Ellie's cry, of that she's certain. That was Ellie and that was her name. She's alive. She's up there. She needs her grandmother.

Grammy is the term of endearment that Annie fell in love

73

with 16 years ago when the first of these grandkids needed a name for her. It would be "Grammy." While friends deliberated and tried out other monikers grandchildren might call them, some cuter than others, she went with the "whatever you want" from the very beginning. And that "whatever" was Grammy.

Now, yes, she certainly heard, "Grrrrraaammmmy."

≈

This Kittitian young man donkey-kicked onto his back on the side of the mountain was a normal teenager not so long ago. The cute, not-so-cute impression that Ellie had about him yesterday on the Frigate Bay beach was right on target. He could be cute, nice, attractive, and then suddenly, erratically, not so cute, even testy with guests, customers, or anyone in his presence, even his own grandmother, the woman who raised him. A streak of meanness is such a turn-off. Seriously, his brain is addled, not just because of Lady's outburst but because something else has a stranglehold on his amygdala, one of two almond-shaped clusters of nuclei in the brain, and known to help a person process memory, make decisions and respond with appropriate emotions.

Kennedy, that's his name, was a local soccer star, and, as Ellie noticed, he's still a teenager. On the crew of the Eagle, a party-boat catamaran that crosses the Narrows regularly with boatloads of tourists, he loved crossing the two miles of open water separating his island from Nevis, its sister island.

Orphaned when his mother died and his father left for England, Kennedy was not named after U.S. President John F. Kennedy. His given name is in honor of former Kittitian Prime Minister Kennedy Alphonse Simmonds, the first person to hold this position after the two-island nation won independence from

Great Britain in 1983.

Our bruised down-on-the-ground Kennedy is hurt, embarrassed, scared, not thinking clearly. The not-so-dumb donkey kicked him that hard. Turning to his side, putting one hand on the ground and then the other, he moves to his knees. It feels as if something is hurt badly inside. He moans but he knows that he must keep moving if he wants to live.

"Boy aye aye. M'ain know," he mumbles slipping into familiar Kittitian.

Here, now, he is in big trouble. He's lost Ellie, the prize that was supposed to buy him a ticket off island. He had made a promise that had to be kept, or else.

"E suit you," he mumbles. "Stoopid. Stoopid."

Go get her. Maybe he can catch up, find her on that donkey's back, meet the man, the boss, before dawn. On this November 19th, the sun will rise at 6:18 AM. He knows this, and he still has time to pull it off.

Kennedy weighs options. But he's foggy so often now. Should he let her go? Pretend he didn't do this. Turn and run back down the mountainside? Too tired. Too dangerous. They know she is missing by now. Police have been called. He knows those guys down at headquarters and they know him. They know his grandmother. No, no, no…keep going up, to the new warehouse.

His initial thought settles itself: Go get her. Outrun that donkey. Get to her before the drug wears off, the stuff stolen from the vet school, the ketamine. Grab her and go. The guy, the man with the money, will make it happen, this chance for a new life. He will pay in cash.

"Moomoo, stoopid," he repeats angry with himself. He starts running in the same direction the donkey went. "Unno kno who e tis u pik."

Kennedy is just as disgusted with himself as his grandmother has been for months. She will hardly speak to him when she passes by on Cayon Street downtown in Basseterre. When he approaches her, she shakes her head in pity. "No more. No more, boy."

And while he pretends to ignore her dismissal, his heart breaks. So stoopid. He knows. She knows. Now everyone will know.

CHAPTER TEN

4:20 AM

Having grandparents who love you more than life itself ought to be every child's birthright. Like bumpers in a baby's crib, they can be there for protection, especially when the going gets tough.

---

*I*t's a grunting, growling, ferociously angry, high-pitchy sound, close, right out there, so nearby that Annie's blood pressure and heart rate jump immediately. Hand to chest, she breathes an "Oh my God." Is it what she thinks it is? Please no. Please no. Not here. Not tonight. Not up here.

The first time Annie encountered a wild boar, she was shocked, no-kidding, she would say later to everyone, truthfully knocked back physically by the gargantuan size of the creature and how aggressive it appeared to be, scaring her to death while she walked a quiet, rain forest trail behind Ottley's plantation house.

77

These crazy pig cousins fit their aggressive adjective, "wild," so well, weighing up to 200 pounds, and humongous at eight feet long and three feet tall. Turning back now to see where this monstrous, muscular, and totally, weirdly prehistoric creature is...nothing like their sweet, domesticated pig cousins in her estimation...she realizes it's right behind her, not more than 10 maybe 15 feet away. Large snout snorting with fangs flaring, staring intently and straight at her, it's obviously been scavenging through garbage cans back there near the end of a long drive. Is this feral hog still hungry? Hungry enough for her? On her left up ahead, she sees a car parked. When in the event of a wild boar attack, one rule is to get to higher ground. The animal won't climb. So go up a tree, anything, just get up and out of bite range. This thing, this big scary boar, perhaps surprised by her sudden entry into his early morning eating orgy, is just as surprised as she is.

It was out at Ottley's plantation that she wandered right into the boar's path in full daylight. There were baby boars rutting in the wet ground, too. The big animal, obviously Momma, stood still, watching her carefully, bemused maybe, making only mildly aggressive movements and Annie was able to quietly back, back, back up and away. Her sisters were along with her in fact and all three of them had been shocked by the size of this creature. This time? She races for that car to climb up on top.

There are 4,285 pigs on St. Kitts, many domesticated, but not all, a population of pigs up more than 60 percent since 2020. What is going on? one might wonder. Annie will later ask the Minister of Agriculture on St. Kitts what the hell is going on? Whose minding all the pigs? Why are they procreating like rabbits?

One foot on the back bumper, hands grabbing a windshield wiper for leverage as well as the corner of the trim, the wiper snaps off easily, but she is still able to push, perhaps to will, herself up and out of reach, should this big creature decide to take her on. But he's still back there, nosing through his pile of garbage, not making an attack move, just rutting, rooting, grunting, and howling. Maybe he saw her as a competitor trying to move his cheese...or eat it. On top of the old car now, she lays back on the roof and looks up at the clear Caribbean night and so many stars.

What else? she asks herself; what next?

Breathe deeply. Stay put. Breathe again. Take your time here, she tells her inner Annie. Rest. Let your heart slow down. Minutes pass and she hears the boar start to move away. The big guy's grunts, growls grow quieter.

Annie sits up, looks around and decides she is alone again. Feet over the side of the vehicle, hands pushing off, she slides down to the cement. Whew. She is sweating, taking deep belly breaths, trying to relax, to concentrate, putting hands on hips to stretch up, out, leaning back now, thumbs punching into those muscles to loosen them, then folding forward and over her knees, she pauses at ground level for a moment waiting for an idea to come, listening for more sounds of life.

Then she hears another animal sound and freaks out, thinking immediately she should go back up on top of the car. But this is an animal running, not as heavy as a boar but pounding the earth, and with a sudden, second, auditory jolt: there is a hee-haw. A donkey's bray? Well, thank God, she is not afraid of domesticated donkeys. These sweet creatures are all over the island too. One visits her yard on a regular basis.

She dashes off, not wanting to lose this lead, tired feet landing lighter now, fed with optimism. Without clear thought or any logic, she just knows that a donkey wouldn't normally be running up here, up above her house, her hillside, unless something was wrong. Donkeys don't usually run, unless triggered by something or someone. They travel at their own pace, not to be rushed unless...

Unless, what? Just go girl. Trust your gut instinct.

❧

Ellie is out cold on that donkey's back, after that second blast of ketamine. She's back in a k-hole. If her grandmother knew this, Annie would probably be just as sick to her stomach as Ellie is, thinking about the way this drug might affect her granddaughter. One of the triggers for an IBS attack is stress and Ellie still has flare-ups. Perhaps at that very moment in Annie's stream of thought, without waking fully, Ellie begins to throw up down the side of the donkey, who accepts this injustice without a whimper or fuss. What was left in her system from yesterday is now gone in an acrid explosion. Unconscious but moaning with stomach cramping and nausea, then mildly, relieved after this uncontrolled purge, Ellie sighs, falling back into sleep: Hmmmm. She begins to snore in relief, momentarily but miraculous.

Lady senses that something is not right, that this human being on her back needs help. There is an unexplainable connection. She starts racing harder and in hurried fear over, across the top of this mountain, knowing only her sense of Needsmust and the need to get there, a place she knows well but not why; the place that feels like home.

❧

Back in the kitchen below, Lizzie and Abigail are still horrified by the sergeant who meanders through the weeds in his brain, picking pieces of garbage up here and then to throw out at them. His infuriating questions go nowhere, add nothing. When did they arrive? Where did they go for lunch yesterday? He asks them for something to eat. Then, Lizzie excuses herself to go to the bathroom upstairs. But that's not her purpose in leaving. She needs to make a call. She had packed her cell phone, the one her parents urged her to leave behind for safekeeping.

On this phone now calling her Pop Pop, she hears the click of a connection and with his voice clear, she starts crying, sobbing in an outburst that surprises her. Where did this come from? Jeez. Totally on top of the bitchy behavior she used on the policeman downstairs, she breaks down now, without warning, not so strong after all, at the sound of her grandfather's strong voice. Maybe his voice was a gateway to the inner turmoil, the horror of Ellie's disappearance, she had been refusing to accept.

"Oh Pop Pop. Oh my God, oh God, oh God," she gasps, trying to catch her breath. "We need your help here. It's Ellie."

It's an hour earlier on East coast time in November, only 3:20 AM there in the U.S. but he's been awake with worry.

"Lizzie, Lizzie is that you? Is everything okay I've been trying to reach your grandmother. Wait, did you say Ellie? What's happened?"

"Oh Pop Pop. Oh my God, everything is not okay," she cries as she reaches for the bedroom door to close it for privacy, not wanting her voice or her tearful breakdown to be heard by the policeman downstairs.

Lizzie's story spews out in a torrent and Buck's mind races forward with this rush of information. Unfortunately, he is not shocked by what has happened. He truly loves St. Kitts but has always been more of a pragmatist than his wife, watching for the dark side of life, expecting the worst. Maybe it's his military training to blame but Buck has been worried and pessimistic about the changes, especially the influx of newly minted foreigners that he's documented on St. Kitts. He's always supported the Kittitian political party in power and still does, applauding how inventive they were so many years ago as the country climbed off a financial cliff and grappled with ways to bring in cash. But, and this is a big but, sometimes the people in power move far too slowly in his opinion. Occasionally, they see something coming their way, duck a little, hoping it disappears, pretending it really isn't happening and when that happy ending isn't there, they might blame it on the other political party. Even voices in the Caricom, the Caribbean Community of 20 like-minded small island nations, had been sounding alarms.

"Lizzie, Lizzie," he tells her, "I know who to call. I know what to do now. Your job is to stay calm, stay there with your sister. Now, walk downstairs and put me on the phone with this sergeant sitting in my kitchen. Don't hang up, my girl. Just walk with the phone down the stairs, into the kitchen and give him to me."

What Lizzie never knew about her grandfather was that when Buck was in the military, he served with the United States Army Intelligence and Security Command (INSCOM), a unit headquartered in Belvoir, Virginia, that conducts intelligence, security, and information operations for U.S. Army commanders. It was not something he was supposed to share with anyone as part of the oath of secrecy he took way back when.

Annie was aware of some but not all his assignments and understood the importance of his secrecy. His children and grandkids simply knew that Pop Pop's work for the United States government was important. They also grew up with the unshakeable belief that Pop Pop always had their backs. If something went wrong, he would try his hardest to make it right. In fact, right there on St. Kitts, he had brought the existence of Ivan, the Russian with the tall tales about his stolen plutonium isotope to the prime minister's attention. This was not something that the St. Kitts' leader Kennedy Simmonds at that time wanted to have on his watch. It was a period of enormous pride for Kittitians because the nation had been granted its independence from Great Britain in 1983 and stolen Soviet nuclear warheads would have been a disaster on all fronts, especially the public relations one when they were building their tourist industry. Buck had intervened quietly, and Ivan had been whisked off the island by helicopter one dark night. Julica, Ivan's favorite bartender at the Frigate Bay tiki bar, even asked around. But no one ever really knew the true story and someone like Buck, sworn to secrecy, would never tell.

Tonight, this Pop Pop knew exactly whom he would call after he had a few words with the sergeant in charge there.

With phone in hand, Lizzie races down the steps, into the kitchen and hands the cell to the sergeant.

"Here, there is someone who needs to speak with you right now."

CHAPTER ELEVEN

4:25 AM

Rabbit hole: metaphor for something that
transports someone into a wonderful or
troubling, surreal state or situation.

---

*E*very so-called "Annie and Buck" trip to St. Kitts, going back decades, no matter how many times in the same year or who...brothers, sisters, aunts, uncles, grandparents... had been invited along, would be punctuated and psychically defined by a sail to Nevis on a catamaran. You stop to snorkel along the way and swim ashore after pulling up to this sister island where a beach barbecue is a must. This catamaran doesn't dock by a deck or on the sandy shore. You climb down a rope ladder into the shallow water and swim or wade ashore. Crew members are always accommodating and wonderful, Annie insists. "They will carry your beach bag and dry towels onto the sand in a dinghy," she assures cautious travelers. "Please don't worry." Dancing on the deck to reggae music comes later, on the trip back. Sometimes passengers hang onto the mast, a pole, something, anyone, anything to keep on dancing above the Caribbean blue water as the boat dips, slips along and sails back to St. Kitts in late afternoon. Looking left or right to water's edge, you might even glimpse a flying fish darting and skipping along just inches above the sea. They do fly but just for a few seconds.

Seriously, you cannot travel to this island destination without getting yourself onto the Eagle, the Spirit of St. Kitts, or the Caona, all double-hulled boats built right there on the island. These kinds of "cat" or catamaran boats are geometrically stable because they are wide and sit shallow in the water. They are not going to tip over or send up huge sprays of sea on deck even when you feel as if you are racing too fast along the southeastern peninsula coast of St. Kitts. You won't even feel the waves seriously enough to get seasick. So forget the fact that you may not be a great swimmer...you'll don a life preserver if you're nervous. Dismiss the notion that you don't like sailing because you've gotten seasick on other boats in other places. And, well, as far as the snorkeling portion of this delightful day, get ready to lower yourself down a rope ladder into blue-green, 18-foot deep, crystal-clear water. You'll float easily with just a few occasional kicks. You can't touch bottom but floating will come naturally. Some friends and family rely on a noodle to stay afloat but all are encouraged to partake in the adventure. And when you put your face into that water and look around through the snorkel mask, like a page out of a Dr. Seuss book, fish will be there: big ones, little ones, blue ones, green ones, yellow stripes, and all, so many different kinds. Annie, who usually performs this full court press to convince first time visitors, promises, "You will not feel sick. You will not drown. You will love it and the day will move your mind out of your current state of sticky affairs. You will really let go of your cares." Plus, she'll usually add, "We love these local sailors. The crew is simply the very best."

Has Annie sailed with Kennedy, our misguided, troubled kid-kidnapper, onboard one of her favorite boats? Maybe so. But if true, he was a different young man from the one you see today, up here, mired in a terrible mess and one that could turn quite deadly, not just for Ellie, the beautiful teenager he drugged and grabbed from bed this very early morning, but also for himself, a teenager in crisis.

♍

The first time Kennedy met the Russian a year ago, the man was so drunk he could hardly stand up on the sailboat.

"Watch that guy," the captain had told Kennedy, one of his most dependable crew members at the time. "I don't want to lose any paying passengers today. That man was already high when he came aboard at 9 this morning."

"No problem, Dusty," Kennedy assured his boss.

Tourists just loved Dusty, the sailor in charge with his sun-blond dreadlocks and super smile, quick with the side stories about the island and a master at making the boat fly almost above the water under the right weather conditions. That day with the Russian, however, there was no wind and Dusty even had to use the engine to get to and from Nevis, "Queen of the Carribees" and the sister island with one of the best beaches in the world. Celebrities, kings, and queens spend time there. Princess Di escaped to Nevis after her official separation from Prince Charles. Alexander Hamilton was born there. It's also where hordes of beach-hopping tourists stop for barbecued lunches daily in high season. Kennedy and his crew know the perfect places to pull ashore.

On that beach as well as on the catamaran, Kennedy not only

watched this Russian like a nervous grandmother to make sure he didn't drown, he also sat with him in the back of the boat for the return from Nevis, at times having to hold the guy's forehead when he puked over the side. Too many Killer Bee cocktails at Sunshine's lovely bar on the beach! Those delicious super-proof concoctions could take even the most experienced drinker down. What a go-to guy was Kennedy, right? He saved this man. The payoff this teenager was envisioning was a big tip when they reached shore and disembarked on the Basseterre port, near the cruise ship terminal.

That didn't happen, at least not that day. The crew had to carry the man off and put him into a taxi with instructions to the driver to carry him into his big house on the hill. They knew where he lived. Everyone on the island did. Kennedy felt bad for the guy but worse for himself because he had been hoping for a nice reward, but this Russian was so out of it that our boy worried that the guy might not even remember him.

A week or so later at the Shiggidy Shack, Kennedy ran into him and realized his Russian did recall that drunken sail with the over-the-side vomiting drama after all.

"There you are," he said pounding Kennedy on the back after spotting him at the bar and coming to stand next to him.

"I vant to thank yu for coming to my rescue."

"Hey mon, no big deal."

"Oh but it vas."

From this friendly chat at the bar centering upon exactly what series of spirits go into the making of a Killer Bee and how many times Igor threw up, the conversation drifted to where

Kennedy hoped to be in his future; in school, in London, or maybe up in the states but certainly somewhere else than where he was, and perhaps closer to his long-distanced father. This guy, the big Muscovite man, could help big time and he liked Kennedy. There it was, unexamined for truth of course, but Kennedy was already pinning his hopes and dreams on one of the rich Russians who had planted himself on the island.

Within weeks, Igor, which was his name, took Kennedy under his wing and into a new scene, so different from the shared bedroom in his grandmother's house down on Durant in Basseterre. He opened doors, month by month, into a young man's nightmare, one that roller-coasted from super drug highs to desperate lows and now included muscle and bone pain, cold flashes, recurring chills, insomnia and gut issues that made his life miserable some days. Igor, of course, could take these symptoms away easily with his bottomless supply but Kennedy had to supply his boss in return with unquestioning loyalty.

Our Annie, putting distance and that boar behind her, stops to look and listen closely. She is nearer the top of the mountain now. That's when she sees it; the building with a light. No, no, not really a building, a shack. Moving slowly toward this place, heart pounding wildly, she recognizes a kind of homemade-decrepit Kittitian structure. It reminds her of one of those driftwood bars that still dot the beaches out on the southeastern peninsula. Visitors and tourists are encouraged to sign their names right on the wooden tables and bar tops. Leave your mark here. Come back, the suggestion shouts. Sometimes, these shabby structures wash away in hurricane winds and water, only to be rebuilt by inventive island owners. She applauds this spirit of enterprise and ingenuity. But why is this shack in front of her and way up here? It isn't a bar or a happy place. It wasn't here the last time she hiked up and over.

There is no sign, no big pig's howl or donkey's hee-haw, or any other sound drawing her to it. No whoosh, crunch, or tinkling glass to be heard either as she did earlier. Her mind wanders back to those strange noises she heard earlier. What could they have been? But never mind. She needs to see what's inside.

Inching closer to check it out, she drops down on all fours, going on hands and knees as she crawls closer. Is she prepared for a fight here? No. She just needs to see and must know what's here. Even so, she checks her pants' pockets and touches the Swiss Army knife as well as that silly little bottle of hand sanitizer to spray into an unfriendly face. This possible defense is laughable, of course. But it might give her a second of surprise.

Perched on cinder blocks, the shack has no glass in the window openings but there is a door with a padlock hanging off the latch, not locked. Why is there a light coming from inside? Close up now, Annie stands up to a window. Thank God she is tall. She'll be able to see inside.

After blasting the oh-so-tired sergeant on the phone out of that comfortable seat in the St. Kitts kitchen, Buck dials another number. The call goes to Belvoir, Virginia, and even this early in the morning, someone picks up immediately when Buck's name is on the incoming cell phone.

"Hey Buck, how are you? It's been too long."

"Not so good Buddy. I've got a problem and I need your help."

"Tell me what I can do," is the instant reply.

CHAPTER TWELVE

4:40 AM

---

*Human trafficking of women...no, let's make it
very clear here...these human beings are often
little girls...is a $150 billion a year business,
second only to illegal drugs sold on creepy,
supposedly untouchable, Internet sites. Russia,
China, and the Sudan are the worst offenders
and Saudi Arabians are big customers with
starting bids as high as $762,789 for a teenage
virgin with the right hair color and
measurements.*

$\mathcal{F}$ or months in 2021, government agencies on several
continents had been making arrests and seizing millions
of dollars in cash and virtual bit-coin currencies
belonging to pimps and purveyors operating on the Dark Market,
the world's largest online site for illegal goods and services. Buck
knew people who knew people, the very same officials in charge of

disrupting this once hidden marketplace where anyone can hire killers, sell drugs, or buy guns, armor, sex and human beings. He was aware of the team that cracked the bit-coin tracking conundrum. Just yesterday at home in Sleepy Hollow, New York, Buck had read a news report in the New York Times and smiled at the quote from Deputy Attorney General Maureen Williams, "There is no dark internet. We can and we will shine a light." He liked the way that sounded… to "shine a light" on this evil and rout it out. Now, on this very early morning of November 19, the existence of this evil is not an interesting factoid anymore for him, it has left a bombed-size crater right in his own life.

Where in God's name was his granddaughter, Ellie? And, while he can only imagine and fear her whereabouts, he also knows that help will be on the way to the island pronto.

He calls Annie again but gets nothing. Where could she be now? Lizzie said she had run out the door heading up the mountain before the policeman arrived but that's all. Was Ellie still there on the island? Oh God, he hopes and prays so. These criminals can move fast. They would keep his little girl alive. She was worth a fortune. But this fact leaves another wake of ill ease and fear in his heart. What would these ruthless traffickers do with a 74-year-old grandmother, his Annie? Their prize was his 13-year-old granddaughter, not her. Jesus Christ, they will get rid of her as fast as they can. What would he do without Annie? His thoughts build to a crazy unprofessional storm. Then, an emotion he doesn't often allow himself suddenly catches him off balance; grief, a profound sadness he knows well, remembering loss and trauma right there, deep in his gut. He recognizes this pain from his time in the military but the other experience with it was very personal; an overwhelming wave had washed over him after their third baby died. What a nightmare that had been but especially for Annie, the mother of his children, the centering force of his life! He had almost lost her as well as the baby girl who did not survive.

∽

Annie was 21 weeks pregnant and gloriously happy to be on her way to becoming a mother for the third time at 37, yes, that age meant she was in an advanced maternal category but, honestly, why should she worry? She didn't feel old. She didn't act old. She was the healthy, working mother of two, ages 7 and 4 and trying to repeat the two miracles she had already experienced; her first born Will followed by Lauren. And yet...

"I feel funny," she admitted to Buck one morning.

"What do you mean by funny?' he asked. Clearly, this was a loaded but legitimate question. In fact, funny is a weird, non-descriptive word to use under the circumstances. Her body felt…well, just quiet that morning. Quiet. That was it. She had none of the symptoms or feelings she had been having just the day, or was it two days before? Was the baby she carried inside her womb okay? Could something be wrong? Was she just being paranoid because it had taken longer to get pregnant this third time? Will and then Lauren had been so easy to conceive. So, what was she feeling? Nothing.

"It's probably nothing," she reassured Buck on his way out the door, "Nothing at all." He was preoccupied with work problems at the time. Thinking of early retirement from his military career and looking ahead to when he might take over his father's construction business. He had put in his 20 years with the service and now it was done, he had told her. "I'm over it. I need to stay closer to home now." Managing two kids during his weeks away from home, traveling overseas where he might be unreachable because of security concerns, had been do-able before but with a third child on the way, this military career of his would have been so much more difficult and too much to ask of Annie.

"I'll call you," she hollered to Buck as he ran out the back door.

Like so many women in the 20th century, Annie once had a love-hate relationship with her body. In her mind, she was too tall for a girl, too big boned, not feminine enough. Now, from her vantage point this night in November 2021, she might laugh about that long-ago distaste for her physical self.

"You are perfect just the way you are," her mother would insist.

"You have to say that because you're my mother," she'd retort.

"No, I don't. And some day you will appreciate that body. It's the only one you have. Stop hating it and beating yourself up."

"But why did I have to be so tall? I had the bad luck to get dad's genes, not yours."

You don't stop this kind of wrong-headed, body bashing without a dramatic turn in your life; a mind-changing upheaval, perhaps a personal tornado. For Annie, this perfect storm of self-perception, driving her towards a better understanding of her body and her life, for better and for worse, came with that third disastrous pregnancy.

So, on that morning of an absolute, heavy quiet in her body, when she drove to the obstetrician's office for an unscheduled, emergency visit, she cleared her head of paranoia and listened deeply.

She heard nothing.

There was no one else there but Annie. She had sensed but set aside intuition, no it was more like fear, but it was true: her growing baby died sometime in the previous day or so. Exactly when, no one could ever determine. But, of course, she didn't want to believe that this little person, much wanted, already loved, would never be. She cried. Maybe she was wrong. Maybe this was just the way a third pregnancy felt sometimes for some women? Maybe, oh God, let it be so, maybe she was still pregnant, her baby fine, just quiet but fine. She held back the truth that came up and went back away in every breath she took, waiting, yes, she would wait, for the official news; a doctor's determination to say that this pregnancy had ended.

At the appointment, the physician, almost a friend now after two previous deliveries, listened closely for the heartbeat and found none. And then, immediately, at her insistence, Annie drove to the nearby hospital for an ultrasound, a rare procedure back in the eighties not available in a doctor's office. Buck met her at the hospital to hold her hand and share the grief.

There, inside Annie's womb, lying on her back...a girl...was the unborn baby who would never become a person.

Chromosomal abnormality? Inadequate placenta? No one would fully explain the end of this pregnancy, especially at 21 weeks. Shocked and teary, Annie tortured herself with what if's, why me's, and what went wrong? She sobbed for the loss of this life. And she kept on sobbing for months, sometimes without warning, sometimes at inappropriate times, always with deep unshakable sadness. She became unable to move out of bed and morose. A prescription, a psychiatrist who specialized in maternal loss, therapy to help her accept this death of her unborn baby, encouragement from all to move on, and time, yes supposedly time would be on her side ...well, nothing worked until Buck booked a family escape to St. Kitts. He had been there before for work. And it was there, staying for three full weeks that she began to emerge, to find a steady state of mind and regain her sense of peaceful security.

"Let's not try this again," she told Buck on their last night of the very first Caribbean escape. They were sitting at the Frigate Bay Resort's Dip and Sip Tiki bar looking at the moon rising across the pool.

"Wait, not come back to St. Kitts?" he asked, surprised because he knew she had been feeling so much better, so alive, almost her old sane self.

"No, I love St. Kitts. Let's come all the time," she replied. "What I meant was let's not try to get pregnant again. We have two perfect kids. No more trying."

At 37, Annie also let go of old worn-out thoughts about her body. Why had she ever subjected it to anger? Why hadn't she applauded it, giving it kudos for getting her around, for growing two healthy, beautiful, brilliant children, and for being there whenever she needed to accomplish something physical? She'd had the perfect body all those years when she bashed it mentally. Her mom was right. Yes, maybe too tall. Okay, and certainly not perfectly proportioned. Look at those legs! But she was strong and healthy.

Now, on this race up the mountain, if she had given herself even a moment to think back to what St. Kitts had given her so many years ago, she might have wondered; did this island give a life, her own, only to take another away?

༤

The phone rings in Reginald Browne's bedroom early on this Nov. 19th morning. The prime minister of St. Kitts had been sleeping soundly, first time in months after an election that followed a fractious period of party politicking and travel abroad. He loves his island, his homeland, and knows there is always something going wrong, never ever a dull moment for Caribbean politicians. Just weeks ago, he managed to push the former PM out of power. That guy had become even too complicated with too many strings that grew during the pandemic.

"Good morning. What is it?" he asks glancing at the time, not even 5 AM, no sign of daylight. Alert signals start firing, too early for this call. Listening carefully, he sits up, turns to the side of the bed, puts his feet on the smooth, chilly, tile floor, and within seconds, is wide awake with this request from the United States government. This is not the kind of call he likes to receive from a trusted partner in his political career as a new leader. But this is his watch and even though he might not have that sign on his door like U.S. President Harry Truman did, Browne believes sincerely in the expression, "The buck stops here."

༤

Our Buck might have laughed if he was aware of Browne's borrowed American motto. But of course, he is much too busy. His mind is racing, adding to-dos. His perfectly spectacular, loving, beautiful granddaughter has been kidnapped. His wife is missing on a mission to rescue her on a dark mountainside. Seriously Annie. How could you? Then another thought; how could you not? This is total, personal chaos and he needs to get there fast.

CHAPTER THIRTEEN

4:45 AM

> *Anyone who has experienced an episode of*
> *hysterical strength in the face of danger and*
> *raced into a rescue, muscles twitching with*
> *endurance, and sympathetic nervous system*
> *going rogue, might recall, I don't know why I did*
> *what I did.*

*T*he scent hits her in an overpowering, nauseating, ugly wave that makes Annie gag. Oh my God. It's sticking to the inside of her nose and going up into her sinuses. Disgusting. Inside this shack is a mountain of mess: overturned furniture, broken bottles, trash everywhere, laced with the smell of urine, poop, and rotten food. Flies buzz and she immediately feels the bite of a no-see-um, those nasty, nearly invisible Caribbean insects. What the hell is this? Her eyes dart around the single room and register where that light had been coming from; a battery-operated lamp lying on its side on the floor.

It's on, battery not dead. Aha. There is no one here now but what in God's name was going on? Is this place connected to her Ellie? A moment of panic passes. Then she spies something that really scares her; a large wire-sided crate in the corner. In a flash, she is away from the window, up the single, cinder block step, through the unlocked door, and into the room itself, racing toward this crate.

Crouching down on all fours to poke her head into this open cage, yes, it's a cage, she's suddenly afraid of what she will find up closer. But it's empty, or nearly empty. Whoever or whatever was in here is gone now. An animal? A person? Her person? Her mind races with questions; what is this place for? Why is the cage here? Who was being held in? And who is gone now? She looks closer now, crawling half her body into it, to check corners and under what seem to be old rags. Picking one up, she realizes that it's a girl's tank top. Dirty beyond imagination, it had once been pink.

Stop right now, she scolds herself. There is no time to waste. If Ellie had been here, she thinks, I would know it, wouldn't I? Wouldn't I sense the presence of my own sweet 13-year-old granddaughter? Wouldn't I? Oh God, maybe or maybe not? And Ellie wasn't wearing a pink tank top when she went to sleep last night. That much Annie knows because when she kissed her goodnight, Ellie was in pink pajamas. This shirt has been worn for a much longer time than has passed this early morning. Goddamn it. This grandmother is so angry now. Get going. Get up off your knees. Where to? She doesn't really know the answer, simply sensing without any rationale that she must head up to the top of the mountain.

❧

Back in the kitchen with Annie's granddaughters, Sergeant

Valamine sits up straighter as Lizzie hands him the phone she used to call her Pop Pop upstairs. Her grandfather is there on the line, waiting and ready to take on this police officer. Valamine takes the cell, looking irked at this insolent teenager, and demands, "Who is this?"

Lizzie, our 16-year-old, now emboldened by the strength coming straight from her grandfather, invisibly but tangibly connected here, replies, "It's my Pop Pop."

Valamine harrumphs, almost laughs at her bold move, putting a grandfather on the telephone. Hah. How silly she is. But he puts it to his ear. The voice on the other end is loud enough to hear without benefit of any speaker button option. The girls can hear their grandfather clearly. Abigail, the 15-year-old, is reading her sister's expression and for the first time in an hour, her sense of dread lifts ever so slightly. She turns squarely, shoulders back, spine straight and glowers at the policeman now holding her sister's phone. Our Valamine, ordinarily efficient and politely correct in his official dealings, is a nice man for sure but inept here after all. Now, he is in for a rough ride that he didn't anticipate at start of his shift. This is no ordinary Pop Pop.

He listens carefully and with a memory jolt, he recalls this Buck fellow, with his big unforgettable voice, from the encounter at the station years ago after his wife's purse had been stolen. A formidable guy, Buck had a commanding set of vocals back then and you can hear it now on this early awful morning. But this is not just a commanding voice. The police officer never dreamed of the intricately powerful connections the American man also possessed. Now he was being told exactly what Valamine had to do, by order of his very own prime minister on St. Kitts. Reginald Browne would be waiting for him in minutes downtown at the main police headquarters on Cayon Street. The distance between anywhere to almost anywhere else on this island, 23 miles around and 8 miles at its widest point, was minor, of course. Browne would meet Sergeant Valamine momentarily with instructions.

❧

Isn't it true that you don't always know why you do what you do? Yes, you have a conscious self but that unconscious inner voice leads you into all sorts of truths and untruths. If logic had been followed on this night...and Annie is ordinarily very logical...she would never have run up this mountain alone in the dark. She would have waited for help. That's what old ladies are supposed to do. She might have screamed, ranted, and called her husband Buck right after phoning the local police. Right? Yes right! But back there at the house and now on the mountain, she is absolutely certain about all this. With every twitching muscle fiber and adrenaline-pumped jolt of mindless endurance, she is compelled to save her Ellie. Like a parent pulling a car off a baby in a driveway, a stranger risking his or her life to rescue another stranger in a fire, or human beings in so many other stories of unexplainable courage in a life and death situation, Annie is up for this challenge ahead of her.

Her sin? Yes, if there is one it's a promise that this trip would be deliriously wonderful for her and the girls, that it would be fun, simply an escape to her happiest of all places in the world after so many months of Covid lockdown. That assurance was hollow.

The words she had spoken to her children and their spouses, "We'll be fine. I can take care of your girls. What could happen after all? St. Kitts is such a safe island. Do not worry." They were only promises after all.

❧

On the street where Annie grew up in Yardley, Pennsylvania in the 1950s, the homes were small, single-story, three, certainly no more than four-bedroom, ranches or Cape Cods. Her family's modest home was just across the road and up from the Delaware River. Her dad built the ranch all by himself, a proud achievement he shared shamelessly with every visitor to the house for decades, offering tours down the hallway from the living room and kitchen and right into each little bedroom as well as the single bathroom at the end of the hall...even when it was most inconvenient.

"Dad please!" Annie would protest as he tried to show one of his basketball buddies around the place, opening doors wherever and whenever.

"I'm getting dressed," she would scream. "Close the door."

Like Buck, her husband, Annie's father had a big voice, but a soft touch even when he was out of touch emotionally. She didn't hate him for these intrusions. She was just annoyed. He was quite a character; tall, dark-haired, handsome, and though his formal education ended after high school, he trained as a skilled tool and die maker, then started his own business after serving in the Navy's Seabees during World War II. He read newspapers from cover to cover and was outspoken on politics, sports, and the lives of his eight children. Always athletic, like Annie, one of his middle daughters, he could "walk" on his hands, upside down with ease, feet in the air, and played basketball on a local team until he was 65.

"Jeez Dad, would you puleassse close that door," Annie would holler back then. Thinking about her father now, who lived until he was 94, makes this daughter wistful for those days when she was building resilience in that pack of siblings. He had loved and respected her. And as a middle child, you never knew what to expect and had to fight for that second glass of orange juice at breakfast or grab the last pancake before it disappeared. It was a crazy, tumultuous sea of family life in small living quarters and Annie was the child who tried hard to make no waves.

Her childhood inside this crowd of sometimes difficult, controlling, occasionally bossy... she would certainly call her older siblings know-it-alls...taught her to stand up for herself, step into difficult situations and recognize her own power. Don't hesitate. Life would never be perfect, she knew, because there is no place on the map called perfection.

She can hear her father now, telling her mother, "Girls don't need to go to college." It was the spring of her junior year at an all-girls' Catholic high school. Her parents always struggled to make ends meet and the budget didn't look promising for including tuition payments. Her two older sisters had gone straight to work in secretarial positions after taking the commercial track in school. Only her big brother had gone on to college in Philadelphia.

"Annie is going to college," her mother insists, using an unusually forceful tone for a woman who always allowed her husband to think he was in charge. There is no debate here; end of conversation. Then, her mom repeats, "She is going to college. We will make it happen." For this and so much more, Annie will always treasure her mother's determined wisdom.

Maybe it was because she had been orphaned at age 12, but Annie's mother had an unmatched, remarkable resiliency. Perhaps Annie inhaled this. Annie never knew either grandmother. Both women were gone by the time she was born. So, there was no personal model or age-old map of what this role would entail for her or how she ought to navigate the next generation of her genes.

Then, within a span of just a few years, more than a decade ago, she had six grandchildren arrive in quick sequence, one right after the other: three amazing girls along on this vacation now and three fantastic grandsons. The boys had wanted to invade this girls-only trip, but she had promised; a girls-only getaway. The boys would get their own, already on the calendar.

Don't you dare think it. Just stop. But she can't; would this have happened if the guys had been along? Why had she insisted on absolute independence here?

CHAPTER FOURTEEN

4:50 AM

The quote is on Annie's bulletin board. She can't remember where it originated, but the command would be perfect for this day.
"The unifying theme is resilience and faith. The unifying theme is being a warrior. It's not fragility. It's strength. It's nerve. And 'if your nerve deny you,' Emily Dickinson wrote, 'Go above your nerve.'"

---

*W*ith tires screeching on the otherwise quiet downtown Kittitian street, the new Prime Minister Reginald Browne's official vehicle pulls up to police headquarters at the same time Valamine arrives. The sergeant is smarting from his embarrassingly inadequate situation. Jesus, did he fail this family tonight? Could he have been wrong about the girl's disappearance? Did his casual attitude irritate the issue even further? The call from Buck sure spelled his Failure out with a capital F. He is also on edge about what the new Kittitian leader has in store for him.

Valamine voted for Browne. Everyone was tired of the other PM. Browne's the new young hero and leader on this island. Getting on this guy's bad side from the start of his power could mean embarrassment or something worse for the police officer.

Yes, he's seriously uncomfortable thinking about this missing teenager, but truthfully, he would prefer to be heading home to bed and not into a confrontation with the leader of his nation. He still suspects that she, this girl, may have gone willingly, sort of, maybe, maybe not, with a young man. But is this a man's way of thinking? Perhaps. Her cousins, those two bossy American girls, with their raging protests keep stopping him from trusting his own preconceived notions. They were insistent. But what does all that matter now? He's in deep now and must fight to stay on board here.

∽

As a Caribbean nation's senior political leader at age 45, Reginald Browne, a husband, father and dentist educated and trained in the Caribbean as well as the U.S., is now the beneficiary of a private driver on call. The guy, Cyril, is an old school buddy. Browne also has a government-issued cell phone with international VIP pre-set numbers and has already been on several calls working with the U.S. Southern Command (SouthCom) to put a plan in motion. Eager to cooperate and make St. Kitts shine brightly for the U.S. government, he knows his independent island is no stranger to these American forces, a unit that brings together the 12th Air Force, the U.S. Army South, U.S. Naval Forces 4th Fleet, Special Operations teams, and several Task Forces, including Bravo. Yes, Bravo, my God. This thought makes Browne smile.

Drug smugglers and traffickers have even drawn Navy warships into the region in recent years. You might accurately describe this military "presence" as more of a "flood" of enforcement resources since 2020. He's seen it on the island and at Port Zante downtown.

Tourists are unaware, of course, but politicians like Browne are pleased. Local leaders have taken note of everything from Navy destroyers, Coast Guard cutters, U.S. Navy combat ships, helicopters, Navy P-8 patrol aircraft, to Air Force craft in the waters surrounding St. Kitts. The Navy vessels, the ones called "littorals" that patrol close to shores and beaches and have gained notoriety for their occasional failures, are capable of speeds up to 40 knots and host helicopters. Let's hope the ones on their way to his shoreline work smoothly today.

He tells Cyril to wait with the engine running. "We'll be right back."

"We?"

"Yes, we. I will have Valamine with me."

His St. Kitts and Nevis Coast Guard held joint training sessions with SouthCom units, a military force with a mission Browne admires; to promote respect for human rights in Central and South America and the Caribbean. SouthCom's new commander, a woman, is U.S. Army General Theresa Bainbridge, and in fact, she just assumed her command on Oct. 29, a few weeks ago and must have flown right over his beloved Caribbean country just yesterday, on her way further south to a three-day visit to Colombia. Browne appreciates women in leadership positions, especially the spectacular women on St. Kitts, hardest workers he knows. Where would the world be without them?

As the new prime minister, Browne called Bainbridge

directly to congratulate her on the new command. "Wonderful news General. I am happy that you will be here keeping watch over our Caribbean communities."

"Thank you so much Mr. Prime Minister. And congratulations to you too! I am pleased and excited with this appointment. I enjoyed your speech at the United Nations a few weeks ago."

"Oh my. You heard my address there in New York? We are both so new in our positions."

"But I wouldn't have missed your speech. I am trying to understand everything I can about the Caribbean nations. I need the insight. You were quite impressive," Bainbridge added.

"I must confess," Browne replied, "I watched the video of your award ceremony and heard your speech as well. Very moving. We are so lucky to have a woman like you in charge of SouthCom. Please let me know if there is ever any way I can be of service."

"I certainly will. Let's promise to stay in touch."

Taking on this top position, Theresa Bainbridge, a mother, and a grandmother, pledged to counter all sorts of threats. As another woman with a mission tonight, Annie would be clapping for her if she knew how important her presence in the Caribbean was at this very moment. On Bainbridge's to-do list is a promise to share information and critical U.S. capabilities to deny transnational criminal organizations and violent extremists the use of established smuggling routes through the Americas. And while the news of an American teenager missing this night has just reached her, Bainbridge certainly knew from her military briefings that well-resourced organized crime groups had been moving drugs, weapons, counterfeit items, money and people, young women in fact, on the smuggling networks.

❦

Minutes after his emotional conversation on that phone with Lizzie and the follow-up with Valamine, Buck had reasoned correctly that this was no ordinary kidnapping his family was facing. It had international roots. Having watched the Russian presence grow on his favorite island, making friends with some while instinctively snubbing others socially, able to sense their unholy ties, he could envision something criminal simmering. There was just too much cash everywhere around a few of these Russians. Buck also knew there was a Forward Operating Base in Aruba-Curacao with aircraft and airfields to support the Caribbean region's multinational efforts to combat this sort of nasty business. What did these Russian racketeers think they were doing on his beloved St. Kitts? He's piqued. No, he's pissed and personally involved now, he is raging with anger and apprehension.

Later this day in fact, SouthCom's Commander Bainbridge would be sitting down with defense ministers in Colombia discussing exactly this kind of despicable human business. Buck had seen this on a briefing report. No, I am not overreacting by alerting military friends, he assured himself. Yes, this was the time to move against these bastards. Here was his very own Ellie caught in their trap. He began thinking of other young women in need of rescue. These people would pay, he thought, gritting his teeth.

"Annie, pick up. Pick up. Pick up please," he says into his phone. No connection. No Annie at the other end. "Where are you? Are you okay? Be there!"

Fearful and frustrated, Buck is growing his must-do-right-now list longer still. Before arranging for his flight to St. Kitts through an old military channel, he must call his children to let them know Ellie is missing and what is happening. At this thought, his heart drops. Goddamn it, how do you open this kind of conversation? Not easily. Then, he thinks, Will and Lauren will want to join him on this nightmare trip to St. Kitts. Is that a good or bad idea? How would it work? Yet this is their parental right. Buck's thoughts race with possible plans of action. Wouldn't it be better if these parents, his kids, delayed their arrival until he knew Ellie's fate and the news was good? No, no, no, he doesn't have the right to withhold this day from them. What would he want as a father? And what about a bad ending here? Do they need to be there with him, no matter what happens?

He picks up the phone to call his daughter, Lauren. She must be first. This is her daughter Ellie.

෴

Something wakes her with a jolt. Ellie senses she has stopped moving and reaches her arm down around the flank of this warm animal. Lady has been breathing hard, warm to the touch from running. Our girl is conscious now with thoughts jumbled. She can hardly stay alert for more than a second. Eyes open. Eyes closed. Please stay open, she prays. Stay awake now. The donkey, is it Lady? Yes, this is Lady, the same sweet burro she met yesterday near the Frigate Bay beach. Moving her head up, Ellie turns slightly and pulls her cheek up to see where she is. Lady farts.

"Oh, my Lady," Ellie laughs. "Your tummy must be exactly like mine, always something happening down in there. Are you hungry?"

The donkey neighs as if she understands. Maybe she does.

Then, the thought lands in a sudden flash of awareness, where is he? Yes, that he, the guy, that awful creep who grabbed her mouth and nose the first time when she was back there in bed, dragging her outside, onto the second-floor balcony, then bumping, banging, lugging her semi-paralyzed body down the garden trellis. It had felt like a dream...no, a nightmare. What is going on? Why is he doing this to her? Then, a bigger, more immediate fear bubbles up; Where is he? Right now? Is he here now? He was just a moment ago. And Lady? He was holding Lady's rope, wasn't he? Yes, yes. She turns her head to look around. No one.

It's quiet and she can sense no human nearby physically, just Lady. Elle leans forward whisper into one of her big pointy ears, "Lady, are we alone here?"

With a shake of her head and a sound that borders on what might be a burst of light laughter, Lady responds with a series of brays and whinnies that feel like happy purring to Ellie lying so closely on her back. This is not a loud, jarring, noisy-donkey bray. There is an innate intelligence that surprises even Ellie, an animal lover. This split second of safety is enough to pull Ellie further into the real world, to bring her back to alert consciousness. Turning her head from side to side on Lady's back and wiggling her body enough to force her legs down, closer to the ground, she begins to free herself from the crudely tied rope that has been holding her on this creature's back.

Ears up, down, making the joy apparent, Lady turns her head back to Ellie, and wiggles her entire body wildly to help her girl get loose, squeaking and squealing in what sure looks like joy. This almost makes our 13-year-old passenger want to laugh out loud. So, she does.

"Lady, what did you do? Fart again?"

The animal's hee-haw response comes back immediately. "Heeeee hawww…heee hawww."

Ellie smiles as she remembers now what happened back there on the mountain. They have traveled some distance but are still high up. Did she really scream at that guy? She was so angry. Then she was out cold with a second smash in the face of his foul-smelling, drug-laced rag. How did they get so far away from him?

"Good girl," Ellie says softly. "You're my Lady, my special Lady."

Off Lady's back, rope falling to the ground but still looped around the donkey's neck, Ellie stands up and looks around, resting one hand on the animal to steady herself. She is on top of the mountain far up behind Grammy's house but can almost make it out down there in the dim, early light. The full moon that she and her cousins had watched rise into the night sky, is lower now. Up ahead, several dark houses are partially hidden in overgrown vegetation, palm trees and cacti. This mountain that was once a blank canvas of Caribbean, has been painted with newcomers and foreign investment. Ellie can see it from here now.

She murmurs to Lady. "Which way should we go?" looking back down toward Grammy's house. She thinks, yes, let's go back down, feeling compelled to head there. But Lady is insistent, braying, pulling away, tugging Ellie in the other direction.

"Why Lady?" she asks. "Why do we need to go that way?"

The rope around Lady's neck swings back and forth with her head as she pushes her nose up to Ellie, telling the girl, "Take it, take it."

Legs unsteady, whole body drained of physical energy, Ellie leans against Lady's flank for a moment. She can feel the animal's warm life force. Lady noses up against Ellie to nudge the invitation further along. Our girl climbs back up on the donkey, holding on to stay on.

"Let's go, Lady," Ellie says, "you lead the way."

CHAPTER FIFTEEN

4:55 AM

Studies suggest that we receive genetic memories
from our parents, grandparents, and ancestors.
Perhaps this is an instinctive effort by their
dynamic DNA to prepare ours for difficult
experiences in the here and now: fear, disease,
trauma, a kidnapped grandchild?

---

*T*he beep-beep of a simultaneous call on Buck's phone interrupts him before he can get a word out to his daughter Lauren. He's at home in Sleepy Hollow, New York. She had been sound asleep, more than an hour away, in her Long Island home. Now, she is immediately frantic because her father wouldn't be calling this early except in an emergency. Lauren likes to sleep in. Something must be wrong. Is it her daughter, Ellie? Her nieces? But she talked to the girls late yesterday on the phone. Everyone was having a joyful time, especially her mother who had been promising the girls this getaway to St. Kitts for months with so many cancelled plans, abandoned airline itineraries. They had worn sunscreen to the beach, assuring her they would be just fine. "No one got sunburned Mom!" Lauren is protective, ever the mother on alert for danger. Yesterday, it was sunburn.

"Dad, what is it? What's happened?" Lauren asks, although ask is a cool verb that doesn't quite match her emotional temperature here.

"It's Ellie," he starts to explain to his frightened daughter, then he stops, unable to ignore the insistent call-waiting beep on his phone. "Wait…wait, Lauren, I've got to take this other call. Hold there. Just hold." This request to wait, wait a minute, just a minute, would be perfectly logical in any other circumstances but for Lauren right now, it's not. Asking her to hold is like requesting that she step into a protracted horror.

"No, no, Daddy please, tell me now. Tell me something. What is it?" She hasn't used a Daddy on him in years but now is certainly the time to tug at his fatherly strings. "Daddy? What? What is happening?"

So, he blurts out, "Ellie's been kidnapped," adding, "but I think I've got help on the other line here."

Oh my God. Oh my God. Lauren is descending into every parent's worst, unthinkable nightmare. Why did she let her daughter go? She is too young to be out of the country without her parents. Isn't she?

❦

In the cool morning air, Annie pauses to look around. This island is so breathtaking, especially from up above where she is standing. She looks around in awe. No wonder generations of Kittitians fell in love with this place even as they were enslaved to the land and its entitled landowners. This view out to the ocean is spectacular in the dawn's light.

She laughs about how many times she has posed family and friends for photographs up on Timothy's Hill. It's a touristy spot with jaw-dropping views of the Southeastern peninsula stretching out dramatically. Friends and family groups have changed from year to year but there were always smiles and poses, sometimes with monkeys. No, no, no, she warns all. Don't get too cozy with those monkeys carrying viruses. These warnings were long before Covid when we all learned more than we ever wanted to about viral misery. So many times, she did this so many times when taking visitors on island tours. But this view today is different. And monkeys, hah, they are nothing compared to what she is facing.

The Atlantic Ocean is down to her right as she heads north. Over on the other side, to her left and down will be the Robert Bradshaw International Airport, where she and her family landed for the first time in the 1980s. The airport has changed since then. Major airlines come and go frequently now, not just on Saturdays. Private jets for millionaires and newly minted citizens, some rich Russians oligarchs, land too but park off to one side, disembarking by appointment into a new private terminal. Ordinary tourists depart into a sprawling air-conditioned two-story terminal that replaced the old tin-roofed welcome center. Sometimes, a steel drum band greets passengers on busy weekends. They don't serve free rum punches any longer. But you can buy a Carib out there on the sidewalk as you climb into your getaway into paradise car, van or taxi.

If she had a moment to reminisce, she might breathe a prayer of gratitude for what St. Kitts offered her on that first visit so many years ago; an end to a heavy hopelessness she experienced for months after her third baby died in the womb. She can't help but still think of her as a baby not the fetus she saw on the ultrasound screen. That was a bad time, a period of life best left behind but not forgotten. In fact, the memory of those first-time-ever weeks spent in St. Kitts with Buck, Lauren, and Will are as clear as where she is heading right now, to Ellie. She doesn't even stop moving to second guess her gut instinct. Just go. And listen.

"Ellie," she whispers, "oh my brave girl, please, please be okay. Grammy is coming. I can do this. No, we can do this together."

❦

Kennedy curses what he wants to believe is bad luck. "F--k. Oh mon, dis is no good." He is so over it all now: the drugs making him sick, the maniacal maze his life has become, the man, that Russian. On the mountainside, he gets up from his knees where he landed after the crazy donkey kicked him and starts running. Damn. This is all wrong. It's been so crazy lately. What the hell is he doing here? And she, this girl, was such a mistake. His biggest mistake? Believing that guy, that cruel, nasty Russian. So nice, so welcoming, so inviting...at first, but then, the dark side opened and it was pretty miserable, he has to admit.

Leaving the catamaran crew to work for this man was so wrong, he knows now, but it felt so good to be rich, powerful, not poor, not island-poor in paradise. Ignore the obvious, he told himself, these girls are just part of the plan, a ticket to ride for him. Denial, of course, was a nice place to be because the Russian had so much money. But this girl, the sweet blonde girl who liked the donkey, the girl from Frigate Bay Beach he met yesterday, well she is different. He should have known when he saw the house, her grandmother's house, on the hillside. Too connected, too loved, too many invisible strings attached. Not a tourist, a stranger to his island. He even warned the boss man.

"You, you there," Igor had admonished. "I don't pay you to think. I do the thinking here. Go get her."

"Okay, okay."

"Bring the little bitch to me. She weell bring big money."

Kennedy, this cute-not-so-cute guy with the sun-bleached blond dreadlocks, recalls those long days sailing on the blue-green water he had loved, on the catamaran with crew friends and fun-loving strangers, from St. Kitts to Nevis, from Nevis to St. Kitts, back and forth along a magnificent coastline that can banish bad thoughts, watching for flying fish, saving drunk tourists from falling overboard. It was all so easy, so effortless. Now he is ruined, done, screwed. Totally.

"So stoopid…"

Even Tata, his grandmother, warned him this move was a mistake.

"Do not quit the catamaran, boy."

She promised that his luck would turn, that he was still young, that the rest of life was ahead. Putting her hand on his soft curls, she assured him that he would find his place, a good place, in the world but not with that angry Russian. Shush to that old-lady logic… Kennedy had brushed her off and turned her knowing ways aside, needing to follow his instincts and go with the money guy, the big dollars and the mansion, a Great House, on a mountain. He was addicted to the power, the cool scene, the people who came and went and of course, the high he could get anytime he wanted.

"No no no, Tata, you know nothing. This man has the cash and he likes me."

"Wrong, wrong," she had argued. "He's using you. He doesn't like anyone, not even himself. He hides a monster in his mind that can break out at any moment. He comes from monsters, many generations of evil. You are special boy. Don't make this mistake."

Jeez, Kennedy had wanted to shout but didn't. Where does this grandmother get her "Tata" power over him? A word from her, a nod, a look of anguish or disappointment and there she will be under his skin, tunneling through his thoughts, wagging her finger. But of course, he fights back. "You know nothing Tata, nothing at all. Yoo spend your whole life right here, going nowhere, knowing nothing, on this nothing island. What makes you think this man has a monster inside?"

"I know Kennedy. I just know boy. Tata always knows. Don't do this."

But, like young people everywhere, Kennedy needed to pull away, to follow his own desires, to make his own mistakes. Sad but true, and some mistakes leave a lasting legacy of misery that can fan out like the miserable Covid 19 virus that was killing so many innocent people in 2021. The drugs now are taking a toll on his body. Where once he felt indestructible and happy, now, his skin crawls, mind jumps, stomach knots and twists, bowels never stop grumbling.

Up here on the mountain, pain in his belly, shaky unsteady hands, body threatening to explode without his fix, percs, greenies, body hurting from a donkey's kick, and mind hurtling toward madness, our Kennedy is going through a nasty withdrawal. In and out of clear thinking, he gets up off the ground, knowing that losing this girl could lose him his life. His Russian, the boss, well, Tata was right. A seriously split personality, he could snap from happy-hour, anything-you-want-to-drink, snort, or down; let-me-help-you-kid friendly to violent and murderous in minutes. Kennedy's bruised-blue right cheek is still healing from the last angry punch he took from this wild Russian up at the big house. And, in the middle of this botched attempt to grab another girl, he wonders if he should simply run downtown to his grandmother's home and beg her to take him back. No. No, he thinks. Try. Pull this plan off the cliff here. Make up for this mistake. Instincts honed on a high school soccer field and polished later working on the catamaran, kick in, his can-do nature still there. It's not light yet. Still time, more than an hour. His head is clearing.

Now, what was it he overheard Igor shouting on the phone yesterday?

Buck ends the call with Lauren. She'll be on the road within minutes. Taking a deep breath, he phones Will to bring him up to date. His children, the parents of his six beautiful, brilliant grandchildren, will not be along for the first ride today. Buck has been through military exercises in his life but they have not and that had made him hesitate to put them in danger. In fact, there is no other option. They were too far away from Stewart International and the military jet, a Gulfstream, and among the fastest in the fleet, that would be there for Buck, after a mad dash up the Hudson River from his home. A public quasi-military air hub in Orange County, New York, this airport is home to the Stewart Air National Guard Base and the 105th Airlift Wing. Buck knew this though it was news to Lauren and Will. Their ride from Stewart would follow his by an hour. Buck would be making the fastest trip ever to his beloved St. Kitts. Like Peter Pan, straight on to morning…in a military, super fast Gulfstream.

❧

Lady stops her farting. Ellie starts. The two are in tandem, gastronomically. Her stomach and entire gastro-intestinal system are so gnarly. What was that drug on the dirty rag?

"Oh Lady," she whispers. "Can you stop to let me off for a minute? I need to go" and she almost says "to the bathroom" out of habit. But of course, there is no bathroom here.

CHAPTER SIXTEEN

5 AM

Families are fragile. Look around, everywhere, in every generation, they fall apart. Children dismiss parents, siblings fight never-ending battles, grandparents are left behind. Statistics on these splits are startling. Misunderstandings run amuck. Forgiveness is set aside.

izzie and Abigail wait.

Valamine waits for his prime minister to finish up important phone calls.

Buck is not waiting at all but driving like a maniac up the Hudson River.

Annie can't move fast enough. She is unable to shake off the image of that dirty shack and the pink tank top. Even the stench stays with her.

Is there a better path up here somewhere? Should she take that narrow-paved road further? It zig-zags, winds, twists unexpectedly into hairpin turns. Perhaps someone is home in one of these houses up here? Might anyone have seen something or someone suspicious? Should she stop to ask? But at 5 AM? The houses on this hillside come with dramatic views and were exactly the reason for purchasing her own. They had rented one once, a big house, to bring all the kids together. Lauren had even hired a steel drum band to play by the pool for a family party. She wanted as many of those good times as possible in her life and this is where she imagined being able to find them.

"Let's buy something here," Annie had said to Buck. "We know this island so well. What's not to love?"

"I know the kids will agree," Buck concurred. "Hey, can you put the house in all our names? A piece of this happy place will belong to all of us," she added.

Was this other, dark side of paradise here all along and she failed to notice? Isn't she always the optimist to Buck's cautious pessimism? But of course, he defends his analytical approach as simply being realistic. "I'm just anticipating problems, Annie."

"Look on the bright side," she used to say.

"But I do," he would argue. "I just want to have a full picture."

❧

This island loves its tourists, and the feeling is mutual. They come in droves from every continent in the world to escape the real world, especially during cold months. So did her family, she muses before this thought turns sour for her, makes her so angry she could scream. How dare you! How dare you take my granddaughter and do this?

Ahead on the road is something that stops her; a building that wasn't there before the Covid lockdown two years ago. A warehouse? It's a simple structure of corrugated metal. Why here?

Reliving the ugly images inside that cage she explored back there, she's wary, worried, anticipating the awful. Cautiously, she approaches the building happy that she is dressed all in black. Does she really believe this will make her unnoticeable? She circles around to the front, looking for signs of activity. No windows. There are two cargo doors and paved concrete. The road going down the mountain to the other side leads off from here. She turns to look down the other side of the mountain and realizes she can almost see the airport beyond Kim Collins Highway, named after the runner, a St. Kitts and Nevis's world champion track and field sprinter. Nice guy, he represented his country five times in the summer Olympics and won a gold medal in the 100-meter. They met Kim at a Kittitian fundraiser.

She stops suddenly. There in the dark is a guy sitting, no leaning, against the closed doors obviously unaware of her nearness. A guard? Is he sleeping? Sure. Annie's heart beats wildly and she tries to turn this inner thumping down. This is her chance to find something out. She just knows it. The adrenaline pumping through her body will be good, after all. Why should she stop now? You will do what you need to do here. You have lived a long life. This is not about you, Annie. You can die. Ellie can't. Not yet. Her life has barely just begun. It's all about saving Ellie.

Inching closer to him, she sees that he looks Kittitian. Could be dangerous? Well, of course. But…well, she believes that at 74, she's in charge here. Not him. Glancing about, checking quickly down each side of the building, she guesses that he must be alone, unless others are inside. And here in this contest of experience versus ignorance right in front of her, she believes without really thinking it through, that her years will get the best of him. She puts her hand in her yoga pants' pockets to make sure that the folding knife from her bedside is still there and checks the other side for her bottle of spray sanitizer. Ready? Ready!

"Good morning," she says loud enough to alert him and then, in her most Grammy-fied, non-threatening tone of voice, she adds, "I'm so sorry to wake you, young man."

Is a simple good morning what she ought to be offering up right now? Since when is being polite ever a successful first move in an encounter with an enemy? Maybe never. Maybe always. Well, who the hell knows, not Annie for sure, but it's her first instinct and she is quite fearless here. She takes a few steps closer and can see that this kid is not fully awake but now very aware of her approach. He looks over, sees this older woman walking towards him and probably thinks; No big deal…old white lady. Should be mindin' her business.

⁓

Lady stops in her tracks so Ellie can climb off to be sick, throwing up and pulling down her pajama pants to relieve herself, right there on the ground. This is awful. This is a nightmare no little girl should have to experience. Then, she vomits violently at the same time diarrhea forces her poor bowels to empty too. Poor Lady. Not even a donkey should be subject to this kind of rider. The Ketamine has wreaked havoc on her sensitive, 13-year-old, IBS-laden gut. Wiping her lips with the side of her hand, she tries to spit out the wretched rancid taste in her mouth. She would give anything for a drink of water. Reaching into her pajama pants pocket to search for a tissue, she discovers that little flashlight with the musical buttons playing Frozen songs. Why not? She tells herself. Pull up your pants. Turn on the light. Push one of those buttons. Maybe the light and sound will alert someone for help.

Lady hee-haws protectively, nodding her head up, down and then around to nudge Ellie with affection. There is no human judgment about vomit or poop here in this animal's affection. There is nothing Lady wouldn't do for her rider. A donkey? Ellie's protector? Who could have imagined?

Ellie can feel this unconditional love. "Oh Lady, thank you so much."

A gentle mewling sound comes back as a "You're welcome."

Unable to hear those far off sounds of Ellie getting sick, Annie walks closer to the young man who is on his feet now. Pee-ewe. This guy stinks — so dirty and unkempt that she suspects he has been up here for days. Is he drugged, maybe hung over? Whatever, she decides his unstable situation is in her favor.

"What do you want?" he shouts.

"Why, nothing at all," she answers. "Just out for an early morning hike." Moving forward while keeping this easy chatter going, willing him to stay focused on her face, she puts her hand into one pocket to retrieve and flip open the well-oiled knife in her palm. Her other hand is holding the sanitizer spray.

"I don't remember this building being here," she says amicably, trying to disarm with sweet, grandmotherly, poisonous chatter. "Was it built during the pandemic? Goodness gracious, whatever for, way up here? You look so tired. How are you managing up here honey?"

"Stay away," he says. "Don't come any closer."

"Well young man, I'm not about to hurt you. Don't be silly. I live right down there." To catch him further off guard, she adds, "Forgive me honey, but you wouldn't happen to have a restroom here, would you? I really have to pee."

His eyebrows jerk up and his gaze goes definitively right as he shakes his head in disgust at this incompetent old lady. He thinks he knows all about her. Appearances do deceive. He doesn't have time for her nonsense. He's expecting people within the hour.

"Go away. There is nothing here for you. No bathroom!"

That eyes-right gesture? Well, it is in that moment, that movement that Annie knows she must move hard, fast and now. Not a second to waste.

If you're sensitive enough to human emotions, you can see guilt and Annie knew he was a liar; his eyes had given him away, and not just about the bathroom. Her sister, a compulsive liar, would always look right when she was about to tell a tall tale. Annie had grown up with lies and shared a bedroom with a particularly gifted liar. This guy wasn't even smooth.

Unthreatened by her easygoing approach — let's call it elderly advantage — he doesn't anticipate what happens next, when Annie sprays straight into his face, drenching his eyes, nose, and mouth with irritating alcohol while pushing a knife into the space in his neck where collarbones meet. Immobilized, he flails toward what is undoubtedly a gun in his pants pocket. He's gagging, gurgling actually and that surprises her. A knife punched into the clavicle area can cause bad things to happen. You've got the brachial plexus nerve there, a subclavian artery and veins with lots of blood, not to forget the apex of the lung. A physician Annie once interviewed told her, "It's not a good spot for a steel blade," even a small Swiss Army knife like the one in her hand. The clavicle is the most commonly fractured bone in the human body.

The next sound startles even Annie. It's her own screaming, screeching, shrieking, and wailing like a proverbial female spirit banshee. It is sudden, but accompanied by her very own powerful shove, pushing him back into the rattling doors of the building. Eyes burning, grabbing for her hand with the knife, he's on the defense when she kicks him in the groin so hard that it knocks the breath out. Annie doesn't stop and uses her right knee to punch down into the groin she has just kicked. Did she learn that move a hundred years ago in that self-defense training session for editors at the magazine? Of course. Did she think she would ever use it? Better yet, remember how to use it? Let's be honest, of course not.

He's schlumping back into the doors while still trying to reach into his pocket, but he is in serious pain. On the ground now, he winces when she jumps hard on his hand, using one foot, then the other. Through her sneaker soles, she can feel the breaking of bone, those small but critical bones in the hand. This must hurt. There are 27 individual bones in every hand, eight carpal, five metacarpal, and 14 finger bones. This was a brilliant but unplanned move on her part. It just happened. It worked. No thought involved. Her fury here on this mountain is beyond her rational control, coming from a deeply disturbed place in her being. Why this guy? How does she know he is complicit in this horrendous story tonight?

Annie, our more-than-simply-furious grandmother now in charge, just knows that he is guilty; he is in on this evil thing.

"Let me inside this building," she demands.

The expression on his contorted face is priceless and painful. He's bleeding down the front of his dirty shirt but still moving. Not dying, she prays. This is shock right up close and personal. He certainly never saw such damage coming from an old woman, someone's grandmother for God's sake.

Eyes burning, still reaching up, attempting to grab her hand with the knife she has pulled out of his neck, he's on the defensive when she kicks him again in the groin so hard that it takes his breath away. Is he going to pass out? Annie keeps right on screaming and uses her knee again and again to punch into his body. She is absolutely furious with an avalanche of emotion that has been building from the irrational moment she realized that Ellie was missing, and she began running up this mountain she had once loved.

He's bleeding so much now that Annie worries she may have injured him mortally. She didn't actually try to hit an artery. Her unexamined aim, honestly, was not to kill the guy. She is guessing that he is just a poor chump working for someone else. In fact, she needs to keep him alive until she can get what she wants; to get inside the building and get information about what exactly is happening here and where Ellie is right now.

"Let me into this building right now," she insists. "Open the door."

"Kay. Okay. Crazzzzee mama. Stop."

"Give me the key to that lock."

"I dunna have the key."

CHAPTER SEVENTEEN

5:10 AM

A 13, 15, and even 16-year-old brain is not fully developed and its prefrontal cortex, that little lobe responsible for executive, decision-making performance, doesn't reach adulthood until age 25. Parents see this all the time, don't we, asking, "Why did you do that? What were you thinking?" Images of developing teenage brains in action show how they make decisions differently from adults, for better and for worse.

*A*t their grandparents' house, Lizzie and Abigail are out on the pool deck facing the Atlantic Ocean. It's still dark on this way-too-early morning but they are watching for something, anything, unsure of everything. The obnoxious police officer is gone. How could he not believe them? Ellie, their adorable younger cousin, is only 13 years old, barely interested in boys, let alone some strange guy who must have climbed up to their second-floor bedroom and dragged her away. They had been asleep when they sensed the movement from the other bed. So freaky.

And then there had been the arrival of Sergeant Valamine! Someone to save Ellie? No. No. No. Grammy had known not to wait. A fool. Jesus Christ, why is it that men of a certain age dismiss the opinions of young women? What else could they have done to convince him to bring help, to go up the hill behind the house, to find Ellie before something awful happened to her?

This morning, these girls, preternaturally at war from birth in their own family brew of combative sibling warfare, are of one mind. But they are alone here. Valamine, the slow-long-talking officer with the British accent, ran off in an angry, edgy huff, looking daggers at them, as he raced out of the kitchen, down the flower-lined driveway and jumped into his official St. Kitts patrol car.

"What the hell was that?" Lizzie had snarled right after he slammed the phone down. She had given her cell phone to him with Pop Pop on the line. Then, his face sunk in shock and he jumped up, racing past them. What was that all about?

"Pop Pop must have really done a number on him," Abigail adds.

"For sure."

"We know how that can feel," they smiled together momentarily remembering the rare but unforgettable times in their lives when their grandfather had felt the need to raise his big voice at them. He could make any of his grandkids stop in their tracks with one of his stern speeches.

"Seriously Liz, I wish Pop Pop were here now."

On the cell phone with their grandfather before she'd handed it to Valamine, Lizzie had been ordered to sit tight, stay with her sister, and told that he was putting a plan in motion. He would have it under control. She could feel the decisiveness, his strength, and she experienced a rise of relief that he could make things right. Both sisters felt calmer for a few minutes. Then, the power of the problem hit them again. Their grandfather was thousands of miles away, their grandmother had run out of the house more than an hour ago to run up the mountain. They were alone and Ellie was missing. What they didn't want to say out loud was that Grammy was 74 years old, not a good age to go into battle. She was old. But the worst ingredient now in their spectacularly all-wrong stew was that Ellie had to be in desperate danger.

"What do you think is happening to her?" Lizzie wonders aloud to Abigail.

"Who?" Abigail asks, always needing complete clarification from her sibling.

"Who do you think I mean?" Lizzie snarls questioning her little sister's sanity.

"Well, I wondered if you were talking about Ellie or Grammy?"

"Jesus Abby, you are so right. I'm so sorry. I am just freaked. Both could be dead by now."

"Don't say that, Liz. Please don't say that out loud or even think it. Don't. Don't. Just don't. It'll be okay."

"Why do you always have to use that lame 'It's going to be okay' line? You don't know that it will be okay. You don't know that at all."

"Let's not fight now."

Still in their pajamas, they stand looking northeast towards the Atlantic Ocean.

"Where are the binoculars?" Lizzie asks suddenly. Their grandfather is a bird watcher and they both know he has a high-powered pair somewhere in this house. "The ones with the night vision," she adds.

"What? What do you see? Why do you need the binoculars?"

"Look there, to the left, way out there. I think I see lights. Boats, ships or something blinking," Lizzie answers.

"Let me get the binoculars."

Some human beings are blessed with superb interpersonal and intrapersonal intelligence, the ability to understand others as well as their own interior selves. Abigail has both, but it's her gift of spatial intelligence that is beyond brilliant. She drives her family crazy, always knowing exactly where everything is located in the places they all occupy. Her need for neatness is overpowering on occasion. But hey, it comes in handy sometimes. Where did that big lobster pot go? What did Grammy do with that extra beach bag? Ask Abigail. Grammy, in fact, hardly ever unpacks on a vacation while Abby takes every piece of her carefully curated wardrobe out of the suitcase and puts her things into the same drawers every single time she comes to St. Kitts. The cousins call her obsessed on occasion.

"You are so crazy," they'll laugh. But she shrugs it right off.

"Someday you are going to need me."

This is that day. Seriously, when something goes missing or can't be found, it's Abby to the rescue. There is never any need to pray to St. Anthony for lost objects. Just ask Abby.

"What's going on out there?" Lizzie wonders turning back to the waves and the dark water as her neat-nick sister darts back inside the house. Abigail knows exactly where those military grade night vision binoculars were stored almost three years ago, the last time they spent a family vacation in this house.

᎓

On the deck of the USS Wichita, off the Atlantic coast of St. Kitts, the commander can barely see the shore in the dark without his night vision goggles. But he knows it's there. Eric Rufson has been here before and knows this island's shoreline. Just a few months ago, his crew took part in training exercises with the Kittitian Coast Guard as part of a mission to engage these U.S. partners here in the Caribbean. This call to action came less than an hour ago. Good thing they happened to be over on St. Martin, just 50 miles away and not at the CSL, a forward operating base further south in Aruba-Curacao. "Saving lives," is an actual bullet point on the Wichita's list of official objectives. So, that's why they are here so fast.

"Can't get any more important than that," he has protested when friends and family up in Jacksonville, Florida, accuse him of living the good life being paid to troll the beautiful Caribbean Sea.

"What a joke," they tease, accusing him of child's play but not seriously. They know he's an important player on the SouthCom team.

"C'mon, it's hard work," he'll retort with a laugh. All put-downs and joshing aside, Rufson loves leading his "Sea Knights," a helicopter sea combat squadron with the U. S. Coast Guard's Law Enforcement Detachment. And yes, more often than not, it really is hard, scary work.

He looks away from the water and back up at the helicopters on board his littoral combat vessel, the kind of ship sailors should love for its ease of operation in shallow water, moving up close and into shorelines. He chuckles thinking about the first time he corrected someone who thought littoral meant literal when in fact, the word littoral simply translates to shoreline. The problem now is that these littoral vessels, eight of the fleet based out of Jacksonville, Florida, have failed one too many times and may be out of commission soon. Too bad. Rufson doesn't like to disagree with Congress or Pentagon moves but he loves the one he's with.

"When were we here?" he asks his second-in-command.

"Last April, Sir."

"Lovely island. Nice people, don't you agree?"

"I would, Sir."

They had spent several days working alongside Kittitian and Nevisian crews and came away with nothing but good will and respect for what this little two-island nation had been able to accomplish as an independent country, the Federation of St. Kitts-Nevis. He surmised that the British government felt bad about losing their colony back in the eighties. A recent stint in poor, troubled Haiti made St. Kitts feel and look like paradise.

Both men have treasured their Southern Command assignments, patrolling the warm tropical waters, intercepting drug dealers, keeping America's southern neighbors safe, which included stopping trans-national crime rings and smugglers. This mission today had come down to them in an emergency call, at 4:20 AM from the higher-up command. It had been assigned so quickly and with such urgency that Rufson was not approaching this day with his usual confidence.

His "Sea Knights" are usually searching for suspected drug dealers. On the bow now looking off again at St. Kitts while waiting for further orders, he recalls the surprise of one of his routine patrols back in May when the Wichita intercepted $12 million in illicit drugs on its way to the U.S. Even after they had spotted this suspicious GFV, the acronym for Go Fast Vehicle, the boat wouldn't slow down. Those pirates were crazy thinking they could outrun Wichita. The crew had to launch its small craft and later fired warning shots from one of the circling helicopters to accomplish that mission. But they managed and it was a real win. His sailors, 40 excellent men and women, smirked about how ridiculous the GFV had behaved. That was an exciting and rewarding day in a challenging situation, Rufson recalls.

Today? Well, this mission is murkier. A kidnapped American teenager? The granddaughter of one of their very own decorated military men? He had only a hint of what might happen next. The educated guess from above was that a Russian mob organization was at the center of a sex trafficking operation. Other young women had been reported to have gone missing and links had been drawn to here on St. Kitts. This felt ugly to Rufson and while he was used to dealing with enemies and criminals, as the father of two teenage daughters back home in Florida, he could sense a different kind of disturbing situation in front of him, one that made him apprehensive about human nature. Who does this kind of thing to other human beings? And young girls to boot? Jesus Christ! He could feel his anger rising. Of course, he knew who did this sort of thing. And it started to gnaw at him as disgustingly awful. He would have to stay calm and keep a cool head here, especially if the enemy was whom he thought it might be.

His new SouthCom commander, General Laura Richardson, now just two weeks into this command leadership post, had insisted on the phone this morning that this was a complex situation here in the Caribbean waters he loved. The millions of immigrants moving up from Central and South America had intensified the problem of smuggling and trafficking in human beings, young women to be bartered and sold. This all makes Rufson very angry indeed.

෯

Passing their Pop Pop's special binoculars back and forth from one to the other on the pool deck at their grandparents' home on the hill, the girls can hardly believe their eyes.

"Liz those aren't fishing boats or cruise ships waiting to dock at all," Abigail says to her sister. "What do you think?"

"For sure. I can make out equipment on deck…maybe a helicopter."

"Let me look," Abigail insists grabbing the goggles back. "Jesus, more than one helicopter."

They turn looking directly at one another. With wonder and a bud of joy they can hardly contain or identify as an emotion yet, the sisters conclude, "For Ellie?"

"For Ellie," they both scream out loud now.

"They are here because of Pop Pop's call," Lizzie adds. "He did it. Oh God. Wow wow, and wow. Who does he know? How did he make this happen so fast?"

"Oh my God, this is really happening," Abby adds. "Oh Pop Pop!"

Yet even with that burst of joyful chorus of Pop Pop cheering released, both girls can't escape grim thoughts of Grammy and Ellie. "This is such a nightmare," Abby says. "I'm really scared Liz."

Looking up the mountain behind the house, they check for signs of movement; nothing or nothing they can see.

"We've got to do something," Abby says. "Being stuck here is not working."

CHAPTER EIGHTEEN

5:20 AM

---

*Can you engineer serendipity? Maybe...but some
say only if you leave room for
randomness...forge human connections...forget
routine...and get off your beaten path.*

---

*K*ennedy has the key, the one that will open the warehouse
door. Racing like the soccer star he was back in school
over in Basseterre, he's also running for his life...and
hers too, the girl on the beach, the pretty teenager who didn't
deserve what he has done this night. Even he knows this.
Goddamn, his brain is a dangerous thing today. It's clearer for a
change. Blame it on the donkey kick, he smiles. Then, Tata's
words ring true in his ears, "You have time boy, time to change
this course." So, he runs faster still. "Your life is long," she told
him. "You can't ever see where your road will take you."

What has he been thinking these past months? Has it been

138

nearly a year? Where was he taking his life? Money! Drugs. Tonight, he is waking up to a thought; not this. This can't be his way out. Something about being lost on a steep hillside has forced him to see clearer. With a sudden brain flash, he stops to notice that he's not in what had become an on-off but certainly familiar, month-long cold sweat. His stomach has stopped churning. His anger is dialed down.

An image of his grandmother flashes in his mind's eye. "Oh Tata...Tata. I am so sorry for what I have done."

✒

Annie starts to circle the building, leaving the clueless, injured guy propped against the doorframe, looking drowsy. Is he losing too much blood? Could he die right here? For a second, she worries that she might have mortally wounded him. But how deep could that Swiss Army knife go? Did it nick an artery? Unlikely. Then she shakes her head in frustration and fury, not regret at all. He deserves exactly what he is getting right here; not only the brutal beating from her, but also the shame from losing a contest with an old woman he had underestimated. How often does that happen? She wants to laugh. Old lady? Grammy? People always assume that because of your age, you are not of sound mind or body. Back there a few moments ago, when she had stopped screaming like a crazy banshee and softened her stance, she called him "Honey," not once, twice, but three times and with this sweet but sour word, he knew who had the power here, after all.

"Stay right here, Honey," she told him. "I need to look around." As if he was able to go anywhere in his condition! Her daughter Lauren always shakes her head in dismay at her mother when Annie uses that so-called term of endearment, "Honey," to shout in anger at a driver who has cut her off on the highway or to complain to a nasty store clerk.

"Mom, you are so transparent when you say honey to these people and mean something entirely different."

"I suppose so," Annie has responded, "but isn't a honey better than whatever else I really want to call them?"

No windows. Fabricated metal siding. Up high on cinder blocks, like so many other quickly-thrown-together, home-grown structures scattered around this beautiful island. They dot the gorgeous landscape like pimples on an otherwise perfect face. This one was not built for roadside rum punch stops or barbecue cookouts, however.

She wishes Buck was here to find a way in. He would know what to do. But he's not here and she is on her own. She must find her own way, as all long-married individuals eventually discover in life. You must survive and thrive on your own, one way or another. In truth, you are better together when there is less dependence. As someone once told her…who was that? …dependency will always breed hostility.

Pacing, fuming now at the back of the building, she throws silent caution to the wind and starts banging on the siding, using two hands. Then she slaps the metal harder and harder before she starts up her banshee screaming once more and kicks the building. It's flimsy. Who the hell cares if she makes noise here? She is a grandmother and her child, this precious grandchild, is at risk, possibly inside.

"Elllllieee. Elllllieeee. Are you in there? It's Grammy. I'm here," she shouts.

Ellie doesn't answer but someone else returns Annie's cries, scream for scream.

"Who's there?" Annie shouts, putting her ear to the side of the building. "Oh Honey," she replies, and this time her use of this sweet name for a stranger is infused with love, not frustration or anger.

෴

In one of the cars speeding out of Basseterre from the police station heading towards the airport, Sergeant Valamine sits alongside his prime minister and is apologetic, embarrassed, sweating, with a churning anxiety. He's been up all night and is now into a new day, one that just might be the worst ever.

"Sir, I honestly didn't know what I was looking at, back at that house," he tries to explain and rationalize his behavior on the job. "To me, it felt like an ordinary boy meets girl on the beach situation. I see that all the time. If I had thought any differently, I certainly would have taken swifter action. Believe me, Sir."

"The St. Kitts government doesn't pay you to act on preconceived assumptions. We pay you to follow a professional code of conduct and rule of investigation. Did you not take the training last summer on human trafficking here in the CariCom area? Did you remember anything from that required course? Have you seen the crime statistics for our Caribbean community?"

"I did. Of course, I do, but it just didn't feel…" He won't dare admit that he was too tired to want to do anything and it felt good to sit in the kitchen of that comfortable home. And while he did take the CariCom training in human trafficking officially, clicking through answers on the computer screen, he had nearly slept through the process, just as weary on that day as he is now.

"Stop right there, Valamine. I am warning you. Do not offer up one single excuse for your despicable conduct this morning, especially not a feeling. Do not. You felt. You felt. Jesus Christ. Your feelings are for sh-t. Didn't you even see the report on that other girl?"

Valamine's stomach lurches. Another girl missing? Oh, he is in trouble now for sure. But he stays silent now.

Their car pulls past the public parking area at the Robert K. Bradshaw airport and stops to the west of the apron in front of the YU Terminal. This new terminal was designed and open to private jet travel in 2014. The facility has been a real plus for attracting the elite, the high-flying, big spenders to his island. These rich people have been buying and building mountaintop homes, bringing their flocks of friends. Built and financed by an offshore company, the Veling Aviation Group with headquarters in Mauritius and offices in London and Qatar, the terminal has been good for St. Kitts in the upscale tourist department, but some officials are concerned, speculating about the underpinnings of this operation. Yes, ownership of the facility was eventually transferred to SCAPSA, the St. Christopher Air and Sea Ports Authority. But even the new prime minister had misgivings; who's really in charge over here? Right now, this PM is ready to curse the Russian oligarchs who have been bringing their much-needed money to his twin islands. Damn, he's only a few months into his term of office and already this has landed on his to-do list, directly from the U.S. government.

Opening the door and jumping out, Reginald Browne races up and inside, taking two steps at a time. He needs to see outside on the tarmac and check the arrival status of private jets. Who's coming in today? Who's scheduled to leave?

"Valamine, come with me?" he shouts back to the sergeant who has remained stiffly, sleepily, in that back seat, afraid to move. "Wake up man. Stay with me."

Then Browne stops. "Wait a minute. I've got to take this call."

⤙

Kennedy reaches the front of the warehouse about the same time Annie starts shouting and banging at the backside. He sees his buddy, yes the bleeding victim is a friend from the big house parties at Igor's mansion on the hill.

"What happened here? What's going on?"

Nearly unconscious and lying on his side now with blood seeping from his collarbone, this fellow traveler on a misguided mission, mumbles. "Arrrrrr. I need help. I'm no good."

"Who did this to you?"

"A lady. An old American white lady.'"

"Are you kidding? Are you useless?"

"Mon, she was so strong. So angry."

"Shut up." Kennedy's heart is beating with the same urgency and anxiety he experienced back there at the house standing beneath the balcony… was it just a little more than an hour ago? Sweat starts to pour, and it feels like every gland in his body is ridding itself of poison. These guys will kill him without a second thought if he stands in their way. He's heard it. Maybe he's even seen it? With a fleeting unspoken plea, he wills himself back to that moment at 3:45 AM and wishes he could take it all back, turn away and not go through this nightmare that is about to destroy his life. He's a good boy, or at least that's what his grandmother, Tata,

143

has always told him. "You are a good boy." But if he were such a good boy, then why did his parents abandon him? Where is his father right now? And what about his mother? Not her fault at all. Not at all. She is dead. He wants to cry. But seriously, why, why, why did she have to get sick, die and leave him? Then, he looks down at this guy, almost unconscious on the ground by the warehouse doors, his buddy? Friend? Well, hardly a friend. He shakes him awake.

"Who is this lady? This old woman? This grandmother? How could you have lost to her?" But of course, he knows the answer to his question and what any grandmother would do under these very same circumstances. He has a grandmother after all. This lady must be the grandmother from the beach.

"Stay quiet here. I've got the key. But before I open the door, I'm going around the back to find her. I will get you out of here. To somewhere safe."

"She had to pee."

Kennedy turns back. "What? What did you say?" The guy's voice is hardly registering. It's a whisper.

"She had to pee."

"Jesus, why are you telling me this?"

"She said she had to pee so maybe she went into the brush to do her business."

"Oh, okay."

At the back of the hastily-built-in-a-pandemic, corrugated metal warehouse, stacked up on cinder blocks, Annie has slipped under the flooring, scrambling on her back, wiggling toward the center, feeling the damp earth, looking for a way up and in through the flooring. She's heard Buck complain one too many times about local construction.

"They cut corners, Annie," her precise, military man has said, shaking his head in distrust of island-style building and maintenance. "Even you could do a better job."

"Oh Buck, not really," she once protested.

"Yes, I do believe you could build a better house than some of the guys I watch. I like them, I do, but I don't trust their work ethic. Would you look at that door frame? It's crooked."

"Stop complaining," she laughed at him. "You are here in paradise. There is no place on this map called perfection, even in paradise. And I love our house! All we have is right here in front of us. Let's live and work with what we have."

So she does, right there on her back under the warehouse, suddenly spotting an opening in the floor.

CHAPTER NINETEEN

5:30 AM

When you invest even part of your history in a
place, perhaps knitting your life into a colorful,
wild tapestry, this knowledge of place...even
things you didn't know you knew...can be pretty
powerful, especially in a pinch.

---

*E*llie was born on her grandmother's birthday. A good omen, right? One would think so. This birthday gift of a new grandchild was a spectacular conclusion to a somewhat troubled pregnancy. They named her Ellie, short for Eloise, one of Lauren's favorite characters in the children's book series published in 1955 about a little girl and written by Kay Thompson. That imaginary Eloise lived a magical life with her nanny on the "tippy top floor" of the Plaza Hotel. Annie, our heroine now lying on her back beneath a corrugated metal warehouse, was over the moon thrilled with the arrival of her Eloise and relieved as well. And Ellie's arrival a week before her due date, on a birthday they would share forever, seemed particularly spectacular.

Thirteen years ago, when she got off the phone with Lauren who had shared the news of the start of her labor, Annie had done her happy dance, confirming, "Buck, she's going to be born on my birthday, tomorrow, I think, I think, I predict. Oh wow, wow, wow. You never know about labor and how long it might take but I just have a feeling. Now, all I want is for her to be okay, normal, healthy. I don't want to believe those prenatal tests. They are wrong too often and scare parents." So, she set worries aside and ran down the hallway of their Sleepy Hollow home to pack for the drive and stay over at Lauren's house on Long Island. Her girl needed to have a mother nearby when this grandbaby came home from the hospital.

Blood tests early in the second trimester of Lauren's pregnancy had indicated a small but significant possibility of abnormal fetal development. Ultrasounds had followed this news to see what, if anything, could be wrong. But all the tests afterward turned up nothing unusual and growth proceeded right on schedule. Yet, underlying anxiety bubbled beneath the surface of calm, especially for Annie who knew intimately what it felt like to lose a baby. So on that cold December, long, birthday night, when a perfectly beautiful newborn baby arrived and earned a perfect 10 on the Apgar score, there was cause for joy.

"Oh my God, Buck, it's all going to be okay. She will be okay."

"I knew it," he countered.

"You didn't know that."

"Not really of course but my sense had been false alarm with that first test warning. Medicine today does raise red flags. I know the doctors are just trying to be safe but seriously they are scaring this new generation of parents. They need to present the false positive statistics whenever they deliver results."

"I suppose so," Annie agreed but not really. She wished she had been given more advance warning about their third baby and the premature end of the pregnancy, but she kept quiet. No need to bring up pain in a time of pure happiness.

Later, in her exhausted mother's arms, little body nestled against Lauren's chest, Ellie, barely 6 pounds, gazed directly into her mother's eyes with what looked like an innate wisdom that surely wasn't there yet but who really knows what infants understand? Clearly, this beautiful baby girl, in that newborn quiet-alert period immediately after the birth…well, this little girl seemed to know how to calm herself from the very first breaths of life. Her parents cooed, smiled and cried with relief. Her grandparents, standing back from the bed, who had faked a confidence they may not have felt all along, were elated.

This first blush of familial love is like a vitamin every child ought to have to survive and thrive. In Ellie's case, she has never proven those initial observations about her personality and resilience wrong. Even, or maybe because of her IBS diagnosis in middle school, she stays calm in a crisis.

So when Lady slows up, then stops beside the narrow road and Ellie thinks she hears something, she stays absolutely silent. The donkey does too. Together, they shift quietly behind the scrubby bushes. Though this 13-year-old might have thoughts of rescue, she's not going to be duped by the wrong rescuers tonight. She knows that someone is out there trying to get her.

⤴

The Gulfstream GF800 carrying Buck is still more than an hour away but flying time to St. Kitts has not been a waste of time. Patched through directly to Commander Eric Rufson on the USS Wichita, Buck has brought the officer up to date on what may be happening on the island. Both men have touched base with Kittitian Prime Minister Browne who is at the airport checking for private arrivals and departures. He's contacted the St. Christopher Air and Sea Ports Authority to learn more about incoming traffic scheduled for this day of November 19 as well as a list of who owns each of the private jets parked there.

"Sir," Buck repeats to Rufson. "I can't thank you and your crew enough."

"No, no. This is our mission. We should be thanking you for the tip-off here," Rufson reports.

"I've watched this flood of Russian money and the growth of economic citizenships on St. Kitts. They call it CBI. It's been worrisome. Illegal drug trafficking, of course, is a huge issue but my mind has refused to go to the human trafficking of young women through these beautiful Caribbean islands. We've been traveling to St. Kitts for decades and it feels like home. But I know that only if we confront this issue and expose these people will it change. This is a huge global human rights issue. Let's go get them."

Rufson gently adds, "Buck, do you mind if I call you that?" He's sensitive that this fellow, a former military intelligence officer and now in a most vulnerable position. He wants to make sure the man trusts him to do the right thing here.

"Of course. Everyone calls me Buck, no need for permission. This is going to be a long day and we need to work as a team."

"Well, we in SouthCom have been watching the growth of these transnational crimes and we welcome precisely the kind of advance insider information you and the St. Kitts government have provided. I'm pleased the Wichita was nearby and we could get here so fast this morning. We're holding off the Atlantic coast near Half Moon Bay awaiting the go-ahead. Also, I must share that my commander, General Laura Richardson, takes these missions very seriously. Our goal is to shut this activity down and it is perfectly clear the American government will not stand for this activity in the Caribbean. Our orders come from the highest command. You may think that what has happened here to your granddaughter is personal, Sir, but we take it personally too. And we suspect this abduction is not the first."

"Thank you. I agree," Buck replied, recalling that first meeting with the Russian back at the Frigate Bay Dip and Sip Tiki Bar so many years ago. Annie had been fascinated by the guy. His moxie at the bar was ridiculous but that theft of a nuclear device was downright insane. Buck had taken his being on St. Kitts bragging about a theft of such proportions personally then and quickly went to authorities to erase him from the island. What he didn't anticipate was that so many more Russians just like him, far worse in fact, would be following.

With the pandemic, Buck had noted Russian-owned super-yachts pulling up regularly to Christophe Harbour out on the Southeast peninsula. But what else are these yachts harboring besides drunk foreigners in need of new countries to call home?

ఈ

Annie hears the buzz of conversation in the front of the building. She's holding perfectly still, praying that no one would ever dream where she has scrambled. She wills those stereotypes of old age to hold up right here and now — weak, stupid, slow — wanting the guys out there to set aside any notion of what she might be attempting. This old woman would never be capable of doing what she is doing right now! What the hell? Even she can hardly believe what she is planning to do. Yet, she knows that was the voice of a child, a young girl, inside this building. She prefers to think of Ellie as a child and well, so is this girl a child too. At age 74, aren't most of the world's people children from her vantage point? Maybe this girl inside is not her granddaughter, but it sure feels like it right now. She heard the voice. She knows she is in there. Oh my God, this is truly evil right here and now in front of her and perhaps worse now that she suspects Ellie is not the only missing girl.

It's dark, dirty; an earthy mix of woody construction and island scents under here, mixed with something else in the early morning damp air. She waits. Lying on her back in the dark, as still as she can, she feels the cold dirt through the back of her body. Her eyes adjust. She begins to see the shoddy, island-style, thrown-together construction. Where are the gaps, the loose floorboards, a way up and in? Are these just pieces of plywood thrown down? Were they even nailed into place? Is that light, even just a little, coming through the floor from above?

⸕

On one of their first visits to the island, Annie remarked to the cab driver, known as Sea Moss Man, that the houses were charming perched right up along the narrow roads but they could all use a coat of paint and many looked unfinished.

"Why don't they paint them in those pretty shades of pink, purple and green?" she asked the driver. "You see those pretty colors in Bermuda. Those are the colors I think of for the

Caribbean."

"No money," he replied.

Buck stepped into the conversation to save Sea Moss and explain that the import duty on paint and construction materials coming into St. Kitts was very high. Ordinary citizens could not afford cans of colorful paint or lumber and nails.

"That doesn't seem fair at all," she had protested. "Why not tax something else?"

"Like what?" Both Buck and Sea Moss had laughed. "Everything is already taxed!"

Annie and Buck still laugh at the memory of this favorite cab driver. They once invited Sea Moss Man, yes that was really his preferred name, to join them at the buffet lunch at what was then the new Marriott Resort. To their astonishment, he went back to the dessert table 14 times, and that was after he had enjoyed a lot of lunch already. Wonderful Sea Moss, a father of ten who took his name from the special brew he made using sea moss harvested from the base of the local volcano in the rainforest. This drink, which was marketed and sold in the local grocery stores, was supposed to guarantee fertility, this father of ten would insist.

"Oh wow," Annie had laughed the first time she was introduced to his green-bottled brew. "Don't tell me what's in it!"

Sea Moss had been so proud of his creation that he painted his taxi van "Sea Moss Man." A fleet of three similar vans are painted proudly with the Sea Moss legacy and managed by three of his sons who follow in their father's footsteps. Annie had seen one of them at the roundabout just yesterday. Was it really just yesterday?

❧

"Liz, we can't just stay here," Abby says, knowing that her sister will want to take the less adventurous road.

"Pop Pop said to stay put. He had put a plan in motion," Liz says. "But I agree. I feel as if we should be doing something, anything. But I think it's too dangerous. The guy who took Ellie could be out there somewhere. Maybe not alone either."

"You're right. And we've already called the only authorities we have here on the island. This stinks," she admits. "This is the very first time ever that I have felt frightened here in St. Kitts. It's always been our happy go-to place."

"I know. But let's get ready for anything to happen. There are two helicopters out there on that boat. They wouldn't be here off the coast if they weren't going to be used for something. I just know that."

"One day, we really are going to have to force Pop Pop to tell us everything, all of it. Not just about today but about all the days he's never shared."

"You think?"

"Yes, I think. Even if he swears us to secrecy! We need to know the story. But let's get out of our pajamas."

CHAPTER TWENTY

5:40 AM

Someone you love will die without your help,
right there, right then. Just imagine. Adrenaline
floods your body, boosting muscles, speeding up
heart and breathing rate, dilating blood vessels,
releasing nutrients. Endorphins light up your
brain.

Could the cascade of enzymes and proteins
create a superhuman experience?

*A*nnie hears the shuffling of footsteps moving into the
bushes behind the building. He's swatting, pushing
branches aside, trying to force her out into the open. He
must think she is hiding in the brush. Hah, she laughs but not out
loud. Just you wait. Just you wait and see now. Do not move a
single muscle, Annie. Hold still. Hold still. Dirt under her back is
damp and lumpy. Garbage has been shoved under here. How lame!

It smells awful down here. The voice she heard coming from inside the building is quiet. Still. Stay still. But be ready. What next? A grumble. Then, there is a young man's voice. He's Kittitian. Footsteps are closer now and then stomping around to the front. Then talking, two voices? Oh thank God, that guy she stabbed is conscious, not dead. They are loud now.

"She's gone."

"Who?"

"The old lady, mon, no moron. The one who had to pee." She laughs. Not so tonight.

"Awww…ooowweee. I am hurting."

"Okay, okay," Kennedy says, leaning down toward this guy to look closer. Is he hurt bad? Maybe. "Think you need help." Then, he quickly changes his mind, "No, no, that won't work. Maybe I can hide you. They'll keell you if they know about your screw up here. To let an old woman into this game." He stops for a moment and tilts his head toward the doors and what's inside. "Have you heard anything? Should I check on that girl inside?"

"She's gone quiet since Igor's guy was up here yesterday. Knocked her out good is my guess."

To save this man's life, Kennedy realizes he must hide him. Drag him quickly into the bushes.

"Help me," he says, trying to get the man to move, to sit. "Can you stand for God's sake. Lean on me. Get up."

"I am not good. Jeez, she broke my hand, kicked me hard, messed me up here," he says grabbing his groin." Then, he goes back to holding his neck.

"Bleeding?" Kennedy checks to see where all the blood has come from. "A knife? She had a knife?"

"Yeah mon. Bad."

"You'll survive, but not if they find you here. Like this."

"Ok. Ok." On his knees now, he grabs Kennedy for balance and together they move awkwardly away from the building. Annie can hear their struggle, feet dragging, one man limping. "Over there. Let's put you over there. Stay quiet." Dragging, pulling, muscling their way, they push into the thick brush away from the road. She can picture almost exactly where they've gone.

"Quiet. Stay low. You'll be okay here," Kennedy says. "You know these crazy Russians."

"Ya, I do."

"Dead."

"Yes, dead quick."

Under the flooring, eyes wide open, hiding, waiting in that 18-inch crawl space reminds Annie of how she would crawl beneath her sister's bed in the three-girl room they shared growing up. Older, middle, younger. She was always the middle and didn't fully understand exactly why her belongings and little treasures would disappear later to be found under the bed beside hers; class photos, favorite T-shirts, trinkets from her top drawer gone missing. There they would be. Whew. It wasn't a mystery how they got there just why. Was her sister trying to make Annie angry? Or did she want pieces of Annie? If so, why? On her complaint, Mom would insist, "Let me handle it, Annie. I'll deal with her." It was always a mystery that should have been unraveled in therapy.

Annie, not under a bed but a warehouse, is wondering how in God's name she got here. Funny but she can hear better than usual, even catching the tone of fear in these young men's frantic exchange about the big boss, the Russian. So, it's the Russians? Aha. That makes sense now. Hasn't Buck been worried about the presence of these guys on the island.

∽

"Valamine," the prime minister orders, "call headquarters and put a team of men out here at the airport to check all cargo as well as passengers on every public and private aircraft in and out today. I've called TSA operations, too," he says sharing more than he has all morning with the sergeant. Browne shrugs with a half-smile, "That TSA director was sound asleep. It's a Friday, never busy today. Hah. But thank God it's not a Saturday that would have created a real nightmare logjam for our tourists. I want to know everyone coming here or trying to leave this island today. From what I understand, these people are planning to make moves today and I want us to be in the best position to stop it, land or sea. We don't want this kidnapping to end badly on St. Kitts' watch."

"Got it," Valamine responds pulling out his cellphone. He's relieved that Browne is trusting him to do anything again. Maybe his career is back from the dead and this day won't end so badly after all. He certainly needs to redeem himself here.

Browne leans up from the back seat now and over into the front to tell his driver where they will be heading next in the big black SUV. He's been in touch with SouthCom and is one of very few officials on the island to be updated on this mission.

"Up there, Sir?"

"Yes, that's where we are going. Is the car too wide for that

157

road?"

"No, I think we can make it, but I wish I had decided on the smaller jeep today." This guy likes driving for Browne. They went to school together here on St. Kitts before Browne left for dental school in the United States and they are appreciating their reconnection with his recent election win. What a difference from the old man who came before.

Browne says, "I apologize. The jeep may have been better suited indeed."

They head out of the airport, circling the roundabout to head back towards Basseterre on Kim Collins Highway before quickly turning left into the Needsmust Demonstration farm. The government of Taiwan started this nursery as a plan to plant Taiwanese roots on the island and it's turned out to be a superb spot for local officials, farmers, students, and tourists. Taiwan handed management of it over to St. Kitts in 2013. The 8.5 acres grows all sorts of local fruits trees: carambola, sugar apple, pineapple, mango, grapefruit, lime, cantaloupe, and vegetables. The scent of the ripening fruit wafts into the open police car window.

This isn't a Martha-Stewart-like perfect garden. But if you find yourself on St. Kitts, go see it. Walk around but try not to think about what grew here centuries ago, sugar cane and profit alongside nasty disregard for human life. Needsmust was certainly home to plantation slavery at its worst; masters, overseers and slaves, whips, lashes, and lives lost. Centuries of history are right there, even for donkeys like our Lady. Past the rows of trees, you can spot the old sugar mill, now in ruins, where Annie took her grandchildren's Christmas card photo. Friends and family loved it. Sugar mills are historically quaint, of course. They stand out in the Caribbean. Don't think too deeply about what they really represent.

That might make you feel sick. And of course, holiday greetings really shouldn't remind readers of the worst in human nature.

∽

On board the C-20, a military version of a Gulfstream IV aircraft, Buck is grateful that his old command in Virginia has taken this personal threat as seriously as he does. The plane, powered by two Rolls Royce engines, can carry up to 26 passengers and is equipped with a secure global communications center. Today it is just Buck aboard with a crew of four. No flight attendant, just pilot, co-pilot, flight engineer and communications system operator. Commander Theresa Bainbridge and others have made this Russian sting on St. Kitts a top priority. Even Buck is surprised by how quickly the plan came together and how much information the military already had about some of these Russian characters on island. It's been on their proverbial radar, in fact. As Bainbridge, there at SouthCom, assured him this morning, "We've been aware of this human trafficking through Central America and up through the Caribbean. Honestly, you presented us with a perfect targeted opportunity today. Let's go get them."

"Thank you, Commander. I am eternally grateful."

"Buck, believe me, this mission is for all of our daughters, not just yours," she responded, "and our sons too, of course. These guys are ruthless. We know them. We've been very aware."

∽

Now up and over the top, with the ocean out of sight, Ellie and Lady sit quietly a few yards from the narrow road. They rest under a tree and Ellie feels good being off Lady's back. She falls back on the ground and sighs with exhaustion. In the nearness of this loving animal, she smells this donkey and feels safe.

"Lady, I wish Pop Pop were here."

The donkey responds with a chortle, snort and slight twist of the head. Her movements are magical. This lady is listening.

"But you haven't even met Pop Pop."

Down in Needsmust where Lady is taking Ellie, where the plantation house once stood out on the hillside, there is no longer a colonial beehive of activity. Centuries of slave quarters were always positioned downwind from the house near the animal enclosures and garbage pits. This classic plantation design was well-known by slavers and sometimes drawn up by French priests, doing the opposite of God's work on these islands. Big house residents, the owners and managers, could breathe easier while slaves choked on kitchen smoke and dung air down below. "Hogsheads" of sugar and "puncheons" of rum were shipped off to England. Check the old records and you'll see how generations of people in Europe fought over their plantation inheritances and territory even after slavery was abolished. You can google this heritage today and check maps of St. Kitts, old as well as new. The very name of this old plantation shouts sadness, Needs Must. For sure.

∽

Back at the hillside house, Abby tells her older sister, "I can't wait anymore." The girls are no longer in pajamas but still using the binoculars looking for something to happen out on the Atlantic Ocean. "You're the one with the driver's license, Liz. Let's go. The car is in the driveway."

"Go where?" her sister pushes back. "Pop Pop told us to

wait. And I've never driven on St. Kitts before. I'm nervous about driving on the wrong side of the road, all that left-side of the road driving here is scary. I'm not sure I can do it."

"You can. I know you can. We'll go slow but I think we should at least try to help. There are two of us for God's sake. We're not going to be any worse than that idiot Valamine, who did nothing. Maybe we can find someone awake over at the Marriott who can help. The night watchman? Someone? Anyone?"

"Okay, you're right. Let's do something. But where are the car keys? And maybe we should take a few of Pop Pop's golf clubs for protection."

"I know exactly where the car keys are," Abby replies. "You go get two golf clubs. I want an iron."

Lizzie looks back toward the Atlantic one more time and starts screaming, "Oh Abby, look. Look. The ship is going away. It's not coming here, Abby. Oh my God."

"Liz, you don't know that. Maybe they were just waiting for a signal to move somewhere else. Maybe they are going to land in a better place. The Atlantic is always rough, here. You and I both know it. That's why we swim over on the Caribbean side. Even the Marriott hotel owners knew that when it was built. That's why they had to put in that rock wall out there to break the waves. Be positive girl."

"Ok," this big sister concedes.

"Good girl. That's it. Now, let's go." Abby shakes her head in dismay at her own use of that "good girl" expression. Jeez, she sounds like her grandmother here and not the little sister. Thank God Lizzie didn't react in fury to it. Whew.

CHAPTER TWENTY-ONE

5:45 AM

Even a country of people at war within itself,
with friends and families fighting about
everything from the wording in a children's book
to who ought to be President of the United
States, can sometimes come together in a crisis;
especially when our children are at stake.

T̶he USS Wichita has its orders; move immediately
to the Caribbean side of the island. "Atlantic is
always rough for a shore landing," Rufson reminds
his officers. "We could do it but the terrain and narrow roads up
that mountain will be difficult. We'll come in from the other side."
The ship will go back out of Half Moon Bay, and go around the
island's southeast peninsula, through the Narrow between St. Kitts
and Nevis and put into port at Deep Water harbor. "We'll be
meeting up with the Kittitian National Guard over there who have
a heads up on where exactly we are heading and the best landings

for our helicopters. Get the rigid hull inflatables ready just in case. Not sure we'll need them, but you never know."

"Yes Sir. Hope there won't be too many cruise ships in port today, Captain. Tourist traffic here has really picked up lately."

"If so, we'll be giving them a wake-up call, a real show of force; Good Morning St. Kitts, the United States of America at its best."

They smile about his Robin Williams-like joke. That *Good Morning Vietnam* still resounds in military circles. But nothing about today is funny here. Lives and reputations are at stake. This is bigger than an everyday drug bust for the crew and certainly no joke. These kids — yes, the crew, both men and women, are so much younger by several generations than Buck, Annie, and Rufson himself — are proud to be here on duty today.

Kennedy is exhausted and sits down for what he believes will be just a moment, maybe two. Sweaty, hungry, angry, exhausted, he thinks his life is a disaster. He is in pain; side is still hurting and his hands are shaking like his grandmother's do at times. But in his case, the shakes are not from age but drug withdrawal. Tata, he wishes wanting too much to ask her; can I take all this back? Leaning onto a tree, he watches his injured partner's eyes close and then snores start. Both have been under the Russian gun, figuratively and literally, for days in anticipation of the pick-up this morning. He checks his watch: 5:45. He has time, enough time to find the girl he lost on the donkey. The meet up is scheduled for 6:18, sunrise. So, he closes his eyes too. They aren't far from the building. He'll hear them coming as they approach, right? Right? He is asleep.

That's when Annie makes her move there under the building. Pushing back on her heels, shoving herself, right shoulder, left shoulder, like a bug moving awkwardly on its back, she inches, squirming and twisting toward the opening in the cheap floor above her. Then, using her hands clenched into tight fists, she pushes up and loosens the entire flimsy piece of plywood. Buck was right. These guys didn't even put down an underlay for the floor when they threw the building together. She's surprised no one had fallen through yet.

Shoving aside the piece of ill-fitting handiwork right there in her face now, she climbs halfway inside — top of her body in, bottom still under — and turns to look around. There is the girl lying on a cot. Poor baby. What have these brutal men done to you?

"Honey, I'm here," she says in a calm whisper while pulling herself all the way up and inside. She almost uses that name Grammy in this greeting, even though this young woman is not her granddaughter. "I'm going to get you home. Away from this awful place." She's by the cot now, putting her arms around the girl who sits up warily, fearfully.

"I heard you," Annie says.

The young woman is dazed, obviously drugged, dirty, disheveled, and astonished too.

"Who are you?" she asks.

"I'm Annie." Before she can stop herself, the words come out and she says, "I'm here to rescue you." Rescue? Really? She's no super-hero. She's a grandmother. She is here to rescue! Hah. Rescues only happen in the movies she laughs at when Buck watches ridiculous thrillers. "How can you stand that stuff?" she

164

usually moans. "Love them," is her military man's retort. But now…well, now is very different and a rescue is exactly what is happening here.

"We have no time," she says to this teenager, about Ellie's age. "Let's go." Is she American? Annie can't tell. She may have detected a hint of accent.

"Where?"

"Under the building. Out the back. Down the mountain," she says, "toward the highway or maybe the airport. Do you think you can make it?"

"Yes, I think so."

"We can do this together," Annie says helping her up. "Over here. I'll go first and be there under the floor to help you wiggle through. It's a tight fit but I've got you. It's scary, I know, but we must go now."

"I know. They are coming today," she says.

"Who?"

"Men. I'm not sure who but I know this is the plan."

"Oh my God," Annie responds. "My Ellie? My girl!"

"Who is that?"

"My granddaughter. I think they have her too."

"Oh no, oh my God no."

"Let's go. Quickly."

Down under the building, the two women, on their stomachs now in the dirt, pull and drag themselves on elbows toward the back. Annie emerges first, avoiding the cinder blocks and trash, and breathes easier outside in the early morning air. On her knees, she reaches back under and helps pull the young woman out alongside her.

"Where are your shoes?" she asks, suddenly realizing that this young woman is barefoot.

"They took them," she answers.

"Oh wow. Those bastards! Jesus Christ! Goddamn them. I'm sorry. So sorry for my rough language! I can't help it. I hate these men so much. Can you walk without shoes? We're going down the mountain to find help."

"I can do it." Can she really? She has been victimized, drugged, abused, must be in a post-traumatic shock here. Was that her pink tank top Annie picked up in the shack?

"No, wait a minute," Annie stops with an idea, silly but still, they might help cushion her feet. "Let me give you my socks." Quickly taking off her sneakers, Annie removes her black anklets and puts them on this child's dirty feet. "They aren't much but may be better than going bare foot. Okay? Whew," she adds, "they stink. So sorry."

Suddenly, with this gesture of kindness, smelly socks and all, this young woman's sobbing starts. "Oh Honey," Annie says holding tightly as tears fall, chest heaves, waves of worry release, convulse, and she tries to catch her breath. "It's going to be okay now. I can't promise anything, but I think it's going to be okay."

A last creepy thought inches into Annie's mind here; is this just her mother's old mantra or could it really be true? Is everything really going to be okay? Don't think about it Annie. Just move. Tragedy is everywhere. Why not right here too? You silly woman.

❧

On the road in front of their grandparents' home, Liz is carefully staying left even though there is no traffic at this early hour. They reach the circle connecting North Frigate Bay with its beach hotels, restaurants, casinos, and shops and the main road up over toward Bird Rock and down into Basseterre.

"Which way do we go, Abby?" The younger sister, Abby, the one with the inner compass, doesn't dare question her older sister's missing sense of direction. How could she not know which way to go around the circle? Jeez. Perhaps, here and now, holding back on her knee jerk criticism is a sign of maturity in their tricky sibling relationship. There will be time later to make fun of her sister. Not now, that's for sure.

"Go left and take the third turn off. Stay left Liz. Stay left. Let's go to the Marriott. Maybe someone there can help. Those security guards are always friendly."

Liz goes slowly, cautiously, oh-so-carefully, but if she were ever going to pick a time to start driving on complicated St. Kitts, this would be it because it's so quiet.

"Look. Liz, look over there," Abby says at the top of the turn, looking toward the water. "No, I take that back. Don't look. Keep your eyes on the road. But wow, that big boat really is moving out to sea. Oh my God. Please come back. Come back. We need help."

167

"What is going on here?" Liz shouts.

Whoooossssshhhh.

They both jerk as a silver sports car races past them coming from the east.

"Jeez. Who could that be?" Abby turns back to watch it go up, around a turn and head back down the other side.

"I don't trust anyone here going as fast as that this morning," Liz says.

"I agree."

"Go around the turn and follow that car. Forget the Marriott."

"Really, you want me to follow it. I don't know Abby. I'm not sure about that. I felt much safer looking for a Marriott Hotel security guard."

"Liz, c'mon. It's for Ellie. Or oh God, we need to think of Grammy, too."

So, the little Avis rental goes completely around this circle now, past the road to the Marriott, and now heads up. They are not going nearly fast enough to catch the speeding car, but at the top of the hill, they may be able to see which way it turns; toward Basseterre? Or out to the airport?

"Where do you think it came from?" Liz asks rhetorically, not expecting an answer, but hoping her sister has an idea.

"Step on it, Liz, please," Abby asks. "Go faster. My guess is that it came from the Southeast peninsula, up over Timothy's Peak and one of those humongous houses. That car has not spent much time on the streets over this side of the hill for sure. It comes from money, lots of money."

❧

Ellie puts her hands on Lady's long soft head, her cheeks, looking into her eyes and then laying her own cheek on the soft fur. This donkey's gaze is bright and clear. The feeling that passes through each of them is mutual. Why don't people know more about donkeys? Ellie wonders. Such sweet and quite brilliant creatures, they surely are. One day in the future, Ellie will learn that donkeys were humans' first form of transportation and domesticated about 5,000 BC in northeastern Africa. Kings, queens, Greeks, Romans, and ancient Christians all treasured donkeys. Sometimes, at the end of a life, these animals were buried alongside their owners. Skeletons of donkeys were unearthed in the funeral enclosures of Egyptian pharaohs. Like Ellie tonight, they realized that life might be impossible without their uncomplaining loyal companions, graceful and unnaturally wise creatures.

"Let's go, Lady."

The narrow road is quiet. Ellie can see lights far below.

"Is this the way home?" she asks the donkey who brays in response.

"Okay, I trust you."

So down the mountain they go, Ellie, sitting upright and holding on tight now, and Lady gently swaying with the clip-clop of her footfalls. They are both calm now, unaware of what lies ahead.

❧

Buck is relieved that the hour time zone difference tonight may have been a positive in his plan. He'd been aware of this earlier zone but as the Gulfstream speeds toward St. Kitts and clocks adjust to the reality of a Kittitian time zone ahead of East Coast America, he can see the shift become a real plus. Maybe he'll be in time. But for exactly what, he wonders.

"Sir, how much longer until landing?" he asks the co-pilot who has checked to see how their single passenger is doing.

"Forty, maybe thirty minutes if we are lucky."

"I am so grateful," Buck responds. "Thank you."

"No thanks needed here. It's our job." Something about his definitiveness here makes Buck recall that slogan for the American military. Were the sailors the first to come up with the rallying cry, "To Go in Harm's Way?" Yes, that's it.

CHAPTER TWENTY-TWO

5:50 AM

---

*Small islands are like small towns. Everyone
knows everything. At least they think they do.
Yet, the world is unhinged with masses of people
moving and migrating everywhere. With a flood
of newcomers, some welcome, others not so
much, all old bets about human nature are off.*

---

*O*n the drive up through the Needsmust garden, in the back
seat of his official car, the Prime Minister of St. Kitts has
a sudden flash of unease, considering an element that
hadn't crossed him mind before; what if? Calm in this crisis up
until now, he senses a danger he hadn't anticipated. As the
amygdala area of his brain sends a distress signal to his
hypothalamus, the adrenaline courses through his body. He's
thinking, oh my God, what if? What if not by air but by sea?

"Valamine," he blurts to the sleepy sergeant seated next to

171

him but slouching toward the window for support. "Have we considered those yachts out in Christophe Harbour? Do we really know anything about them? Where they've come from? Where they're going on from here? Who's on board? Or who are these owners bringing on board?"

"Not sure what you are getting at, Sir. Of course not."

"What I'm asking is, what if these thugs, these Russian pimps, aren't flying in and out of our airport with these young women? What if they arrived by water?"

Browne is a politician first, but also a father. Now considering a sea escape, he realizes a plane would probably have proven too complicated. Yes, they may have parked a private jet out there on the tarmac or even arrived by air, but what if they simply leave with their bounty by sea? Yachts would leave with fewer questions asked, and if the young women were cleaned and dressed up, they might appear to be willing young women off on a holiday, right?

"Who's in charge out there at Christophe?"

"Sir, I know a man out there. Let me call him now."

Christophe Harbour is beautiful. You catch a first glimpse of this newly developed area from land and high up as you drive over the mountain and out the Southeastern Peninsula. It was once just a big salt pond with a wedge of land sticking up on its Caribbean side. Now, with brand new vacation homes being built into the hillsides and berths for anchoring yachts provided courtesy of the Kittitian Citizenship by Investment Program, the harbor is a wonderful place to stroll, shop the art gallery and have a quick bite to eat. The management arranged with the government to offer its own on-site customs and immigration clearance. There is no standing in long lines for passport checks or security pat downs. It's an easy, stress-free place to arrive and depart. This perk is now figuring large on Browne's worry list. What if? What if these kidnappers have taken advantage of this official welcome mat out there? Yes, there is a government office in Basseterre charged with vetting all new citizenship applications, a way to check new homeowners at Christophe Harbour. But, these people pay other people to make themselves look clean. And high-rolling renters could probably come and go with ease through Christophe. Right? No, don't think that. No.

Valamine responds. "Good thinking, Sir. I'll get my friend Sam on the phone." Sam Odama has been Valamine's friend and accountant for generations. Sam couldn't believe his good luck when an old friend asked if he would take on the paperwork for the incoming and outgoing yachts on a part-time basis. The job, which required little effort until recently, came with a free office rental at the harbor with a beautiful view.

"Just keep your eyes on the numbers, Sam," he was told. "Don't pay attention to these people out there. High rollers, the rich and famously extravagant can be strange. You and I both know that."

So, when Sam's phone rings on this early morning and he hears his old friend Valamine on the line asking questions about comings and goings, he's relieved. Something has been troubling him for weeks now. Something not quite right…just a sixth sense and question that has been keeping Sam awake at night; an overheard conversation that he should never have been allowed to hear.

❧

Kennedy jumps irrationally, forgetting for an instant where he is. He's been snoring. Gone for only minutes, he is awake with a raw prickly awareness. How the hell did he let himself fall asleep? He checks his partner there on the ground nearby, putting an ear to this guy's chest to listen for breathing and then eyeing the wound at his neck for signs of fresh blood. It's clotting. The guy is simply out and perhaps better than before. He checks the man's pockets, locating the gun and fishes it out. He may need it. On Kennedy's reconfigured mission now, he knows he will be in danger and not from the old lady who had to pee. Our young man is living up to his namesake for the first time in months. Yes, an overload of stress can deplete someone, but stress and its effects on the body are also at the whim of how controllable the situation is. For our Kittitian teenager right now, this is eustress, the opposite-pole positive cousin of distress. Right now, he sees clearly that the demands of his situation may be too great to overcome. Is he a fool? Maybe so, but he'll die knowing he will never be the creepy Russian's bonehead again, certainly not today. He's up and running toward the warehouse doors, fumbling for the keys to those doors he's had all the time.

Inside, there is no one and nothing… the other girl is gone. But what the hell? a hole in the floor? He walks over, gets down on his knees and shakes his head in wonder looking down into the dark. The old lady? The grandmother? Is she the same grandmother he knew from the beach yesterday? Oh mon. What she won't do for her granddaughter! Yet, he knows grandmothers very well indeed. His own Tata? What will she say? What would she do for him? Everything. Anything.

Out the door and around to the back of the building, he races to check the area where the two women, younger and older, sat so recently on the ground. There are footprints and one set is shoeless. Oh boy. He wonders why they paused to sit even for a second.

They should be running for their lives. Time is short.

Oh mon. Oh mon. Stop thinking. Go.

Making sure that the gun is safely shoved deep into his pocket, he takes off down the steep hillside, keeping to the side of the road in case he needs cover for hiding.

❧

At the top of hill, with the Conaree Hills to their right and the road over to Bird Rock to their left, Lizzie and Abigail have convinced each other that leaving the house against their Pop Pop's orders was a good idea after all. The speeding car they are chasing is out of sight screeching around the bend, going much faster than Lizzie's new driver instinct will allow her. She's so unnerved, truly weirded out, about driving on this "wrong" side of the road. There was nothing about this sort of thing in the American driver's manual she memorized to pass her driving test just a few months ago in New Jersey.

"This feels so weird," she admits.

"I know Liz. Believe me I know. But we had to leave. Doing nothing back there at the house was getting us nowhere. And I think we can make a difference. Grammy needs us. I just know it."

"What about Ellie? Don't you think she needs us too?" Liz's instinct is to jab her sister immediately with a counterpoint. She isn't even aware of her verbal digs most of the time. Call it sibling stew, loving but with a sharp taste. They have years of practice going at one another.

"Of course, I know that, Liz. I just have this sixth sense that Grammy is even more in danger right now."

"You do not know that."

"I agree. I just have a feeling. Let's not fight. We need each other."

"Okay."

᪥

It's a big house one street up from Annie and Buck's place on Half Moon Drive. The address is officially Sea Mist Drive. There are few street signs on St. Kitts so you might never know that unless you had a street-marked map. You need to know where you are going anywhere on St. Kitts. You can't just google an address. Good luck with that. That could take you in circles. For this house, go up Fairway Rise, but don't turn right on what is officially known as Sea Mist. Go above to the unpaved road behind and take a steep right turn. Confusing? Of course! This is island knowing. The path will curve up and just before you reach Bay View Terrace, you'll see this place nestled into a grove of trees and bushes, professionally designed for privacy landscape. Not many people do see this place. You go only by invitation for sure with just a few regulars who have been in and out a lot in recent months, jetting in by air and sometimes arriving by sea. Kennedy and his injured cohort back there by the warehouse know this place very well. It belongs to their Russian boss who is preparing to exit the private driveway right now, heading toward the rendezvous. Funny word to use here he might admit. There is a Rendezvous Ridge community nearby where construction has stalled, perhaps already abandoned early in its genesis. Did those developers know Igor and his pimps had anything like this rendezvous in mind? Of course not! They are too busy trying to raise cash.

"Get in," he barks to his bodyguard. "We don't want to be

late."

Instead of turning toward town or Kittitian Village and the Marriott, the car goes left toward Dolphin Rise. These two thugs, yes, let's call them what they are, are aware of the roads that can lead nowhere up here. These little roads are concrete, weedy slabs but you can travel up and down the mountain if you are careful. Poured by contractors, the brainchild of developers, the roads are in place to attract new homes, new citizens, and new money from foreigners seeking peace and privacy; all good ideas, of course, especially when St. Kitts teetered on bankruptcy, but these slabs have also now paved a path into an unexpected nightmare.

The car is an Aurus Senat and Igor had it shipped to his new island in 2020. He doesn't always use it in town, but tonight is different. He wants to impress his buyers. Shown for the first time at the Moscow International Automobile Salon in 2018, Igor's car choice is a full size, luxury sedan. He didn't go for the armored limousine. His is the civilian version but it still has that Porsche and Bosch engineering. Nice. On most days, heading to the beach or the casino, he uses his Audi. The Aurus is usually way too flashy in his neighborhood.

They are off and not for the first time to this location. Igor has been working this deal, an exchange of goods he might call it, for weeks now. He expects, as it has before, that everything will go smoothly. His upfront deposit has cleared and is in his bank account. He checked the bank app just a few minutes ago. All he needs now is to pick up the girls. His buyers will be pleased. So young. So perfect.

"Good to go," he announces.

Annie and Silvie, the girl she pulled out of the warehouse through the floor, are on their way down the other side of the mountain. The sound of the Atlantic Ocean is in the distance. There is mist this morning. She'll take Dolphin Rise down the hill and make her way over to the airport. That's the plan for now. The path through Needsmust is one she knows well. Silvie will go along with anything, this poor little girl, wearing only Annie's sweaty socks, her shoes long gone. Goddamn those monsters who did this. Annie doesn't ask any probing questions, simply giving her reassurance. There will be time for answers later, at least she hopes so. They hold hands.

"We can do this, Silvie. I won't let you go. You have my word. I am so angry at these men who took you and who have my Ellie, my granddaughter. You can't imagine what I might do or say. I am furious. I can do this. We will get out of here."

This girl had hardly spoken a word. Where in God's name did she come from? How long have they been holding her like this?

CHAPTER TWENTY-THREE

6:05 AM

*Why is it that women are too often stereotyped as
the weaker sex? If this were honestly true, why
do women have a longer life expectancy in every
society of the world?*

On the Gulfstream, Buck places a call to both Lauren and Will. The communication system on board makes this easy. His children are waiting at the airport in Orange County, New York to catch the next available military ride to St. Kitts.

"I will call you as soon as I have any word," he tries to reassure them. "At this point, I expect to land by 6:20, St. Kitts time. We received word that American forces are moving into place. This plan is in motion."

"What forces Dad? What are you talking about? What plan? Who is this we?" Lauren is obviously frustrated with her father. "I

179

need to know. This is my daughter who is missing. Do we know where she is? Do we know who kidnapped her? You keep talking about we."

Will tries to calm his sister.

"Lauren, give Dad a chance here. Let's listen."

Buck can picture this big brother with his arm around his sister. "Lauren, Dad is doing everything he can."

"Honey," Buck says, "I will tell you everything when I can. Right now, I just can't. I'm relying on people I've known and have worked with before."

"Who are you, Dad?"

"Lauren, you know who I am. When we get Ellie back safe and sound, I'll tell you my story, as much as I can. Honest, I promise."

He could hear her crying; not tears of anger or frustration with him as much as at this situation with a deeper fear that her baby girl could be gone forever. This is a parent's worst nightmare.

"I am doing my best to get Ellie back to you Lauren. You've just got to trust me now."

"Okay. Okay."

Yet, this father and grandfather was blowing only promises her way, promises that even he wasn't sure he could keep. What he did know was that he had to keep Lauren calm enough to survive and not panic in the next few hours. Anxiety is okay. Anxiety can offer information or sometimes push a person to know and do more. That's what one of his commanding officers used to say.

Use your anxiety. On the other hand, panic can paralyze. Lauren, in truth, knew this only too well. This is his girl who had gone through a period of panic attacks her first year of college. Her bouts of rapid pounding heart rate, shaking so hard she couldn't function, body moving quickly from chills to sweats, and inability to breathe had frightened him to the core. But she had learned to cope and could do it again here. Right?

"We will talk later," he insisted. "I will call you as soon as I can, as soon as I know anything, anything at all." With the call disconnected, Buck experiences one of the deepest fears of his life. He suspects this will all end badly, and his children will blame him.

"How long until we land?" he asks the co-pilot who has come back to check on him, the sole passenger on board.

"Soon, Sir. We are making better than excellent time. Landing will be at 6:18 AM sunrise on St. Kitts."

"Well done. That sets a record for flying time, doesn't it?"

"Yes, Sir."

⊰

Children like Ellie metabolize Ketamine faster than adults and the half-way point of its effect on her young body had passed. Kennedy, who had knocked her out twice, took no note of exactly how much he was administering or how long it might last. He was simply following orders and the Russians up there at the house above Sea Mist seemed to know a lot about their drugs. The second dose was minimal. Ellie feels a little bit better now. Her head is clearing. The nice part about Ketamine is that this analgesic can enhance or at least maintain normal skeletal muscle tone and even stimulate a body's cardiovascular system. Nearly an hour after that second smaller rush shot into her face, she is more awake than she has been since last night. Thank God.

"Lady, I love you girl. Let's go faster. We need to get farther away," she whispers to her new best friend. A donkey nasal-woof-harrumph in return makes Ellie laugh. She understands. She is talking back! How spectacular is that? Sitting up on Lady's back to look around from the top and down the steep hillside, the view is spectacular. She can see the ocean way down to her right and on the other side of the ridge to her left...well that must be Needsmust down there. She's been to that garden with Grammy. And she can almost make out the old sugar mill she climbed with her cousins. Then, the two of them head off, taking untraveled paths that force her to duck away from branches and push back at old wild bushes and scrubby trees growing up here. There's even a bit of sugar cane. This plant, like the people who grew and harvested it, refuses to give up.

Donkeys don't really talk, of course. Ellie knows that. Bible stories about Balaam, Eeyore in *Winnie the Pooh*, the funny animated donkey in the movie *Shrek*, and Ellie's favorite, Puzzle in C.S. Lewis's last volume of *The Chronicles of Narnia* are magical exceptions to this rule of reality. Yet, as an animal lover, our girl has suspected that these creatures have emotions and let's call them thoughts as well. So, when Lady answers with what sounds like words, Ellie is not surprised but rewarded for her belief in a world of sentient creatures like this simple loving donkey.

There goes Lady again. "Heeee Ooooo Hawwww... Oooo Elllliiiieee Elllieeee."

On Lady's back, Ellie can feel lungs working hard to push more air into vocal cords, trying to get these animal "words" out. Well, maybe not the English language but words, nevertheless. Her ears flap wildly. Eyebrows and lids move in communication, and nostrils flare. Lady uses all in her power to talk back.

"I know you love me, Lady. I love you too. It's going to be okay," Ellie assures, laughing out loud about the fact that she has used her grandmother's go-to expression, "It's going to be okay." Well, I hope so, she thinks. Who really knows anymore?

As one unit, they start galloping as fast as Lady can go through the brush and rocky mountainside. Ellie laughs but holds on tight. At a steep section alongside Dolphin Rise, they take an unmarked road down and around in a stroke of luck. Maybe this ridiculous mantra, "Everything will be okay" brings real luck at that moment and not just the thought of it. Why? Because Ellie and Lady could not have known that Igor was speeding toward the end of his roadway and about to take a left onto Dolphin just a few yards above them. They miss each other's presence by seconds.

Lady has a destination in mind and wants to head closer to the area she knows well buried in her inherited genetic history. The terraced area of the two Conaree Hills lies high above where the old Needsmust mountainside compound had been. Our two girls, one human, one equine, race through this maze of trails, pushing through whipping branches and vines into what looks like a dead end on the map of St. Kitts. But Lady knows where she is going.

On the deck of the Wichita, Rufson has readied the two helicopters, an armed MH-60S Seahawk and another, the MQ-8 Fire Scout, ordinarily used for surveillance of traffickers in nearby waters. Crews have been briefed about what they might expect and are aware that these are not drugs being moved but young women. Unnerving for sure.

"We are working under orders from our new Commander of SouthCom," Rufson had told them. "She's had this operation on her radar and now we are in a position to intercept. Any questions?"

While it was certainly a special assignment, the crews were ready and familiar with St. Kitts. They had been here before after all, just a few months ago, but none had ventured into the Needsmust Demonstration Farm or the Royal Basseterre Valley National Nature Reserve nearby.

"Sir, do we know where the young girls are being held?"

"We have pinpointed coordinates for a newly constructed building up there on the mountain, possibly the rendezvous, but there is no possibility of landing on that steep mountainside. One of you will put down in the Nature Reserve and the other will head to the airport nearby for now. We suspect activity and maybe a Russian presence there as well. You have your orders. Let's go."

❧

Annie is getting as far away from the warehouse as possible. Silvie is alongside and keeping up. She had been held up there for some time, first in a filthy shack and then moved to the warehouse with that new hole in the floor.

"Are you okay? Can you do this with me? My poor beautiful girl," Annie says, stopping to give her a hug. "Don't think about where you've been right now. That is over."

But of course, it's not over for this young woman and even Annie knows her young life has taken the kind of turn no woman should ever experience. In any nightmare of rape and abduction, Annie has read, the prefrontal cortex of a human brain is impaired.

184

Silvie's situation and future mental state could be tenuous. She certainly needs medical care at this very moment, this much Annie knows. But in the moment, this safety of Annie, reaching out, touching, encircling with genuine affection, will have to get her through the next few hours.

"You are safe now," Annie assures her again. "Safe. And almost home. So stay with me here."

"Better," was all Igor had said at the time of Silvie's move from one dirty hovel to the next. It was the first time Silvie had seen the old Russian and he took a long, intrusive look at his captured prey before checking out the new digs. He poked her, grabbed her by the chin, twisted her head from side to side. She was crying, fearful then of another round of raping.

Letting her go, he said, "This will work well for future arrangements," obviously pleased with the place. "Good access to the highway down there and the airport."

Silvie continued crying, alert and aware for the first time in days. They had been drugging her. With hands tied behind her back, shoeless, dirty, exhausted, fearful, she was a mental and physical mess, nothing to them, just someone to sell, just a body, a woman for sale. They had unloaded her from the jeep to the warehouse like a piece of meat, pushing her onto the cot.

"Shut up."

"Keep her quiet. Give her more. Don't mess up here."

"Got it."

Now with this strange woman, this Annie, in a hardly credible turn of events, she was free, racing alongside someone's grandmother and desperate to phone home, her mind flipping uncontrollably back and forth, from then to now.

"Annie," she asks. "I need to make a call."

"Oh gosh girl, so do I but there is no cell service here, at least not on my poor international plan. Why do they sell this kind of option to tourists? We'll get a connection when we get further down. Who are you going to call?"

"My mother, and my grandmother. We were on a cruise together and spending the day out at Reggae Beach. A week ago? Maybe longer? I can't think clearly. The cab driver picked us up on Port Zante when we got off the ship and dropped us off there. He said it would be a fun day."

"Oh my God. Your mother? Your grandmother? They must be sick with worry."

"I know. They thought I was just having a rum punch with this cute guy." Then tears start falling again.

"Listen, you did nothing wrong. Having a rum punch with a cute guy in a Caribbean beach bar is not your mistake or your fault. Jesus, those bastards would be better off dead. I could kill them. Goddamn."

It's a thought. Kill them? Just a thought. Or is it?

CHAPTER TWENTY-FOUR

6:18 AM

There is a biblical belief that revenge is never the appropriate course of action. Well yes, of course, but some crimes...maybe the inhumane kind...simply cry out for a get-even response, don't they?

---

*T*he quality of light at dawn on what will be a beautiful day on a small Caribbean island is unique. Ocean breezes push through clouds and the not-quite-there-yet sunlight hesitates, breaking and peeking through for those few minutes before really bright light shines. The wind whistles into hillsides and stirs up palm trees. Open the door carefully to that rush of ocean sounds if you are near the windy Atlantic on St. Kitts. Really breathtaking, literally as well as figuratively! That's why ocean front hotel rooms cost so much more. So windy that you soon understand why trees grow crookedly leaning back away from those gusts forcing crooked angles. On some days, it can hit with a force of nature inclined to change lives, and not just growing trees. All that shoving and smacking takes its toll, of course. Trees grow up but not straight, sometimes at right-angled sideways.

Ellie's stunned cousins, having been hit with this nearly unnatural wind-driven force this very morning, are on Frigate Bay Road in the rental car on the other side of what Grammy calls paradise. They are not sure they would agree with that term anymore and are heading towards the circle that leads into town or out to the airport. Take your roundabout pick.

"Liz, this is just crazy," Abby says as they follow far behind the expensive car. Lizzie is too road-focused, going faster than she's ever driven, to respond. Eyes on the road, stay left, stay left.

"Where is that car going?" she asks.

"My guess is the airport. Look, it's heading onto Kim Collins Highway. So go right up there. I'll tell you when to turn."

Re-configured and enlarged to ease traffic in, out and around an always busy intersection that hubs two sides of the island together, this traffic circle is a seriously circuitous trip if you don't know exactly which of the eight options to take arriving from the Frigate Bay area. And, if you are not accustomed to driving on the left side, like Lizzie, the trick of taking the correct turn off is even harder. Even drivers like Annie have gone around the circle more than once realizing too late that a turn has been missed.

"Buck, this reminds me of that Chevy Chase movie," she laughed first time she took it after the new construction was completed. "In busy traffic, you could get stuck going around and around, unable to inch through rushing cars."

Whaaack. Whaaack. Whoop. Whoop.

The sound of helicopters above surprises the girls.

"Don't stop, Liz. Keep going."

This too-loud-to-think-straight clicking and whooping is called thickness noise and is deafening. The morning air is actually being beaten up by the copter blades. Then floodlights spread in front of the girls on the road. Abby unbuckles her seat belt, rolls down the window all the way to lean out and look up.

"Jesus Christ. Oh my God, Liz. Did Pop Pop do this?"

"Whoa. Where are they going?"

"The same direction as we are, the airport."

But as they race along this stretch of highway, with hearts beating wildly, one of the helicopters turns right toward the Conaree Hills up and over the old sugar mill, the one on their family holiday card photo.

"Abby, which way should we go now?"

"Stay left first. Then take the second turn."

"You crazy girl, how do you remember all these turn offs and circles."

"I don't know. It's just my brain. I can't help it."

Racing down the mountain, Annie swats the no-see-ums.

"Damn these things," she says to Silvie, adding, "Are you

okay?" Annie knows Silvie is not okay and may never be, at least not for a long time. Being victimized as she has been, could scar and warp this young woman. Is this her granddaughter's fate as well?

"Yes. I am okay." She sounds a little better.

"We can do this," Annie says putting one arm around Silvie's shoulders again. "We can do this girl."

Annie's mind races. Can she do this? How did she get here? Why in God's name did she put her granddaughters' lives at risk for a frivolous vacation? Can she blame Covid? The pandemic certainly did unearth a deep vein, or was it an artery of fear, frustration, and anger in the world. In those months of isolation, she dreamed and planned more time with these kids and grandkids. Time is so precious when you start numbering years left in life from your seventies. She followed the government protocols with no complaints, washed her hands incessantly, shopped for groceries remotely, kept to her own house, took long walks alone, zoomed with her children, and wore masks everywhere. But she had almost put these precautions and fears behind her. They were safe. They were here. She had even promised her children that they would eat only at outdoor restaurants and stick to beach side activities. They would not share breathing space with strangers. Hah, what an empty promise that is now. And yet, they were going to one of her safest places in the world, her home on St. Kitts.

"Wait a minute," Annie whispers to Silvie. They stop. Turn. In fear now.

Behind them on the road, they hear the slap, slap, slapping feet of someone running down the incline towards them. And before they can duck away to hide, he's upon them.

"Hold on," he yells. "I won't hurt you. I want to help." He's close enough, maybe 15 yards away. He looks familiar.

Annie eases into her grandmotherly soft-style defense mode. It worked before.

"My goodness. What are you doing out here at this time of morning?" She's smiling. Silvie is cringing. This girl has certainly seen this man before. She's experienced him at his worst, knows what he has been capable of doing, to her. Grabbing Annie's arm, she starts pulling away, wincing, whispering, "No, no, no. Please let's go."

"No, no. I won't hurt you. I know what's coming down here, what's supposed to happen." The kid moves closer to the women and turns toward Silvie with recognition, in a horror of memory. "I am so sorry. I am so, so sorry."

"Why are you sorry?" Annie asks. She reads into this apology…and sees guilt.

"Woah," he says, eyes moving back and forth in surprise. There are two women here, not three. "Where is the other one? The blonde?" Then he adds, "Wait. Where is the damn donkey?"

"Donkey?!!!" Annie screams. "Do you know where Ellie is? You are a disgusting piece of sh-t. You took her. You are the one who dragged her body from bed last night." She runs toward him with fists raised and starts hitting, slapping, and kicking him. "What have you done with her? Where is she?" She is reaching for her knife.

"Lost her," he says trying to protect his face with hands. "I lost her up there when the donkey ran off."

"A donkey?" Annie recalls that hee-haw sound on the

191

mountain. So she hadn't imagined it. It had been donkey after all. She pulls out the little knife. "Sit down here you creep. Get on the concrete right now. Face down." He does and she immediately grinds a foot into his lower back. He winces. "Don't you dare. You have no rights here. Start at the beginning. Who are you and what have you done? What are you up to?"

"Not just me," he protests, head turned to the side, cheek down. "I had orders."

Silvie inches closer. "I know him. He's with them."

"Who are you with? What is this all about?"

"The Russian," he explains. "He told me to grab the girls. He sold them." Pointing back up the hill to the warehouse, he winces in pain as Annie's foot crunches his back again.

"Oh my God. How could you?" Now, she leans down and punches his ear. He takes it, no longer trying to protect himself. She hits him again, considers the knife in her hand, and then stops, realizing. "I know you. You worked on the catamaran. You took us sailing. Oh my God." Trying to picture the easy-going, cute kid he once was, she asks, "What happened to you?"

"Please," he begs. "I want to make it right. I'm here to help you. I'm okay now. I was a mess. The drugs. We've got to find her before they do. She was tied to the donkey, knocked out with drugs, special K."

"What? What kind of drug is that? She's just a child. Only 13."

"Not sure. Igor gave me the stuff. Showed me how to use it."

"What's your name? I've forgotten."

192

"Kennedy. My name is Kennedy."

"Oh jeez, were you named after our American President?"

"No, after our Prime Minister, Kennedy Simmonds. But I want to help. I need to do this. I am sorry, so sorry. But we've got to find her before they do. She will be taken off island soon, very soon. She was sold. There is not much time."

"Sold? What do you mean she was sold? Who's going to take her? Where?"

"I've got a gun," he says.

"Good, I may need to use it," Annie says emphasizing the I here. This sounds so natural coming out of her mouth. Yes, she will need a gun. Right? Yes, her brain is careening into a get-even encounter.

Grabbing Silvie's hand, she asks, "Can you do this with me? We need to find Ellie."

She nods and then Kennedy says, "I have an idea about dis donkey."

How many years ago did Buck make her take that gun use and safety course? Would she even know what to do?

≈

"Can you go any faster?" the prime minister asks his driver. Traveling up the mountain, they can hear helicopters and see floodlights.

"No, Sir. And I'm not sure I've taken the right turns up here. The roads are a mess. It would be easy to lose control."

193

In the back seat, Valamine's phone rings for the second time and his friend Sam is on the line.

"I'm out here at Christophe Harbour and it looks like a super-yacht arrived last night after I left. Do you want me to try to check the papers on it? I may know something, overheard people talking."

"Yes, see what you can find out. Who was aboard? When will it be leaving? Can you see anyone out there on the boat now? Would they have had their own vehicle aboard?"

"All quiet there. And yes, it's big enough to carry almost anything, even a car. There are two large tenders aboard to ferry people and vehicles."

"Sam, you have the prime minister's permission. He's here with me now. If you need access codes to immigration and customs sites, let us know."

"Okay."

CHAPTER TWENTY-FIVE

6:18 AM

The perception of a woman speaking softly,
tentatively, is that of weakness, isn't it? But the
truth for so many smart women, generations of
them, is that sometimes speaking softly can carry
a big wallop of power.

---

*E*llie sighs. Her gut growls. Not with hunger. Oh jeez. She needs to go again? Not now. She thought that had passed. Hold it. Her body is a knotty mess. She's itchy, dirty, but well, seriously, seriously relieved. Should she be? Is she safe? Crouching off the side of a narrow concrete road in the bushes, hand stroking the warm donkey's flank, she wonders; what next? Was it just two days ago that she landed here in St. Kitts with her cousins and Grammy? Two days? That airport is just down this mountainside. In awe, no shock, at her predicament; outside in her pajamas on a mountain, she considers the short but so-very-crazy-long time it has taken to get here to this moment. A little foggy (no wait, this is dizzy) with each turn of her head…this is called vertigo, right? From that drug? Her friend with the bone cancer described this weird sensation last year on a Zoom hospital visit.

"Ellie," the eighth grader friend had admitted. "It's the strangest feeling. Totally head-spinning."

Now here she sits in her own kind of dizzying danger. Ellie remembers saying back then in the hospital during visiting hours, "You are so brave."

To which her friend protested, "What else can I be? No no, I'm not brave. Not really."

"You're right. You've got no choice. You just keep going?"

"Yes, just keep going."

Vertigo? That's what this is. Exactly, she thinks wondering about the drug that the creepy guy shoved over her nose and mouth? Then, she smiles recalling the image of him groaning on the ground.

"What a kick, Lady. Good job. You whacked him good. Who knew you could kick like that?"

The donkey chortles and snorts as this girl gets back up onto her, not tied anymore but upright and simply holding on around her neck. A memory of ET, one of her favorite movie creatures, pops into Ellie's head just then. They had watched the old film during the pandemic. "Phone home, Lady. I need to phone home." That little space traveler with his crazy large head, enormous blue eyes and bird like feet had traveled to earth from another planet, made a mistake, and was as much in the dark as Ellie is right now. She thinks of him hiding in the dark inside Gertie's closet amongst the stuffed animals.

Phone home. Phone home. But where and how?

Lady nods her head and twists back around, trying to nudge Ellie, as if telling her where and how.

෯

The Gulfstream carrying Buck is coming in for a landing at the Robert K. Bradshaw International Airport and he looks out the window at this oh-so-familiar place. It's been more than two years since he last landed here. The island is green, mountainous, and welcoming in its morning-mist distance. He is on edge for sure. This is the kind of thing that happens to other people, right?

Is his granddaughter already gone, whisked off into a dark web of worldwide human trafficking? Where is Annie? There's been no word since his good night last night. Will this plan in motion really work? Old military connections have come through but what if? He knows that if you harbor a thought, especially a negative one, and keep thinking it over, and over again, you jinx yourself. Welcoming catastrophe into your frame of mind is a bad idea. So, he compartmentalizes. He can do that. And with this smoothest-ever, wheels-down landing on the Kittitian airport tarmac, he shoves failure aside. Jumping up to race to the plane's door, he takes a last look out the window.

A helicopter is landing. Eyes watering...tough guy Buck gets teary. He's overcome with pride in the American military he knows so well, and this takes him by surprise. Vulnerability comes with grandparenting, of course. Or is there something else here? Is there an emotion that he tries to push aside? He is a man not used to being out of control, not knowing the answers, not being the go-to, get-it-done Pop Pop, a man with a to-do list that is rarely ever too long or insurmountable. He is out of his realm, no comfort zone anywhere.

❧

On the side of this mountain, Annie and Kennedy make a plan to return to the warehouse. Silvie can go no further. Her initial relief about being out of bondage, away from the nightmare of that warehouse, has worn off.

"I need to rest. I'm so sorry. I don't feel well," Silvie says. She's breathing hard, queasy, leaning over her knees, one hand on her stomach. Annie's socks are also no match for concrete.

"Oh my gosh girl. You have been so strong." Annie crouches, putting her arms around the girl as any grandmother would do. "You've been through a nightmare and now I'm putting you through more of it. Stay here. Hide. We will come back for you. Over there. Head over to that side and stay out of sight." Both Annie and Kennedy help Silvie to the side of the road, out of sight.

"I thought I was going to die back there. It was horrible," she says looking directly at Kennedy accusingly, so very brave here confronting a captor, one of them, one of the ugly men. "Why did you do this to me? How could you?"

Annie turns and with lips pinched in anger, shouts at Kennedy, "You rapist!" She punches him in the face. "Did you rape my granddaughter too?" Yes, she delivers a punch.

"No, no. No one did. I lost her. On the donkey. The donkey took her."

"I don't believe you. And if I find out you did, I will kill you. She is so precious. When did you last see her?"

198

"No, no, I took her from the house, the bedroom. That's all. I tied her to a donkey. I know the donkey," Kennedy tries to focus only on what they need to do, not his guilt, not the girl right there in front of him. Jesus, then he thinks back to the misery he even inflicted on the poor animal, the donkey he whacked, beat up, this past week as well as this girl and the other. That pretty girl from the beach, with the long blonde hair, yes he made her so sick with the drug.

"What did you say?" Annie demands, glaring at him. "Tell me."

"I tied her to the donkey."

"Oh my God. I know. You already said that. A donkey?"

"Yah." Then in a childlike voice, he adds, "the donkey likes her," not mentioning that this animal kicked him so hard this morning he could hardly think. He can still feel that pain in his side. That crazy donkey likes this girl a lot.

"She took off fast when I lost the rope. I know where. De animal goes there all the time."

Annie cringes thinking of Ellie bound and tied to a donkey's back. "Where?"

"See that big cut? Up over there?" He points to a familiar piece of Annie's landscape. She can see this gouge in the range of hilly mountains from her backyard.

"Damn donkey. So stubborn. Always heads up dat way to the other side. Somethin' in de head; a memory, a place. Always find her in there heading down to old Needsmust. Tata told me that the plantation house stood high on the hill."

"Who's Tata?" Annie asks.

"My gram. My Tata."

"Kennedy," she says, switching to a gentler tone. Maybe it was the mention of his grandmother. Maybe just her instinct here about what is supposed to happen. But she changes course in her mind.

"I need your help Kennedy. We've got to turn back, go up to that warehouse. That's where the exchange is going to take place, right? You stay right here Silvie. I will come back for you. I promise. Hide now. Stay out of sight." For better or for worse, Annie has decided she needs this Kennedy, sensing an ordinary Kittitian kid there inside somewhere, a boy who has gone astray. She needs him and he certainly needs her if he is going to survive his Russian nightmare.

They start running back up. Annie feels exhilarated, not tired, not old, but determined to beat all the odds here in front of her.

On one of the last turns up the hill and in the range of the warehouse, they spot headlights coming from the other side.

"Got to be Igor," Kennedy says. "Hide." He checks his watch. It's time.

"No no no. We are not hiding from any Russian monster here. I don't care how dangerous you think he is. I will not give him that. This is my safe place. Not his. He will not own it. He will not frighten me or you away," Annie insists. "I am here. I can do this. Kennedy don't be a fool. Stand up strong. We must deal with this man, together. He may know where Ellie is."

If he had any hope of avoiding his worst enemy, Kennedy

has none now. But for some reason, he grows infinitesimally more confident. Is it this old lady? A grandmother? Even while he still believes she is totally irrational, he says, "Ok. Ok but mon. Sheeet." One of her favorite bad words sounds so different in his Kittitian slang. She almost laughs out loud.

"We are not in trouble. He is in trouble. We've done nothing wrong. He has. He's the criminal. He's the one who should be frightened. Sent back to Russia, his mother country. Hah. I hope he dies. Only a coward steals young women, little girls, for rapists' pleasure, to make money, to sell as slaves. Do you realize that's what was going on here?"

Kennedy hangs his head. "Don't you think he preyed on you too? I hope he dies here tonight."

"Let's move. Come on." She starts running toward the front of the building and the car's headlights. Kennedy follows, a few steps behind. "Wait a minute," she says stopping and facing back to him. "Give me your gun."

"Oh wom'n you don't know. Tata, please," Kennedy responds, slipping verbally into the mistake of whose grandmother is here. "Be careful. He can kill, without thinking. You don't know him, these men. You don't know them."

Annie looks at him. "I do know. I know a lot more about life and death than you do and we cannot let him win here. We fight back. This evil must stop here. Come on."

She grabs the gun he holds out to her. Rounding the side of the building, the two slow their pace in the immediate glare of a car's headlights.

The driver jumps out of the car, looks surprised and says,

"Whoa…who you?"

"Well, sir, I should be asking you the very same thing. Who are you?"

She slips quickly into her simple-grandmother-out-for-a-walk-this-morning mode. She goes with the sweet, gentle, outspoken, candor to kill, take off guard, and keeps right on talking in simple, silly sentences. Her words are a stream of ridiculously soft punches into the air of confusion.

"I don't recognize this building from my last hike up here," she goes on and on, still chattering easily, moving closer and closer. "Was just wondering what it's for? Is it yours?"

From the back door of this very fancy car…a Russian-made Aurus Senat with a nine-speed automatic transmission, she will later learn…Igor emerges. Dressed in black, wearing an expensive sports jacket and pressed, my God pressed, slacks, he has lathered on his awful after-shave lotion and Annie can smell it even before seeing his face clearly. The scent is just like that other ridiculous Russian, the one she met on St. Kitts at the tiki bar years ago. What is it with these awful men? Do they think they can cover up their stink? Do they believe they are invincible?

"I know you," she says emphasizing the word know but in a very pleasant tone of voice. "Hey, you're my neighbor. The man who loves the local rum, right? Is it the Coconut that's your favorite flavor? No, I think it's the Vanilla."

He's stopped moving towards her and is standing still. What the hell? Is she crazy? What in God's name is this old woman talking about?

"Last time we met you were at the Marriott lobby bar. That

was a fun night. Remember?" Igor looks weirdly at her, taken absolutely by surprise here by her pleasant neighborly banter and his favorite bar scene. Actually he does recall the evening when the old lady seated next to him insisted on chatting. So off guard now, looking for his lackeys who should have been at the warehouse doors, he is unaware that Annie is reaching into her pocket where she tucked Kennedy's gun, the one he grabbed from his friend lying somewhere near here in the bushes. Kennedy stands behind and out of Igor's sight, hoping his boss won't register a failure to follow orders here.

"Gud eeeevning," Igor begins to play along with the pleasantries, stalling until he can figure out what's going on.

"Or are you a coffee lover?" she asks Igor. He pulls his chin and head back in a shake of confusion. She continues, "Have you tried that Shipwreck Lime rum yet? I honestly believe you will like it as much as the Coconut."

Time stands still.

CHAPTER TWENTY-SIX

6:20 AM

---

*Empathy…that capacity to experience the
emotions of others…makes us human. But what if
you can't feel empathetic? What if something
along your path…and who knows
what…destroyed this part of your humanity? Will
awful people, who may have suffered awful
circumstances, keep right on hurting others over,
and over again? Are they redeemable?*

---

*T*he image in Annie's mind…and she sees it
clearly…is not of Igor, the Russian menace right
here; not his driver standing alongside the sleek car,
hand on gun; not Kennedy, the Kittitian kid directly behind her
hiding like a shy toddler. This picture is of Ellie; her beautiful 13-
year-old granddaughter just launching life as a teenager, not even
fully aware of where her body will take her in life. She is being
raped, over and over, and then over again by ugly, despicable men,

taking turns, laughing, pushing, bruising, smacking, and sexually abusing her. Her thighs and vagina are bleeding. Her insides are in spasm. She is crying, whimpering. This just-emerging-from-childhood body is being defiled, destroyed perhaps forever to the sensations in a normal loving sexual life. Annie believes this is a crime so vile — and she has never been raped — that her mind is made up. Rapists deserve the worst, so undeserving of human life. She can do this. She will do this.

So…well she is not nervous at all about what she's decided; what she sees there in her mind is only an image, of course, but what if? What if? And now this thought has created a need for action. If she takes no action here, now, she knows she will regret the inaction for the rest of her life. Like the Nike commercials still say, "Just do it." She can also hear the long-ago roar of a crowd at an ice hockey rink when her Lauren played on a team. She shoots. She scores.

The gun, the one Kennedy just gave her, is there in her hand.

While Igor wonders if this woman — this crazy old lady who will not shut up, standing before him at close range — is insane or simply stupid, she pulls up the weapon and aims the gun at his midsection, then slightly down directly at his groin. *What the f--k,* his mind screams. While hers prays. *May you never ever be able to use that penis again.* Imploring her own brand of almighty justice, she asks, *Let that penis be gone, torn off in this blast.*

With an agonizing, explosive cry, this foul man fouls his pants with blood, feces, urine, and falls to the ground as his driver rushes toward Annie. She sees this. Clearly. Calmly. She knows what she has done. She's relieved in fact. It will be okay. Right?

⌒

In the oversized official car, with a driver, an old school mate upfront, and Valamine to his side, the prime minister reaches the top of the mountain near a warehouse he has never seen before. They hear a shot. A gun has been fired.

"What's that?" he asks no one and then points to the building. "Let's move quickly. How long has this thing been here?"

He can hear the Atlantic Ocean down there from the open window and sees another car's headlights. Then, his phone rings there in the backseat. "Yes, Sir." His timing is perfect. This is the kind of opportunity every new leader of a small nation indebted to the United States of America would dream about.

"Let's go," he tells the driver who is halfway out the door, following the sound of that gun shot. Browne turns to the sergeant, still seated comfortably back there. "Valamine, do you have a gun with you?"

"Yes sir, but…"

"Bring it," he interrupts while opening the back door to jump out and head around to the front of the building. "Are you coming man? Hurry up."

He's alongside his driver now as they race forward. "You didn't sign up for this kind of action," Browne says.

"But of course I did, Sir."

Though Valamine, who is near retirement, certainly did willingly sign up for this kind of action, he sighs, moving slowly, letting others take the lead, not wanting to die or be injured tonight, wishing once again that last night hadn't been his night for overnight duty. Why couldn't this have happened on another night?

❧

Helicopter lights flood the Kim Collins Highway ahead of the girls in their rental car. Abby watches one copter veer off to the right heading away from the airport to rise higher in the air toward the Conaree Hills. The other is down, out of sight and has obviously put down at the airport.

"Oh Jesus, Liz," Abby says as the speeding car ahead of them turns, not left into the airport circle, but right, almost directly below the helicopter's skyward path.

"Turn up here by that Needsmust sign. Go right," Abby says. "Quick, we need to follow the car and that helicopter."

"Ooooo Abby this makes me nervous. Are you sure?"

"Yes, I'm sure. Go go…turn right. Up there. See the sign?"

"Okay."

"I think it's a Maserati."

"How do you know that?" her sister asks.

"I went to the car show in New York with Pop Pop."

"Jeez. Seriously?!"

"What should we do?" Abby wonders as Lizzie pulls to the side of the bumpy lane that goes through this Needsmust memorial garden.

"Abby, I think we should wait here. This is just too dangerous. What can we do even if we are able to catch them? All we have are golf clubs. I'm guessing they have guns," she says reminding her sister that their only real weapons are from Pop Pop's favorite golf clubs, the set just shipped down for this winter season: an iron and a driver.

"I know. You're right. That Maserati GranTurismo can go almost 200 miles per hour."

"You, little sister, make me crazy sometimes." They sit for a moment. Then, Abby says, "I have an idea."

"What?"

"Let's pull the car up over there, face directly into the hillside and keep the high beams focused on the mountain. We may be able to see something."

"Like what? Another speeding car? A helicopter crashing?"

"Oh jeez. I don't know Lizzie. Yes, maybe. Something, anything, someone!" Why does her sister always have to second-guess everything she says? Is this a first-born, know-it-all trait? Can't little sisters know best? At least occasionally?

"Good idea."

Touche, Abby wants to say but holds back. Instead, she reaches over to her sister's arm in a gesture of love. Sibling relationships are complicated.

∽

At the airport, Buck runs toward the helicopter on the tarmac nearby and grabs the outstretched hand of the man he has known only as a calm voice up until now. This must be Captain Rufson.

"Oh my God, am I happy to see you here."

They huddle and Rufson brings Buck up to speed with what is happening and what his unit knows. This Caribbean situation has been on military minds for some time. A crew is already in the helicopter waiting and salutes Buck as he climbs aboard.

Liz pulls the car farther along the bumpy farm road, turns onto the grass, then goes left, to face into the slope of the mountain. A few houses line the new road up there but it's early in the winter tourist season and there are no lights yet. They quickly realize that even with the high beams on, the focus of their headlights is low and too narrow to see much. What are they looking for after all?

"I know what you're thinking Liz. This is a lame idea. But let's just try it."

"It's not lame Abby."

So, in the front seat, side windows open, listening to slapping of helicopter blades up high and feeling the warmth of this Caribbean morning sunshine, they wait. Up there, the speeding Maserati dips in and out as it travels up the labyrinth and switchbacks of roadway.

"That guy is crazy," Abby says. They catch a glimpse of his headlights every so often.

"Or late for something," Liz adds. "Did you see if there was more than one person in the car?"

"No, it was going too fast and too far ahead. I bet you couldn't have seen inside anyway. Tinted glass."

"Oh yeah. For sure."

The car continues up with its occupants obviously ignoring the overhead helicopters, two of them now. Stupid men do stupid things. These human beings inside that car…perhaps we should not include them in the human race category…don't even notice the young girl on the donkey going down a side path. Why would they? They are single-minded. They've come too far to let this deal slip away. One guy keeps dialing Igor and cursing island cell service.

Minutes pass. The girls see both helicopters circling above the mountaintop now. The drift of a screeching loudspeaker reaches them. Then, below, right in front, they spot something coming through the field at the base of the slope.

"Do you see that?"

"Yes. Yes. What is it?"

"It's moving faster now, coming toward us," Abby says. "Oh Liz, I'm scared."

"This is a first," she laughs. "You scared? Let's just wait a minute."

They keep looking. Should they be afraid?

"It's not a speeding car," Abby laughs as gut instinct sends both a no-fear message. This whatever-it-is, a hundred yards out now and approaching, is obviously coming toward the headlights of their car, and seems to signal no danger with its direct, definitive but non-threatening approach.

"What the heck?" Lizzie says.

CHAPTER TWENTY-SEVEN

6:30 AM

According to the World Health Organization,
one-third of all women had their first sexual
experience being raped or assaulted: a statistic
worth weeping about.

*A*nnie looks up to the sound of the helicopter above and then floodlights encircle her. Woozy with a what-did-you-just-do sensation, she's holding this gun in her hand as her mind floods with images of Ellie being raped. What happened or is happening to Ellie is perfectly clear and ugly. So horrible that she can see it right there…but only in her imagination.

Kennedy, perhaps empowered or more likely frightened by the consequences of what Annie has just done, steps from behind to her side and shields her from the driver who is about to shoot. With one arm raised, he is pointing his pistol at her. One helicopter is noisy and directly above. Air whips around on the ground. Her short gray hair blows. Annie can't hear anything distinctly. Sound has been dampened by the bullet blast: time and space are now in a muffling mix. Then, one rope, and another dangle from the copter and a loudspeaker voice blares, "Put down your weapons. This is the United States Coast Guard."

Weapon? Yes, hers. She hands the gun to Kennedy who has put his arm around her in a grandson-to-grandmotherly touch of protection. And with this touch, she wakes to the worry: Where is Ellie? Oh my God. She is not here.

Down the ropes, U.S. military operatives drop to the mountaintop and race toward this scene; a man, the bloody mess of him, on the ground. Maybe dead? Annie is stunned but not surprised and not apologetic. She wonders, where did this help come from? American military? Buck must have received word. How else could this be happening? Then, from a side road behind, she hears the approach of another vehicle.

Our Annie turns to Kennedy, the kidnapper, and is about to say something as he takes back his gun and looks wide-eyed with fear, or is it shock? at her. Before she can open her mouth to say anything, the Prime Minister of St. Kitts, the Honorable Reginald Browne, is behind her flanked by two men, one with another gun in hand, facing off with the driver who has stopped moving toward her and dropped his weapon.

Facing around to Browne…Annie has only seen him on television after the election when he spoke at the United Nations. Such a young man, she thinks. He is the same age as her Will. It's only then that she glances down and really sees, honestly takes in the consequences of her actions, the bloody Russian, the man she shot, now lying in a fetal position right there at her feet, bloody and moaning. Moaning? Yes, not dead. He's making sounds. Oh good, she decides, surprising herself. Yes, she wanted him to suffer, to experience retribution for his crimes, but maybe not die.

"Ma'am, let me help you sit down here," someone says. "You've been through quite a shock."

More men and women in uniform swarm around her, not paying inordinate attention to her there or the details in the immediate confusion. A medic turns Igor…is that his name? Did she hear that somewhere…over to check and tend to his injuries. Annie blinks back tears of emotional overload, not remorse. No, no, she is not sorry she took her shot. Could this be considered a defensive response? What grandmother wouldn't take the same action if given the chance to right a wrong, the rape of a precious granddaughter?

"But where's my Ellie?" she asks no one in particular, but everyone nearby. "Where is Ellie?" No one is listening in the confusion. "Where are you, Ellie?"

⚚

Buck is in the second helicopter now circling above the warehouse nightmare scene. The other has taken off downhill. He catches a glimpse of Annie down there on the ground slumping against a warehouse door. His heart leaps. She is alive.

"Landing will be impossible, but we need to show force from above," Rufson explains. "We do this often at sea, scares the bejesus out of slick but stupid drug traffickers. Sometimes that is almost, but not quite, funny."

Buck nods, unable to smile right now at this observation of tough guys being frightened silly. "I can see Annie down there. Thank God she's okay."

"Oh my God. That is good news about your wife Buck. We'll catch these men, Sir. There is no doubt about it now."

Looking down again, he sees no sign of Annie now. And where is Ellie?

Rufson looks at Buck and reads his thoughts, "We'll get your granddaughter back safely Sir."

Can you really guarantee that? He wants to say but doesn't. He knows what can happen. What might have already happened.

❧

Two sisters, less than two years apart at birth, were babies in the same sandbox fighting over every toy and every move. These battles of "Mine…No mine" were frustrating to those around nearby: parents, grandparents, aunts, uncles, cousins. Would they ever be able to work together, did they really love one another? It sure didn't seem to be true. And yet, those sibling war games might have prepared them for days like this when the only way forward was by working together.

"Liz, I think it's an animal," Abby says. She has leaned as far out the car window as possible.

"You're right. It's a pony or horse…no wait, it's a donkey…with someone on its back."

Jumping out of the car, running to make sure their eyes are not deceiving them, the girls start screaming, "Oh my God. Oh my God. Oh my God! Ellie, is that you?"

This feels like a morning miracle.

"It's me, Ellie. I'm here. Yes, yes, I'm here," their cousin

214

shouts as she closes the distance, gets off the animal and rushes into the hugs. The donkey, well, this crazy, lovely, loving animal whose name may or may not be Lady tries to nuzzle into the threesome to make it four. Her brays and whinnies mimic the young women's voices in a nasal, hyena-like laugh of hee-haw, hee-haw. If Annie were able to hear them, she'd be reminded of the piercing screams all the little girls make at birthday parties, on the softball field behind her house in the states, or whenever they play boisterously together. Seriously, it's not just Annie. Everyone knows girls scream louder than boys. The high-pitched banter is pure joy here this morning.

"Where were you?" Abby asks, pulling back to look into Ellie's eyes.

"Up there," Ellie says, smiling and pointing to the mountain.

"Oh girl, we've been so worried, so sick, so scared for you," Liz says. "Wait," this oldest cousin now asks, "Are you alright? Are you okay? Did they hurt you?"

And in the word hurt, all three read an assumption none wants to say out-loud. That word is raped. It lies there unspoken between the girls now hugging tightly.

"I'm okay. Or, I think I'm okay," Ellie shares quietly, speaking softly, perhaps starting to exhale this fear that wasn't her fate. "He drugged me, two times. I think I heard him come in through our sliding glass bedroom doors. Then, I can't remember. I was so sick up there." There is a pause, and an embarrassed moment pops out. She chuckles, "I had to poop and then I threw up in the grass. You know me. Always something going on in my gut." She smiles a little, sighs and looks squarely into the faces of her favorite girl cousins. She is so happy to be here with them and the sweet relief pours into this moment. "That was a mess," she

215

laughs now. "And poor Lady here, I think she needs a bubble bath. I retched right on her too."

"No toilet paper, huh?" Abby adds.

"Oh my God, Abby, how could you ask that?" Liz counters.

"It was a joke."

With the return of this sibling sparring that Ellie knows so well from their years of playing together, all three start to laugh hysterically.

"Of course, it was a joke. I was kidding," Abby says.

"I knew that." Ellie insists and laughs about one of their grandmother's idiosyncrasies. "You know how Grammy always reminds us what to pack?" They all know only too well about their grandmother's advance travel planning to-do lists. "This wasn't one of those trips where Grammy insists that we bring our own roll of toilet paper. And I certainly didn't have time to pack carefully," Ellie continues. "But look what was in my pajama pocket that I played up there in the dark." She pulls her Frozen flashlight out of the side pocket of her dirty pink pajama pants. "Remember when she told us to pack a flashlight just in case we needed it in the dark? Well, here it is. I needed it and I hoped it helped."

"I know it helped," Abby agrees, not honestly convinced that a Walt Disney toy really helped in any way. This is clearly the difference in thinking between a 13-year-old and a 15-year-old, one still believes in the magic of toys, the elder not so much.

"Well, I'm just glad I had it with me. Where is Grammy?" she asks. "Why isn't she here with you?"

"She told us to stay at the house," Liz says.

"And she ran out the back door to rescue you."

CHAPTER TWENTY-EIGHT

6:45 AM

---

*The new gardeners of Needsmust leave a gentle,
logical touch in this valley, taking a relaxed
approach to pruning, planting, and nurturing
what grows naturally here. What once was a
place of horror and pain is gone. This is not a
place of death anymore. Or is it?*

---

*I*n the helicopter, hovering above the warehouse now,
Buck asks, "Can you drop me down too?"

"Are you sure, Sir?" Rufson cautions. "This
could be a tough climb down for someone your age. I usually let
my younger generation go ahead."

To this, Pop Pop laughs just a little, not derisively but in a
tone of reassurance for Rufson. "I can do it. Trust me." He walks
toward the open copter door and takes the steady arm of a young
man handing him the rope. "I'll be okay here, Son. I've got it."

Buck has done this before, a long time ago. He knows the ropes.

On the ground next to Igor, the medic has determined that Annie missed her mark. This man's penis is still partially in place but the bullet traveled dangerously down the inside of his thigh and into his calf. Her shot at close range ripped through critical veins and possibly arteries. He's bleeding badly and a tourniquet is being tied to try to stop it. He did soil his pants, however, so there's a mortifying clean up taking place too. His neatly pressed slacks have been cut off. Several medics are now working on him. They want this man alive. Other sailors have the driver/bodyguard under restraint, hands tied.

One of the helicopters is heading back down the mountainside in the direction of the airport to follow what has been spotted from the air; the speeding car, a Maserati trying to maneuver a turn-around on the narrow road. They watch as it nearly plunges off the side of the steep hillside. Obviously unfamiliar with this area of the Conaree Hills, the driver doesn't know that there isn't room to hide at all. Everyone in St. Kitts knows almost everything about everyone else, especially in the light of morning. If Annie knew of their plight, she'd be gleeful about what is about to happen. But what she doesn't know is that all three of her granddaughters are directly in this race car's path.

∾

The girls stop laughing and rejoicing in the field. They see the copter heading back down, following the headlights of that crazy car.

"It's those guys Liz," Abby says.

"Who are they?" Ellie asks.

"Not sure but they were in a huge hurry to get up that mountain. We were trying to follow them," Liz explains.

"Let's get out of here," Abby says alarmed. "Quick. Hurry."

Lady also starts snorting and stamping in warning. She flicks her head.

"What is it, girl?" Ellie asks.

"Can she really understand what you are saying El?" Abby asks.

"Yes, she can. For sure and something is wrong here. Let's get away."

"Liz, move the car over to those old picnic tables so it's not so out in the open," Abby asks. "Ellie, let's go."

And once again, Ellie asks her Lady, "Which way should we go?"

⁊

Without a word to anyone, just a glance toward Kennedy who is busy answering questions, Annie walks slowly, casually toward the side of the warehouse. For anyone wondering where she is going or what she might be planning, she would have said, "Have to pee. Be right back." No one asks. No one notices. Hovering helicopters, Coast Guard officers, Russians, and the arrival of the prime minister are big deals.

At this moment, Annie is experiencing a gnawing, agonizing fear, a premonition that something awful is going to happen if she doesn't move immediately. The weight of it is huge enough to make her leave her sense of duty behind here. She should stay to share her side of the story, but she simply can't. This scene is now under control, she tells herself. Like any parent and grandparent, she compartmentalizes, too. She must do this now. She will deal with all that other stuff later. For now, there is only one thought; Ellie. And, she has this hunch triggered by something Kennedy shared. Her instinct is whispering; where might this donkey have gone with her granddaughter on its back? Yes? Maybe?

To be honest, Annie will not remember much from this incredible sprint down a mile-high mountainside from Conaree to the fields below. She doesn't feel tired. She doesn't feel inadequate. That will come later. She can do this right here and now.

So, out of sight now behind the warehouse, she starts running, and not on the road. She won't take those stupid concrete roads...damn them...with their switchbacks and impossible hairpin turns. The light of day now sends her straight down, through brush, vines, and slippery grass, not even following any old trail. What fans the flames of her determination is a promise made to her children and grandchildren that this trip would be safe. Oh my God. How wrong she was about her Grammy getaway! Was it a hollow promise made by an old lady? Yes, but seriously, don't all grandmothers make these claims every single time they babysit or send parents off for weekend getaways? "She'll be okay. We'll have fun. Everything will be alright." And why not say these things to ensure confidence in a safe happy future. The alternative?

In truth, how could one possibly go through life focusing only on what could go wrong? To never make a wrong turn would call for never making a move, jumping off into an adventure, even going with the flow. If you never plan a trip, travel far, go anywhere, see the world from others' perspectives, or jump into life, then can you call it living your best life? You've only got one, after all. And should your fears be allowed to hobble not just yourself but your loved ones with what can be overwhelming, perhaps real but maybe unrealistic fears? All she knows right here is that she alone has this time right now to right a wrong.

From the moment she dives into the brush, shoving aside some branches and crushing ahead on her way down, her destination becomes immediately clear.

Needsmust, like so many eighteenth century sugar plantations, was once architecturally spectacular for its time with buildings featuring stone ground floors, high timber ceilings in the main, stately, great house reserved only for owners, managers or rich visitors. Overseer's homes, storage buildings for processing sugar and rum, trash buildings for the dried cane called bagasse, a separate kitchen, maybe a hospital called a hot house, designated villages for slaves and of course, stables for animals. It was all here. Donkeys worked hard grinding and hauling cane though working not nearly as hard as the slaves who labored day and night during crop time in extreme heat and dangerous conditions. Lady's legacy of genetics is a happy one. She simply knows this as home. Not so for human beings. Back then, if you were enslaved, you might even end up with the job standing by with a cleaver ready to chop off someone's limb that had been inadvertently dragged into or caught by a machine.

To forget, to minimize or lose this scary, painful history would be a mistake, of course, especially here on St. Kitts where repurposed plantations welcome tourists. You need to know what these places are all about. This need to remember, to commemorate and keep this legacy alive is critical to moving forward, isn't it?

Just look at how spectacular Reginald Browne, the Prime Minister, is here. Is his ability to confront Russian legal incursion into his island home born from generational strength? A collective consciousness is surely at the heart of it right here on St. Kitts. Well of course, Annie will muse later when her ordeal is over; the theory of collective consciousness believes that human beings are linked to each other and their ancestors through shared experiences.

For Lady, this must be true, too. For some weird, and yes questionable but deeply buried genetic memory, she keeps on returning to her roots. She heads for home whenever she can. And that home is Needsmust. Magic.

❧

Buck, on the ground now, steps over to the prime minister who has been questioning Kennedy and asks quietly, "Can I use your vehicle to get down the mountain?"

"Of course, Sir. It's been a pleasure to meet you here even under these circumstances. I will catch up with you later this morning. Take my driver right now," Browne answers, then adds, "and this young man who may be of help. Bring him along. His name is Kennedy."

"Wait, I think congratulations are in order," Buck interjects. "Both Annie and I watched you in the news reports from the United Nations last September. You were great. We love your island. Honestly, we're proud of St. Kitts and the roots we've grown here. If it weren't for the ingenuity of you and past prime ministers, St. Kitts might not be as solid and successful as it is. I must say, keeping your financials afloat is one mighty task."

"You're right, Sir. It's always a tough balancing act. Thank you for the compliments, it's been a whirlwind for months," Browne admits. "And now this."

"Yes, this," Buck emphasizes. "This is a nightmare."

"But especially for you, Sir."

"Please call me Buck. I know. This is perhaps a grandparent's worst nightmare."

"Buck," Browne adds, "do you want me to come along now?"

"No, I think I've got it. And I know there will be people waiting down there to be of assistance. Better that you stay on top of this now. I expect there is more to come up here."

"I'll stay put but keep in touch. Use my driver's cell phone if you can't pick up a signal on yours."

Into the big official car, Buck climbs, taking the front seat, and adding a "Thank you," to the driver. Kennedy, who has introduced himself to Buck, not mentioning his part in this predicament, jumps into the back.

Heading down this narrow, concrete, twisting road, the car slows near the spot Kennedy remembers leaving Silvie, the other young woman held captive.

"Over there," he points. "We told her to stay put, that we'd be back to get her. She's been through a lot. Her name is Silvie."

Kennedy jumps out. Then Buck follows. "Silvie, you can come out now. You are safe."

Standing up unsteadily from inside a thicket of wild shrubs, she says, "I wasn't sure you would come back." Then she looks around. "Where is Annie?"

❧

The girls are running toward the old sugar mill when they spot the Maserati speeding down the mountainside.

"Those guys are in trouble," Abby says. "Are they coming for us?"

Ellie looks up.

Lady whinnies, nudges her girl with alarm.

"El, how well do you know this donkey, girl?" Liz asks now, grinning.

"Oh God, Lizzie. If it weren't for Lady... what if she hadn't been with me this night?" Her tears start falling. "I don't know if I'd be here. This Lady is my lifesaver."

Running through this field on an early morning on November 19, all three sense the intelligence in Lady and a connection none could have imagined just the day before. If Liz and Abby had thought their younger cousin was just a wee bit animal-crazy yesterday, today they know this was her saving grace. This morning, it becomes perfectly clear that when this hungry animal gobbled Ellie's ketchupy egg sandwich at the beach, a bond was secured igniting a life-changing link.

CHAPTER TWENTY-NINE

6:50 AM

Annie's story, especially her what-ifs and regrets on this early morning, could belong to every loving grandmother. Make a plan...a grand get-away, let's-all-do-the-happy-dance plan...then, hold your breath, anticipate disappointment, envision joy, and wonder about how it will all work out.

It doesn't feel good in the Gulfstream speeding Will and Lauren from Orange County, New York, toward St. Kitts. Lauren, Ellie's mother, had believed that simply climbing on board and getting on the way to where her daughter might be would make her feel better. It would stop the shakes, the internal pound-pound-pounding, breath after breath of what-ifs and why-didn't-Is. But it hasn't. She may even be worse because she's stuck inside a metal tube going faster than the speed of sound. It's another Gulfstream airplane, military version, among the fastest in the world. However, the critical word here is stuck.

Mothers act. They race, dive, go directly into danger when children are in the path of disaster, don't they? When they can't, it's a muddy, quicksand mess. Mothers run into their child's danger zone. There's no holding back, even from a burning building or accident scene. Would you stop if your child were inside, underneath? Of course not. Go mom, go. It's this dreadful unknowing, immobilization, not being able to do anything at all, a frozen-in-time panic that is sickening. Lauren gets ready to vomit.

"Think I'm going to throw up," she says to her big brother, the sweet handsome guy across that aisle in the plane. His Lizzie and Abigail are there in St. Kitts too but out of danger, he believes.

"Grab the bag," he says. "It's right there in the seat pocket." But he's also unlatching his seat belt to come to her side, to pull out the bag and hold her forehead as she leans into it and retches. He's always loved his little sister. She is immobilized and now physically sick with her regrets and never-ending thoughts; how stupid was it to allow her 13-year-old daughter to go off without her? Why didn't she insist on traveling with the girls on this get-away? How could her work have been more important? If only she had been there. If only. If only. But could she have prevented this? And then, she goes where she really shouldn't in her thoughts of blame, why the hell did her mother get the girls so excited about this grandmother getaway? What was she thinking? How could she have promised? Will she ever be able to forgive her if Ellie is gone? Is this her own family's Shakespearean tragedy unfolding? She's already growing angry with her mother, damn her stubbornness, wanting to have her grandchildren to herself. So selfish!

Too much time has passed since these worried parents spoke to their father, their can-do-anything dad, the powerful Pop Pop who arranged this fast flight miraculously. He had promised to call them. He hasn't. What is he planning to do today? Will is uncertain, having always believed in his dad but with a tug toward logic and reality. The guy is not superman. He's really old now, in fact. Always the less optimistic sibling, Will relives a disaster he can never forget from his high school years. The reassurance of happy endings died for him on a night-out of partying with friends in senior year when one of them ended up dead at the bottom of a hillside, having slipped on rocks when drunk and standing high up on top. His friend. His best friend. Gone before high school graduation, only three weeks away. This memory is embedded in Will's psyche. People, even people you love, can die and suddenly. Yes, it happens. Happy escapades like the one his grandmother planned for the girls can turn lethal, leaving a deep distrustful gouge right there inside, haunting all the days that come after. Will knows this so well. You carry this pessimistic, let's call it realistic, attitude with you always, never able to throw it off, change that tune, discard, or wash it away. Will knows this oh so well. He checks his surroundings here and now. But he looks back to that high school escapade and sees the bad, the ugly, and the wound left behind on his happy family.

"Will, tell me it's going to be okay. Tell me that Ellie is alive and safe," she asks.

"I can't tell you that Lauren," he cautions but gently. He wants to touch his baby sister with a light brush of optimism on top of this truth. "We don't know anything yet." And this not knowing is all that they have here. He wants to remind her that bad things happen to good people, but he shuts down this cliché before it can escape his lips and leans in to give her a kiss on the cheek.

"I can't stop thinking the worst," she admits. "We are not in some fairy tale here and these guys are really bad." With that, her sobs start up. "They have my daughter, my Ellie."

"Take a deep breath," Will insists. "We know nothing. We know nothing, yet." Then, he thinks of that mantra on his mother's refrigerator. What does it say? Something like, "worry is like sitting in a rocking chair, rocking and rocking. You can rock all you want, but it gets you nowhere."

"Set this down now," he whispers to his sister. "We can do this."

An officer on board comes down the aisle of the near empty airplane to give these parents the update.

"We'll be landing within the hour. Hang in there." He can't help but see the tears and read the emotion in these parents. "We've got this. I can't promise you anything but can assure you that we've got a plan. We know who these men are."

❧

There's a crush of stones under the wheels as the prime minister's car, minus the prime minister, speeds down the mountain with Buck, Kennedy, and now Silvie. It turns left and then right and then left again, perhaps going way too fast on these mountainside hairpin turns. They catch glimpses of another car heading down but to their left, not even taking the best road down, the one with fewer potholes and drop offs. They must be on the remains of an old cart path. How crazy.

"Who are they?" Buck asks the driver.

"Not sure, Sir."

"I'm so sorry but I never caught your name back up there," Buck adds.

"It's Cyril," the driver says. "No problem. Busy morning here."

He takes the comment literally, smiles turning to the back seat to check Kennedy and Silvie and repeats, "Quite. Busy doesn't really describe it."

This jokey conversational exaggeration breaks the tension, and it feels good; unfinished, edgy but still good.

"Keep your eyes open," Buck asks, looking ahead.

Kennedy adds, "Yes, this is where the damn donkey goes down … all the time."

"How strange," Buck says. "Why do you think? What was here for her?"

"Home. My Tata…my grandmother…says she's always heading home."

Buck smiles at Kennedy invoking his grandmother's wisdom. Always looking for parallels in this role of grandparent that Buck loves so much, he thrives on reassurance that his generation can share wisdom.

"Do you think Ellie is going to be there?" he asks point blank.

"Yah."

"But why?"

"I know this donkey. And she liked the girl yesterday. I saw it. They connected."

And this is where Buck's ears perk up. This kid saw Ellie
and the donkey together? What's up with this? In fact, where does
he fit in here? But it's a line of questions he doesn't have time for,
nor want to pursue at this moment. He will get to the bottom of the
story and this young man's involvement soon enough. After all, the
prime minister recommended he come along. Kennedy is in his life
because the leader of this little nation of St. Kitts/Nevis put him
here. There must be a good reason.

The centuries old, abandoned, crumbling, stone sugar mill
with its thick circular walls, is cool inside. The sharp, earthy scents
shouting old, damp, mossy are everywhere, but there is a touch of
sweet sugar cane lingering too. Even with weeds growing from
gaps and gashes in the decaying mortar between the rocks and
crevasses, it's still quite majestic, towering up to at least 30 feet
high in its ruined state. This structure is fully open at the top to
sunshine, but there is a side window up there too. These girls can
remember looking out that window years ago before the steps had
fallen apart and the platform disappeared. Pop Pop had helped
them climb, so Grammy could take their picture looking out the
little window for her holiday card. There's a safety here inside.
Momentarily. The girls look at one another and heave sighs of
relief.

"Do you think I could take her home?" Ellie asks.

"Who?" Liz and Abby ask in unison.

"Lady?"

"I don't know what U.S. immigration customs would say
about that," Liz laughs. "But you never know. Pop Pop does have a
lot of pull with people who know people."

"Watch that hole," Abby warns balancing on the rocky floor. "Loose stones here," she adds. Machinery once occupied the center of what was a floor of cogs and iron wheels that turned to press, pound, and pulverize cane stalks to be soaked into sugar.

The four of them, three cousins and a donkey have climbed up what was once the same incline where stalks of sugar cane were lugged to be processed. Lady had to be pulled along gently, unwilling at first to leave the safety of familiar ground outside. Ellie, coaxing the animal, explained why they needed to stay out of sight. But it's also Abby now who drapes her arm around Lady cooing, "It's okay girl. We've got you here. We won't let go." Yes, she knows this place, the mill where her ancestors carted the stalks from neighboring fields and now inside, from the sound of her snuffling in approval and hee-hawing too loud, she feels at home.

In one of the helicopters, Rufson has stopped circling above the clearing around the warehouse. The situation on the ground is under control. These Russians will be moved off island as soon as possible to a secret but designated location. It's been done before in tricky international criminal situations. And he knows where to take them. Igor needs medical attention, of course, but he'll receive no sympathy for his situation anywhere here and the local hospital is inadequate. What about that kid in the bushes with the neck wound? Well, he must have an interesting story Rufson has yet to learn. He's told his story to the guys on the ground, but it hasn't made its way up to his command yet. Right now, his mind is focused on where the young women could be; two of them, Buck's granddaughter and another missing tourist. The military assumption had been that the girls, the young women abducted and for sale, would be in or near that warehouse. One had been spotted and was being observed from above via satellite, this morning.

Inside the building, however, it was obvious that someone, just one? had been held captive. Then, the hole in the floor had been the big surprise. Who did that? And who crawled through?

The second helicopter has been ordered to head back to the airport. But Rufson has decided to take his down as close to Needsmust on the ground as possible...if he can find a flat enough area, free of overhead wires and large enough to land safely with his crew. Looks possible.

"Sir, are you sure about this landing?"

"Yes. Trust me. I've found worst places to land. It's tight but do-able. Let's go. I see movement down there."

On the way there, he checks the whereabouts, once again, of the sports car careening down through the maze of switch backing concrete on the side of this undeveloped piece of St. Kitts.

"Get directly above," he says. "Hold there. Shake them up. Flood them under our search lights. Let's scare the hell out of these guys."

CHAPTER THIRTY

7 AM

---

*The history of the world as told most often from
the male perspective, sometimes misses half the
story. Women are certainly not passive
bystanders, especially not older women. Look
around. Ask a grandmother.*

---

he mountainside east of the Robert K. Bradshaw
International Airport on the island of St. Kitts this
morning is like a board game with too many moving
pieces…Chutes and Ladders? Certainly not. Candyland? Nothing
sweet or fun at all. Clue? No, we know who did it. Such a crazy,
complicated scene gone haywire with speeding cars, yes, that
Maserati Abby identified and the big black Escalade belonging to
the prime minister; helicopters above, one about to land ever-so-
carefully to avoid power lines near the Needsmust field, another
flying over to the airport; and there are also Kittitian coast guard
vehicles moving along the Kim Collins Highway toward the turn-

off into Needsmust. Residents in nearby neighborhoods are out on the streets now and at roadside intersections, shaking their heads in a what's-going-on hew and cry. Kid you not. This much was true. No one could miss those helicopters.

The chatter is typical. "Hey mon? Was' up?"

"Dunno."

"Drug bust?"

"Me-be so. Me-be no."

Annie, the additional element of surprise on this mountainside but not on anyone's radar, is single-minded with only one thought; get to the sugar mill. Get Ellie … get there before anyone else does or anything else happens. Her grandmother inside voice tells her so.

"Elllliiieeee. Elllllieeee!" she starts screaming irrationally so far out of anyone's earshot more than 120 yards away. Okay, so she ran track in high school and has completed marathons. Let's give her this strength. She needs every bit of energy and muscle memory she can muster. For God's sake, this is football-field length, and she will close the gap ahead or die trying, unaware of exactly what is happening above, behind or at a distance. Perhaps the word here is die.

Inside the sugar mill, the girls have been ratcheting up internal alarms, listening to the sounds of confusion and danger coming closer.

"Oh my God," Liz whispers.

Then, there's another loud cry out there, "Ellie. Ellie."

"That's Grammy," Abby says. "I know it is."

"Are you sure?" Liz questions.

"I'm sure."

Before Annie reaches the mill…

Before the girls cross to the doorway of the old stone structure and look out…

Before the car carrying Buck screeches to the bottom of the hillside and turns left heading into the Needsmust nursery gardens…

Before Commander Rufson's pilot lands the helicopter safely…

Well …the Maserati with its testosterone-addled Russians skids off an unexpected, 90-degree bend when the driver misses a hairpin turn going 177 miles per hour. The expensive sky-blue car with these two men inside is airborne, free-falling for a few brief moments, with its passengers experiencing zero-gravity effects in fact. Even if they attempt to unbuckle seat belts…Would they have been wearing them? Probably not. Can they jump clear of the car before it starts to tumble in its gravity-assisted, mountain-road disaster, with their imminent deaths surely inescapable? You simply can't jump from a car going that speed on a mountainside and live to brag about it. Perhaps they are alive inside long enough to experience the explosion when the vehicle hits the side of the steep hill once, twice, and then starts hurtling down; upside, right side, back again and then skidding across the open field heading toward the sugar mill.

The grass here is dry. There hasn't been enough rain during this past year's supposedly rainy season on St. Kitts. An unfortunate truth of climate change because the tumbling, twisting, upside-down Maserati is a ball of flames now skidding out of control through all the parched perennial grasses so perfectly ripe for fire. Shocked residents in the houses on the hill are now out on porches and front decks to see the flames following the vehicle that refuses to stop. You can only imagine what's happening inside. Do these creepy guys die immediately or are they alive and on fire?

Annie can sense imminent disaster approaching from behind…she hears it, feels the heat, in fact…unsure of exactly how far ahead of this blazing car she is with no time to waste by turning back or thinking. She's just shouting one name and going as fast as she can.

"Ellie Ellieeeee."

At the sugar mill, three girls, not one, stand on the old stone ramp, apoplectic, shocked by what is heading their way, not just Grammy but a car skidding and setting the field on fire.

"The Maserati," Abby says. No one is listening.

"Run girls, run," Annie screams. "I'm here. I'll be with you. Get out of the way. Now. Run. Get away. Go, go, go."

Closing the distance, Annie realizes that it's Ellie, Abigail and Lizzie with a donkey running down the ramp, out of the path of disaster, going toward a tool shed. This donkey is leading the way; girls running along right behind the animal.

Almost there, almost there now, Annie has a 74-year-old heart beating so wildly that she might wonder; is this a heart attack worth dying for? She can see them and an overpowering longing to hold them close propels her forward to the end of her long night's journey.

Near one of the garden's sheds, with views of the sugar mill, the teenagers stop, huddle, and turn to see their grandmother, running toward them. Abby shakes her head in wonder, "Oh Grammy," she mutters. "Wow wow wow. How did…?"

She's there; sweaty, strong, catching her breath, pulling all three around, close to her…and then sobbing with emotion. Our Grammy can't stop the tears of relief, perhaps tears of sorrow, anger, guilt for what this day has brought upon them. No, for what she brought upon them, right here in their beloved St. Kitts.

"Oh my God, girls. I am so so so sorry. I love you so much, so much, so much." And in this midst of tears, fears, exhaustion, confusion, she sees these beautiful granddaughters anew. Alive. Here. Now. Not gone. Spectacular children! They are her life's longing for itself. These children of her children! They have lived to tell this tale. And that is good, all by itself.

"What is happening?" Abby asks, looking around at the chaos; toward the crumpled car in flames at the base of the unscathed sugar mill, at the helicopter that has landed safely in the field, and at the big black car that has sped up the Needsmust Estate road toward them and come to a quick stop.

"Oh girls, I only know part of this crazy story."

At that point, the sound of a fire truck racing into the garden adds to the turmoil. Car doors open then and a familiar voice calls out.

"Pop Pop?" Lizzie asks.

"What? How?" Annie whispers. "Your grandfather. Here too?"

"Pop Pop," they shout when they see him. "How did you get

here so fast?"

"I have my secrets," he says, with a sly smile as he hugs them. "I promise to share some of them with you very soon."

His arms are around Annie now and he's asking, "How did you do this? Annie, my love, how in God's name did you run all the way here?"

She's laughing. "Oh Buck, how could I not?"

"But..."

"For heaven's sake, you know these St. Kitts' police. They mean well...but hurry, well, let's not go there. Hurry is not a speed in their wheelhouse."

The girls are wide-eyed in wonder at their grandparents, still in love after all these years, all these kids.

Then Liz gets his attention, "Thank you Pop Pop. Thank you for picking up the phone in the middle of the night. I didn't know what else to do, who to call."

He smiles knowingly, not ready to share everything yet.

Abby asks, "But what I want to know is who did you call, Pop Pop? Seriously, who do you know?"

"Later," he says laughing. "I promise to tell all later."

"Really?"

"Well, maybe not all but enough."

Ellie is quiet. At peace now, Ellie looks straight into this multi-layered catastrophe of fire, smoke, death, and family all around and sees her kidnapper approaching. This boy is different from the one she first encountered yesterday at the beach and early this morning on the mountain. This cute-not-so-cute face is calm, subdued, fearful, guilty. Good, she wants to say but stifles the urge. He's been holding back, standing out of clear sight, let's call it hiding, behind Cyril, the prime minister's driver. Ellie realizes that he's hiding from her. More resilient than ever, the youngest here, she has been no helpless victim tonight. Like her grandmother, she knows how to face a traumatic event and instinctively, stoically move through it or at least get past the vomit part. She also has an idea here now.

This kid, yes Kennedy is his name, comes forward to face her now. This boy knows what is true about this girl Ellie. She won. He lost. This girl is wise, far wiser than he certainly is. He can hardly look at her, eyes turned down, while she stares directly at him, chin held high.

"Why did you do this to me?"

"I am so sorry," he answers. Everyone stops to listen. "I was sooo stoopid, so messed up, sick," he adds as a possible but lame excuse.

"It's not okay. And you're not forgiven...yet."

Then, she turns to her grandmother and grandfather, and asks, "Grammy, Pop Pop, this is someone who needs your help."

⌒

The happily ever after ending this morning isn't a happy occasion for everyone, of course. We've got a couple of dead Russians in a burning car, local kids who conspired with this horrific kidnapping game plan who will need to be rehabilitated, other Russians, one bleeding, others sitting out on an oligarch's super yacht in Christophe Harbour, who will need to be removed from the island to a secret location pronto, and perhaps the big boat impounded? For a place that sells serenity and get-away from the real world to tourists, St. Kitts has remedial work ahead. Yes, it's quite a laundry list of to-do's for the new prime minister. But he's up to these tasks.

Browne, still up on the mountain at the warehouse, wants this Igor and the scandal he engineered to disappear immediately from the island. The U.S. has done this before for its Caribbean neighbor, with ordinary drug traffickers. It will happen again here. Quietly. Secretly. Simply. No news will be good news. Perhaps the explanation of an awful traffic accident for hapless visitors who missed a turn. Were they tourists gone wild? Nothing new. Seen it before and will see it again. Today is no different. That will be the official story.

On the phone, Browne takes a call from his driver. "Good news down here; the girls are here and safe with their grandparents. Bad news; Needsmust Estate fields are on fire."

"I'll head right there."

"Do you need me to pick you up Sir?"

"No, I'm going to take this Aurus Senat parked right here."

"Oh really? I've always wanted to drive one," Cyril admits.

"You're up next. I've got the keys."

CHAPTER THIRTY-ONE

7:20 AM

Can you escape adversity or trauma in a
lifetime? But would that be the perfect life?
Perhaps it is only by falling, by failing, or by
facing catastrophe and then getting back up that
you become wise.

A heavy blanket of calm…knowing that she has accomplished something more important than anything else perhaps ever, in her life…overwhelms Annie. She's silent, sitting on the ground inside the Needsmust greenhouse with her granddaughters. They are all looking out to the controlled madhouse on the grounds of this centuries-old estate. The gardener showed up for work a few minutes after 7 AM, opened the doors and confronted with the cataclysmic disaster in his small green world, he welcomed this family inside. A fire is still burning nearby. The sugar mill will survive and may stand there proudly for another century.

"Come. Come inside. Stay safe," the kind man had said unlocking the door. He is the epitome of all (or most) of the people Annie knows here on St. Kitts: kind, welcoming, supportive.

They watch as another fire truck arrives, men race to stop the spreading flames, and the sports car burns to a mangled mesh of metal and cinders. Annie thinks she can smell burning flesh in the noxious mix. Who were those awful men? Looking over to her girls, Ellie, Lizzie, Abby and now Silvie too, she is not as sad as she ought to be for the loss of human life over there. What happened to her empathy on the way to this moment? Let it come later. For now, she wants to gloat.

Exhausted as never before, she's at peace knowing she isn't in charge here and starts crying and not just a few tiny tears. She is sobbing. Yes, she cries too much, her older sister always says. Lauren agrees. Yes, she probably sheds too many tears for someone in her seventies, the decade when we're supposed to be stoic. But these tears today are not of sadness but relief welling its way up into an explosion of emotion.

"Oh Buck, it was so awful. I was so scared. So worried that I had brought all this upon our family."

"Annie, this wasn't your fault."

"Yes, it was. It is my fault and it would have brought an end to so much I love in my life. If it weren't for my plan, this ridiculous vacation I insisted on taking, Ellie would never have been in danger. I know what I did."

"You didn't cause this to happen, Annie."

"But..."

"Believe me, Annie, there is evil in this world, and this was surely evil but you are not evil."

"Oh my God, Buck. I never would have forgiven myself if..."

"Don't go there, Annie. If there is an if here...you responded to that if, took matters into your control and stopped the if from going forward. It was you. As a matter of fact, what exactly did you do up there?"

She laughs. "Oh my. Can I tell you later? In detail, I promise. But do we all have to stay here now? Can we answer the authorities' questions a little later? I just want to go home. I want all of us to go back to our house, our home here."

"Of course."

"I know I have my share of explaining to do and not just to you," she says laughing. Oh jeez, is laughing about wanting to maim a man, to shoot off his penis, the right emotion? If so, she really is screwed up but maybe just momentarily. But she can't stop laughing in a delicious, superb release. The girls join in.

"What's so funny Grammy?" Ellie asks, petting Lady who has joined them here in safety.

"This was all too crazy!" Ellie adds, pulling out her Frozen flashlight with the musical buttons she begins to push.

"Yes. Yes, that's what I mean. Too preposterous. Now I remember where I heard that music," Annie points to the toy. "Honestly, if we try to tell the story of this day, people will be laughing out loud. A toy? A 74-year-old grandmother to the rescue? Russian kidnappers? How did we survive this catastrophe? Ellie, I heard you calling me with your flashlight and the music, the sounds of ice crushing from the movie, too."

"Oh Grammy, I kept hoping you would hear, that you would come get me."

Even Lady snorts here, hee-hawing and turning her head into Ellie with affection, begging to be petted. Remember me, she seems to be saying.

"I forgot to add Lady, our donkey heroine, to my list of all these wacky, unlikely elements. Do we dare ever share this real story?"

Turning to hug Ellie in her dirty pink pajamas while shaking her head side to side with a definitive no, Annie adds, "Let's get you cleaned up." She takes a sniff of Ellie raising her granddaughter's armpit to her nose. "Pee-yoo. You too Silvie. You both need tender loving care and bubble baths."

With her own arm raised to sniff herself, she adds, "Whew...girls, I stink. Look, I've even got blood on my hands. Oh my God, do I need a shower and then maybe a long soak in our pool."

"Of course, you girls can go but I need to stay for a bit," Buck explains. "Maybe Cyril, the prime minister's driver here, can give you a ride back over to the house."

"Wait," Lizzie says. "I can drive us. I think Grammy's rental is still where I parked it. At least I hope so."

"Lizzie, you drove the car over here?"

Looking sheepish," she admits. "I did. I had to."

"Oh, my brave girl. I'm so proud of all of you," her grandmother says.

"Wait a minute," Buck adds. "I just need to check the time, but I think you'll want to change your minds and stay nearby, maybe head over to the airport in fact. We have a surprise."

"What kind of surprise?" Ellie asks.

"You'll see soon," he says smiling. "Let me take this call first."

∽

Arriving air passengers on St. Kitts are almost always run through a gauntlet of officialdom by well-meaning public servants. It was no exception this morning for Lauren and Will who had landed in another military Gulfstream coming from Orange County, New York. Like everyone else on this busy Friday morning, they were sent into the arrivals terminal to wait their turn. In fact, because standard immigration forms or any instructions for downloading a new arriving passengers app hadn't been available on their superfast military aircraft, they had to fill out forms manually at the counter inside. The good news was that their father had called with the very best news, "Everyone and I do mean everyone, will be waiting outside when you emerge!"

"Is this business or pleasure?" Lauren asks her brother second-guessing questions about the purpose of their visit on the form. How strange to have to categorize this lightning-fast trip to St. Kitts? There is no way to choose either of these options.

"Wait. I hope it's purely pleasure," he laughs. "Though I didn't pack my bathing suit. In fact, I didn't pack anything. Did you?"

"No, I didn't either. This is a first time for that. I usually have to pay extra for overweight bags."

Outside the white steel, window-less doors, a dirty, dusty group waits on the wide cement sidewalk. A few are down on the curb too tired to stay upright any longer. They are laughing and asking one another. "Who wants a Ting? Does anyone need a Carib? I know it's early in the day, but what a day this is!" Annie shouts. Cabbies jostle for customers. Vendors line the wide sidewalk. Vehicles idle waiting for pick-ups. It's an ordinary busy Friday morning at the Robert K. Bradshaw airport on St. Kitts.

Annie waits, sitting, sipping a Carib beer, the earliest in a day she has ever dared do this. She doesn't ordinarily like beer in fact. However, today these calories and the touch of alcohol are perfect. Her granddaughters are laughing and very much into loving their green bottles of Ting, their favorite grapefruit soda made right there on the island. Buck watches carefully, everything and everyone. He's still on duty, she muses. And thank goodness.

Then, her children come through the big doors into the sunshine. "Lauren! Will! We're here. Over here," they shout waving over the throng of people and signs carried by cab drivers and hotel greeters. The hugs, kisses and relief for these parents and children are palpable. Annie can taste this exquisite relief. But she stands back letting her children be with their own children, an ordinary miracle this morning.

She starts to cry again.

"Grammy," her children say. "It's okay. It's going to be okay." They have learned this optimistic mantra well, for better and today, for worse. Right? Is this a good thing to pass along to the next generation?

But wait, and her mind wanders back to the full extent of her journey today. She allows herself to think pessimistically. Oh my God, I may have killed a man today. Or certainly maimed him. The fleeting thought is now carried along by guilt. Who is she?

"Oh my God, Buck, wait. We've forgotten something," she says turning to him in the happy chaos of reunion where a new panic is populating her brain. "We've got to get our boys here, our grandsons, and our daughter-in-law and son-in-law! They must be frantic."

"I've stayed in touch, Annie. I've called them. They are coming. I couldn't command yet another military Gulfstream ride today, but they are all set with tickets on the commercial flight leaving from Newark first thing tomorrow morning. I got lucky with the flight schedule. It's direct and there were seats available."

"Oh God, thank you, thank you. Do you think of everything?" She shakes her head in admiration.

"No," he laughs and throws out a question that always makes Annie frustrated about her husband. He has been known to forget this date. "What day in March is our anniversary again?

"I know, but do you?" she asks.

"Yes, I am kidding. I do remember. It's always March 3."

"Now," he says addressing everyone, "let's get you all home. I think we need two vans here. Should we call Sea Moss Man?"

Standing there on the airport sidewalk surrounded by family, Annie realizes that in a world ravaged by wars, floods, fires, kidnappings, political and economic strife, even goddamn Russian pimps, there is no such thing as a perfect place. This momentary safety of family surrounding her may be as good as it gets, right here in the sunshine as she finishes her beer in her St. Kitts peace of place. This is the island that rescued her decades ago with the first whiff of sugar cane and a rum punch in an airport paper cup...the place that nurtured her with its laid-back, rush-slowly temperament...and now the island that helped bring her granddaughter back safely. Here, now, taking a deep breath of clear clean air with a touch of ocean breeze, she realizes that this is as perfect as possible, just one moment in the time of her long lucky life.

EPILOGUE

F irst-degree kidnapping and/or sexually assaulting a victim can result in prison sentences of between 20 years to life. Fines may also be imposed. While this fictional crime on November 19, 2021, did not occur within U.S. borders, both young women who were victimized were American citizens. This would have been important if it had really happened. The relationship between St. Kitts/Nevis and the U.S. is historically solid.

The two countries work as a team according to the U.S. Department of State's Bureau of Western Hemisphere Affairs. The U.S. established diplomatic relations with Saint Kitts and Nevis in 1983, following its independence from the United Kingdom. Since then, the U.S. has sought to assist Saint Kitts/Nevis to enhance security, promote economic prosperity, and strengthen democracy in its parliamentary form of government.

A State Department report on Sept. 13, 2023, explains, "Strategically located in the Leeward Islands, near maritime transport lanes of major importance to the United States, Saint Kitts/Nevis' proximity to Puerto Rico and the U.S. Virgin Islands makes the two-island federation attractive to narcotics and human traffickers." To counter this threat, the government of Saint Kitts/Nevis cooperates with the United States in the fight. The countries have also signed "a maritime law enforcement treaty, later amended with an overflight/order-to-land amendment, an updated extradition treaty, and a mutual legal assistance treaty."

In December 2021, just a month after our fictional kidnapping might have occurred (and it really didn't happen), the St. Kitts/Nevis government Citizen by Investment Unit (CIU) began to question and withdraw acceptances to a large group of Russian, Ukrainian, and Belarusian applicants. The measure was even retroactive affecting individuals who had already been approved and had paid their price. As of October 2023, St. Kitts had also decided that there were no legal provisions for reimbursing or returning funds that were already part of the government's budget.

St. Kitts/Nevis is just one of 23 countries on several continents that offer Citizenship by Investment (CBI) including Antigua, Barbuda, Cambodia, Dominica, Grenada, Malta, Moldova, Montenegro, and others.

Brinley Gold Shipwreck Rum was founded, nurtured and has flourished on the peaceful island of St. Kitts. The company is proud to be from St. Kitts and making genuine, small batch Caribbean rum right on the deep-water port that is sold all over the world.

AND ON A FICTIONAL FINAL NOTE

Annie was not charged with any crime.

With the intervention of Buck, Kennedy's involvement was pardoned. Annie took him under her wing, and he eventually attended Montclair State University in Montclair, New Jersey.

Igor and Russian co-conspirators were transported off island to await sentencing in a secret location. In the cemetery above Basseterre, the remains of two burned beyond recognition bodies were interred.

The government of St. Kitts/Nevis impounded the superyacht owned by a shell company belonging to a well-known Russian oligarch. The big boat sat in the waters of Christophe Harbour collecting fees for months before being sold along with all properties owned by the criminals, including that great house on the mountain. Proceeds were spent locally on good works.

OTHER BOOKS BY THIS AUTHOR

Through the Motherhood Maze (Doubleday 1981)

Maternity Style (St. Martin's Press 1985)

My Feet Are Killing Me (ghost writer, McGraw Hill 1987)

Jackie Cochran (Bantam Books 1987)

Medical Book of Remedies for People Over 50 (Publications International 1996)

Are We Having Fun Yet? The 16 Secrets of Happy Parenting (Warner 1997)

The Everything Pregnancy Book (Adams Media 1999)

Fat Chat with Tamara (Contemporary Books 2000)

Oh Boy, Mothers Tell the Truth About Raising Teen Sons (Warner 2002)

https://www.maryannbrinley.com/.

ABOUT THE AUTHOR

I am an experienced writer interested in the wisdom of women, in parenting, families, science but most important of all, in the incredible power of words. As poet Emily Dickinson wrote in *This is My Letter to the World*, "I know nothing in the world that has as much power as a word. Sometimes I write one, and I look at it, until it begins to shine." I have written and published nine non-fiction books but spent most of my career in the world of magazines. I was a senior editor and writer at *Ladies' Home Journal, Good Housekeeping, Family Health, McCall's*, and *Woman's Day* magazines from 1972 to 1989. More recent experience was as a writer and publications editor at the University of Medicine and Dentistry of New Jersey (now Rutgers University). I retired at age 65 to work as a free-lance writer and for our family business, Brinley Shipwreck Rum.

My husband Bob opened and operated a factory making electronic temperature sensors on the Caribbean island of St. Kitts for decades, the setting for ***Annie's Redemption***. My children were young, Zach and Maggie, when we started our adventure there and we have always felt right at home on this stunning island, slipping easily into a St. Kitts' state of mind. In 2002, our family also started our rum company, a labor of love and family affair led by our son, Zach. My roots are deeply planted on St. Kitts, one of my favorite places in the world, just like my heroine's.

You can learn more about me at, https://www.maryannbrinley.com.